WOMAN OF SUBSTANCE

ANNETTE BOWER

SOUL MATE PUBLISHING

New York

WOMAN OF SUBSTANCE

ANNETTE BOWER

Cover Design by Rae Monet, Inc.

Published in the United States of America by
Soul Mate Publishing
P.O. Box 24
Macedon, New York, 14502

ISBN: 978-1-61935-225-4
eBook ISBN: 978-1-61935-110-3

www.SoulMatePublishing.com

For Cam

Acknowledgements

To the Canadian Storytellers' Writers Workshop at Notre Dame College, Wilcox, SK, Terry Jordan, facilitator and the fellow participants where I first imagined Robbie in disguise.

To the Bees: Byrna Barclay, Linda Biasotto, James Trettwer, Leeann Minogue, Anne Lazurko, Shelley Banks, Brenda Niskala, Rod Dickinson, Kelly-Anne Ries.

To the Saskatchewan Romance Writers.

To Lawrence Hill for distant mentorship at Booming Ground, UBC.

To The Saskatchewan Writers Guild.

To Catherine Bush the Fiction Colloquium Facilitator, Sage Hill Writing Experience.

To Brenda Novak's Annual Online Auction for Diabetes Research.

To Deborah Gilbert of Soul Mate Publishing, who donated a valuable critique, which resulted in an offer to publish this novel.

To my husband, sons, daughter-in-laws and granddaughters, my parents, extended family, and friends, who sustain me through their love, understanding and humor.

Chapter 1

The golden leaves in Wascana Park slipped to the ground around Robbie Smith. The sun added perfection to her field study adventure.

Four girls on roller blades sped around a bend, charging right at her. One yelled, "Get out of the way, Tank."

Robbie's foot slipped, and the bulk around her middle sloshed to one side. She flung out her arms to break her fall. *That was a waste of time*. She raised her head, then spit a leaf out of her mouth. "Get back here and help me up," she shouted.

She pushed on her hands and got her knees under her. Thank goodness the park was empty when she hoisted her rear end into the air. *I'm fat, I'm fat. Remember I'm supposed to be fat. How can I not remember? I can't get up.*

Stuck. Someone's coming. Oh love a duck and save a rose. What'll they think? She peered around her shoulder, and then under her arm. She couldn't see anyone. Her borrowed polyester slacks snagged on dry brown grass. Her thighs rubbed against each other when she struggled to stand. She looked around and saw a garbage can. She could crawl over and pull herself up.

Footsteps crunched through leaves, before the breathless words, "I'm coming," reached her ears.

Her breaths came in rapid pants. In her twenty-five years she could count on one hand the times she'd felt trapped. *I'm not trapped, just slow-moving. Think. Think.*

At least help was on the way. Perspiration rolled from her forehead into her eyes. Her face was probably a mess.

Was her disguise ready for close inspection? She blew out a frustrated breath. *Figures, the first time I venture out with the polyester body suit, and I get caught.* She'd taken every precaution, and even spent forty-five minutes on her makeup, but did her face appear proportionate to her over two-hundred-pound body? She could explain this situation if she had to. It wasn't catastrophic. Sure, it was a glitch in her research but not the end of the world.

She lifted her head and saw the old man from the park bench. His black earflaps pulled tight to his head.

"Here, try this," he said, handing her a cane. He stood with a wide stance and seemed to sway in a gust of wind.

"You sure you can spare it?"

"Don't waste time. Just get up."

Robbie steadied one leg under her. The aluminum didn't slide or sink when she pushed hard on the cane. *Come on. I can do this. It's just like getting out of a squat position, which I've done a thousand times.* With a heave, she stood. "Thank you." She handed the cane back to him.

"You're welcome." His palm wrapped around the curved handle.

Her wig felt like a visor on a cap. She reached round and gave it a quick tug. "Did you see those kids? I fell and they didn't even stop."

His breath wheezed in and out before he spoke. "Young hooligans. Nobody's safe."

She brushed dry grass and leaves from her coat and slacks, and glanced over her shoulder to see if all of her body parts were aligned. "I look like I've rolled around on the ground."

He leaned closer. "Can't be helped. If you land in the dirt, some is bound to stick." He plodded through the leaves with his head bent as if watching that each foot found a safe landing place. "When you came into the park, you reminded me of my Mabel. I was hoping we'd have a chance to meet."

Robbie heard the longing in his voice.

"Name's Frank Proctor. Frank by name and frank by nature."

She clasped his outstretched hand. "Robin Smyth." It wasn't an untruth. Robin Mary Smith was on her birth certificate, even though most people called her Robbie, but the slight surname change was part of her strategy. The tip sheets for maintaining a secret identity suggested the deception should be close to the truth. The truth was she didn't have to alter her stride to match her steps to his as they shuffled back to his bench. The bulk of her thighs helped considerably.

"I haven't seen you around the park before." He bent at the waist and lowered himself to the bench.

"I've been here." She'd waved to him many times when she'd run past him without her disguise. She just hadn't introduced herself before today. When she sat down beside him, the extra inches on her behind almost bounced her back to her feet.

"Relax. Enjoy the sun." He pulled a bag of cold toast from his pocket and passed her a piece.

As the geese began to paddle to the shore, she said, "The geese trust you."

He teased the bread into crumbs with bony fingers. "These here birds know me. I like to be outside. I live over there." He turned toward a seniors' care home, where she'd often seen men and women sitting on benches and in wheelchairs around the front door.

"How's that working out for you?" she asked. The man's legs looked like pencils covered in black socks extending from under his pant legs and into his Velcro-fastened running shoes.

"Not bad. There always seems to be too much food, so I share." He tossed the handful of crumbs toward the birds. After a brief moment, he spoke longingly. "I remember when my mouth used to water as soon as my hand touched the back doorknob of our home. My Mabel sure knew her way around the kitchen." He breathed deeply. "But Mabel, the kitchen, and the aroma of a good meal are all gone now."

"I'm sorry."

"It is what it is." He brushed crumbs off his hands and reached into his breast pocket, pulling out a worn leather wallet.

The guard goose honked an alert, and the geese waddled back to the water. A man about six foot two came toward them. His dark eyes focused on Frank. Frank gripped his cane against the man dressed all in black.

Robbie straightened her back and watched his quick feet and long legs nimbly sidestep the goose poop on the sidewalk. She held onto her cell phone. *Come on. Give your head a shake. I've been in this park many times and I've been safe. Just because this morning I was bullied, all of a sudden I'm ready to fend off the enemies around every corner.*

"Granddad," the man in black called.

"Jake?" Frank rubbed his eyes.

"Yes, it's me." The words held a smile.

Frank clamped his fingers on the bench rail and stood. Robbie watched as the stranger's two long arms swooped around Frank and wrapped him close to his chest. Seconds before his warm brown eyes closed, the stranger's five-o'clock-shadowed jaw relaxed and a smile pulled across straight white teeth.

Witnessing the love between these two men, she felt as if her heart grew larger, like the Grinch's Christmas heart that grew three times its size. With her hands supported on the bench, she stood. Should she wait and say goodbye, or should she just slip away? The stranger's brown eyes opened and his brow furrowed.

"When did you get here?" Frank asked his grandson as he slipped back onto the bench.

"A couple of hours ago. Just enough time to pick up the car and find you. Who's your friend?"

Frank turned and blinked.

Robbie extended her hand. "Robin Smyth."

The man reached past Frank, gripped her hand, and gave it a quick shake. "Jake Proctor." He drew his eyebrows together and met her gaze. She felt a glow of warmth readying her lips for a welcoming smile.

But then she watched him look down to her chest, past her protruding belly, to the length of her tree trunk legs and finally down to her black oxfords. She tugged at her jacket where it stretched across her chest. Was he going to ask her why she was wearing a costume? Halloween was last week. *Stop cowering. If he asks, I'll tell the truth.*

Instead, Jake turned away from her and squatted beside Frank.

Perhaps he didn't notice anything was amiss. Robbie was caught between pumping her fist into the air and whispering an enthusiastic "yes" and wondering when this man in black might ask her for an explanation. All of the hours she'd spent in the costume designer's studio getting the torso fitted and natural-looking, and the padding on the leggings which helped splay her legs at the proper angle had paid off. The hours she'd mixed colors in the theatrical makeup department dedicated to creating the illusion of a larger face and securing the right amount of wax along her gum line. The three different fittings to have a latex mold made for her neck had actually worked. Perhaps she appeared ordinary. Or didn't he really see her? Didn't he notice her curly auburn wig, her purple bling-encrusted eyeglasses? He wouldn't know that her eyes were a different color because he hadn't met her before. So she'd give him that break.

She put her arms on her hips. *Look at me!* she commanded silently. *See me as I am.*

Okay, Frank might have eyesight challenges because he wore glasses, plus his age and his apparent physical fragility wouldn't help. This Jake had the telltale fold that ran from his nose to the corners of his mouth that appear during a person's thirties. He didn't wear thick glasses, or if he didn't see well, his shoes would be spotted with goose droppings. He also said he had a car so he wasn't sight challenged.

She stared at Jake, but he only nodded at intervals as Frank spoke. He reached over and picked up Frank's open wallet from the bench.

When he looked at her, his eyes narrowed. "Do you meet my grandfather often?"

"No." She studied the bridge of his nose. "We've just met."

"Let the woman alone." Frank held his hand open for Jake to return his wallet. "She reminds me of your grandmother when we were young and still went to the movies and dances. Those were good days. After I convinced her to marry me, they only got better. You find a good woman yet?"

"Granddad, I worry about you." He raised an eyebrow at Robbie.

If it wasn't such a nicely shaped brow or, if his hair didn't fall playfully on his forehead, or even if he didn't have the broad shoulders that filled out his leather jacket, she might be worried. But most of all she enjoyed his height. For some inexplicable reason, she shifted and wondered how far she would need to stretch so their lips could meet. *Hello, Robbie, Frank's talking here.*

"You live too far away to worry very hard," Frank said.

"I'm here now." Jake nodded toward the worn billfold. "And your wallet is on the bench in plain view."

Robbie's cheeks burned. "You, you think I'm asking Frank for money?" She forced herself to stand straight and gripped her hands so she wouldn't brush at the dirt clinging to the front of her jacket and kept both feet on the ground so she wouldn't kick him in the shins. These solid shoes would give him a good bruise.

"For starters, you look as if you could use some clean clothes. There's bread on the bench. And there's the open wallet and a frail, old, man." His clipped words and flashing eyes when he nodded toward each item left no room for doubt as to exactly what he thought.

Struggling between her outrage and the genuine concern in Jake's eyes, she said, "Ah, Sherlock Holmes, I presume." *Nincompoop. Just goes to show a well-fitted jacket and height can disguise real character, too.*

"No." He put his hands behind his back and jutted his chin forward. "I'm a concerned grandson."

"Stop it, both of you," Frank growled. "Here's the picture of Mabel I wanted to show you before Jake turned up out of the blue." He handed his billfold to Robbie. Behind yellowed plastic was the image of a woman with dark curls smiling at the camera holding a baby wrapped in a blanket.

"That's our Mabel." He looked from Jake to Robbie.

"Yes." Jake stood behind Frank and his hands hung loosely at his side.

Robbie felt a sense of relief. She turned toward Jake and pointed at the baby. "You?"

"No." Jake sounded resigned. Robbie understood that sometimes a person just has to allow the story to be told.

"Girl, your glasses need cleaning? She's holding this boy's mother." Frank chuckled. "Mabel looked young until the day she died."

Jake reached toward Frank and spoke gently. "The nurses asked me to bring you back for a rest."

"Guess we'd better go. Don't want to rock the boat. They might take away my privileges." His lips were blue.

"Let me help you." Robbie felt his bird-like arm through his coat sleeve. "One good turn deserves another."

He patted her sleeve. "Maybe I'll see you again, Robin Girl," he said as he leaned into Jake.

She crossed her arms over her chest. "I'll watch for you. We'll protect each other against hooligans."

Jake's arm wrapped around Frank's back, making him appear protective and reassuring as he shortened his stride to match his grandfather's. The autumn light played across Jake's black leather jacket and dress pants as they moved toward the care home.

Robbie turned the opposite way toward the path that led to her street. Perspiration formed on her upper lip. Under her breasts, a rivulet of sweat trickled to her navel. While she placed one foot in front of the other, the breeze ruffling the sleeves of her jacket, she thought about the way Frank clung to his grandson and the familiar tone of the banter between them. She was fortunate she lived only eleven miles from her parents and often shared meals, ideas, and memories. She wondered why Jake had been away and why his return surprised Frank. From Frank's point of view, Jake had been away a very long time. Jake had the tanned look of someone who spent a great deal of time outdoors.

The flip of a curtain at the edge of the picture window across the street indicated Mrs. Mitchell wasn't quite as involved in her daytime TV. Robbie raised her hand and waved. The curtain dropped. *I'd better talk to her now or she'll be phoning the police when she sees a strange woman coming and going from my door.*

Robbie rang the doorbell and thought about what she might tell her neighbor. *The truth works or as close as possible.*

She heard the thump of the walker as it hit the floor in the front hallway. The door opened as far as the safety chain would allow. "Can I help you?"

The odor of stale air escaped and assaulted Robbie's nostrils. She reached up and rubbed her nose. "Hello, I'm visiting Robbie and she asked me to tell you not to worry when you see me coming and going."

"Don't try to fool an old lady. Are you friends?" Mrs. Mitchell's hearing aid squealed when she turned up the volume.

"Yes." *Truth. I am probably my own best friend right now.*

"Tell Robbie to give me a call when she gets home."

"All right. I will." She turned to leave.

"What did you say your name was?"

"Robin Smyth," she replied loudly.

"Oh. Pretty close to Robbie Smith, though you certainly don't look like her." Mrs. Mitchell adjusted her eyeglasses tighter to her eyes.

"No, I don't. I'll give Robbie the message." Robbie continued down the stairs and crossed the street before she heard Mrs. Mitchell's door close firmly.

Now I'm committed. Three people know me as Robin Smyth. She would have told Mrs. Mitchell the truth if she had opened the door and showed any sign of recognition. *I'll call Mrs. Mitchell later and tell her I have company staying with me or one day I'll open the door to our men in blue because she will have counted the times a so-called-friend unlocked my door.*

Robbie rummaged at the bottom of her jacket pocket and found her keys. A quick twist and the deadbolt slid away. *Home safe*. She stepped across the threshold and collapsed onto the stool. People accepted her and didn't question her appearance. All the time, energy, and money she had invested in her disguise for her master's thesis and just putting her head down and doing the work appeared to pay off today.

After kicking off her shoes and hanging up her coat, she slowly climbed the stairs to her bedroom. *Ha! I'm going to have to work harder to be stronger.* She slipped off the sweatshirt, threw her slacks into the hamper, then reached around, unhooked the bra, and unzipped her body suit. She let out a sigh of relief as she slid the last of the heavy padding from her arms. *Much better.* Now she knew that she'd need the cooling packs when she was indoors. Seeing body parts, the polyester torso with careful stitching around foam pendulum breasts, an apron belly, and the stuffed and dimpled leggings strewn on her bed was creepy. She arranged her wig on the stand, removed the latex neck roll, and finally rolled the wax away from around her gums and discarded the wet mass into the wastebasket. She felt the hot furnace air against her neck, then pushed her fingers through her sticky hair and reached for her dressing gown.

For months, she had felt something was missing from her research about women's weight and body image. Then Nadine, her professor's office administrator, challenged Robbie when she said, "You can research all you like, but you'll never understand what it truly means to be fat. You're tall, slim, with that cute short hair and amazing hazel eyes. It's different in your world than it is for some women."

Later on the same day, Robbie had opened the heavy door and pressed the bell for the meeting room. The security door had unlocked. She could still see the light reflected on the high-waxed tiles. The three women had been seated at a round table. Robbie had slumped into her chair at her meeting with the women who had volunteered to be part of her study. She looked around and said quietly, "A friend told me today I won't understand what it's like to be fat until I am."

Mavis shook out her shoulder-length sun-streaked hair and nodded. "Hello to you, too."

Sharon sighed and shrugged her shoulders, then crossed her thick calves and ankles, wearing her ever-present white socks and runners.

Margaret's fashion ring flashed while she drank from a glass of water before she said, "We agree. We just didn't know how to tell you."

"Sorry. Hi, thanks for being here." Robbie held her palms up on the table. "What am I going to do? I'm too far into this, and I need to defend this thesis by December." She thought about the hours of interviews, the writing and rewriting of her thesis statement.

"I'll wear one of those listening devices just like a PI, and you can hear what some people say to me," Mavis suggested as she flipped her hair behind one ear.

"Thanks, but you really can't count on someone being rude or insensitive every day."

The women looked at each other. "Oh yes, we can," they said in unison.

"But according to all of you, I still won't be close enough."

"How about you eat a lot?" Sharon asked. Sharon had been the first woman to volunteer. She wore white v-neck T-shirts and jean Capri pants even on the cool days.

"I couldn't gain enough weight in such a short time."

"How much do you like ice cream and brownies?" Mavis offered. "Baking is my passion." Her bangle bracelets chimed as they rode around her wrist while Mavis pretended to stir a mixture in a bowl.

"What about dressing up to look like you're fat? Men do it all the time. The movies are full of those characters. Whenever there's a costume party, men seem to find triple D bras and stuff them." Sharon stood and struck a pose showing off her assets. She flipped her chestnut braided hair across her shoulder and the end tipped toward her cleavage in the V of her shirt.

"I've been at those parties and watched the movies, too. It could work. Where would I start?" Robbie brought out her pen and paper from her backpack.

"You know you'd be doing something unusual, don't you? Women don't usually dress to look bigger," Margaret pointed out. She always appeared with full makeup and color-coordinated jackets, pants, shoes, and purse.

"I wonder why we don't want to take up space. They used to in the past. Remember bustles on skirts." Robbie tapped her pen on her teeth.

"But how about corsets? Haven't you been listening? It's hard in our world." Sharon stuffed her hands into her jean pocket.

Margaret leaned forward in her chair. "Or the new shape garments as they're calling them today. Have you ever seen a robust woman model one of those elastic numbers? The other day on a runway show, I could see the model's pelvic bones through the so-called shape wear and don't tell me they are designed for models. But you know I was tempted."

"Skinny wasn't exactly easy either. I was called chicken legs. Hmmm, is that why I took up running?" Robbie lifted her pant legs up showing how her childhood legs had been replaced by firm calves.

"Yeah, try fatty, fatty two by four can't get through the bathroom door so she pooped on the floor." Margaret mimicked a child's voice. Her blue eyes seemed brighter than minutes ago.

"Or, 'save some food for Biafra,'" Mavis added.

"Okay, it was harder for some of us than others. If I'm going to do this, I need to get started. My defense is the end of this semester. Any ideas?"

Sharon laughed. "We can lend you clothes but we have to brainstorm how you will fill them out."

Robbie sat straighter and leaned forward. If anyone could help her solve this dilemma, Mavis, Sharon, and Margaret would. They were talented and had many years of experience as plus-sized women.

"For your height, you could add another seventy-five pounds and still move around comfortably," Sharon suggested. "Watching the different women at the gym, you could be that size easy."

"Adding the appearance of over seventy pounds would bring me up to approximately two hundred and ten," Robbie calculated.

"Perfect. You start throwing around numbers over two hundred and people cringe," Sharon said, flipping her braid down her back again.

"I'd give my eye teeth to be two hundred and ten," Margaret added, snapping the closure on her black patent purse.

Robbie's cell phone alarm rang. "Time. I promised I wouldn't ask for more than two hours a meeting, and we're there."

Sharon rubbed her hands together. "This will be fun. We'll call the project, 'Fat like Me.'" Sharon paused. "I suggest we all go home and email Robbie our ideas. On Friday we can compare notes. I'll use my lunch hour for a little research."

Friday came and Margaret, Sharon, Mavis, and Robbie sat around the table in the meeting room and discussed their findings.

"How bad do you want to do this? It could be quite expensive," Sharon said. "I've found places where you can order a custom-made body suit by the same people who make the costumes for the sitcoms. They're not cheap." Some of her chestnut hair had escaped from her braid and she started to unwind it.

"I've found something closer to home. The costume department at the Globe Theatre has a line on a female robust torso we could alter. But it will cost," Margaret offered. "I asked Hubby if we could contribute to the project. He said he'd think about it, if you need extra."

"I've been researching as well, and I've decided if we can find a place to rent a suit, I'll spend my inheritance from my godmother. She hoped I'd use it for a trip after I graduated, but I can't graduate if I don't pass," Robbie said. "Thank you, Margaret. That is very kind of you to offer."

"Looks like we have a plan," Margaret said. "Do you want to call the Globe Theatre or should I? I might have an in, I used to volunteer on opening nights."

"I will call and if I have trouble I'll get back to you, Margaret. I'll keep you up-to-date until our next meeting with emails. Thank you for using your time for this."

"Are you kidding? It's our pleasure. This is as important to us as your grade is to you. This may be significant to many women out there. You never know who you will touch with just a little thing like putting on a pair of panties others would sneer at when they see them hanging on a clothesline or in a department store," Sharon said. The others nodded in agreement.

In the alcove, which had housed a buffet in her house's earlier days, Robbie typed in her password on her computer and transferred money for the project into her checking account. Then she called the Globe Theatre's costume department who were helpful and completed the order for the woman's torso and added speedy delivery. Robbie squeezed the alteration appointments into her busy schedule. The leggings had to be made to her height and the torso fitted at the shoulders and buttocks. The drama makeup students at the University of Regina helped create a latex chin roll. The 'Fat like Me' group booked a special meeting and shopped for a wig at The Hair Affair Salon.

"You should get a long wig. It would distract from your chin." Mavis plucked a blond wig from the mannequin.

"I disagree. I've been reading about people who disguise themselves to do undercover work, and they keep close to the truth, if possible. So I think a wig, similar to your own hair, but of course, fuller to balance your body." Margaret held a curly auburn wig over Robbie's head.

"Allow me to assist you." The salesclerk positioned the wig.

"Will it breathe? Do I have to have it styled?" Robbie asked. "I don't have a lot of time."

"This brand is very light, and you just have to shake it out and fluff it with your fingers. The curls bounce into shape." The clerk scrunched the curls between her fingers.

Sharon's white runners squeaked against the tiled floor. She handed Robbie dark-framed eyeglasses. "These are a fashion statement, no magnification. This salon has everything."

Mavis's bangle bracelets clattered when she twirled the chair and inspected Robbie from every angle. "Too bad you didn't have brown eyes. You would be perfect."

"I know people often comment on my hazel eyes," Robbie said. "Okay, time to brainstorm again."

"Your budget still okay?" Margaret asked. Her diamond rings shone in the store lighting.

"I'm okay. I'll have to buy some plus-sized clothes, of course," Robbie said.

"Would you consider splurging on a pair of tinted contacts?" Mavis glanced at a pamphlet from the counter.

"Good idea. I'll check with an optometrist and get some advice."

"You be careful. You wouldn't want to hurt yourself for this," Margaret called from the settee.

"I will. It isn't necessary. It's just an added dimension,

right?" Robbie repositioned the glasses on her nose. "Maybe I'll get fitted frames, too."

"A common eye color and a pair of fabulous glasses with a little bling would synch the disguise." Robbie stepped back tilted her head.

"If something is a little off, people may just ignore it if you look put together," Margaret added, smoothing her navy colored jacket.

"A woman once said to me she'd never met a fat pair of eyes." Margaret pushed herself out of the grips of the valor cushions, glanced into the mirror, then applied lipstick and blotted her lips with a tissue.

Robbie stood behind Margaret and scrutinized Margaret's blue eyes in the mirror. "She was right. Eyes show many things, but body weight is not one of them."

Robbie swiped her debit card, keyed in her PIN number, and paid for her fabulous wig.

After they left the shop, Robbie said, "Mavis, Sharon, Margaret, you've been terrific. Anyone want to go for coffee?" The fall wind scattered the leaves piled in the corner of the entrance.

"There's an English Tea House on Second Avenue. We can meet there."

"Mavis, you're always in the know." Sharon opened the car door.

"Anyone want to ride with me?" Robbie asked.

"We're good. We all came together. We'll just meet there," Margaret called from the back seat of Mavis' van.

On a Friday afternoon, the vehicles moved steadily through the traffic lights.

Robbie parked next to Mavis's van. She opened the door of the Tea House where flowered teapots and china were displayed on cabinets and shelves. She inhaled the exotic aroma of spiced teas and fresh scones.

"Mavis, how did you beat me here?" Robbie asked.

The three women each had a bone china teacup and a teapot covered in a tea cozy in front of them.

"Good karma. I hit all of the green lights." Mavis brushed her fingertips on her shoulder.

"It's too bad Erin and Nicole couldn't be here," Sharon said, unshed tears glistening in her brown eyes.

Sadness drifted over the table.

"I know we're doing this for all the Erins who die trying to be thin," Sharon said, picking a piece of scone from her chest.

"I just know Nicole will come back and look us up again someday." Mavis tried hard for her expression to match her sun-streaked hair.

"We can hope." Margaret looked out the window as if the possibility existed that Nicole would walk across the parking lot at this very instant. "She's my friend on Facebook. I receive updates on her timeline. She seems to be just going along as best that she can without her best friend." Margaret dabbed a spot of tea from her silk scarf.

"I'm glad," Robbie replied and concentrated her attention toward the list of teas available until her eyes cleared of the momentary tears. "I'll have the chocolate mint oolong." She passed the menu to the matronly woman hovering at her elbow.

After the server left, Mavis brought a shopping bag from under the table. "We pooled our resources and brought this for you."

"Don't go all misty-eyed on us. We're a team," Sharon cautioned as she passed Robbie a serviette.

Margaret reached over and patted Robbie's hand. "This is temporary. We want all of the items back."

"Okay then." Robbie put the gift bag on the floor and parted the tissue paper. She lifted a teal blouse. "This was Erin's favorite color. Thank you."

She removed the next item and said, "I remember your amethyst ring, Margaret, thank you."

"You're welcome. You'll need something to balance your hands."

Peeking at the last item in the gift bag, Robbie said, "I can guess who lent me the slacks. Thank you, Mavis."

"We're about the same height, and there's an elastic waistband so it will sit comfortably."

"Reach down deep. There's something else."

Robbie reached into the bag beneath the pants and drew out an animal print scarf.

"Got to get your sexy on, as Erin used to say." Margaret blushed.

Emotion threatened to clog in her throat, so she shot to her feet and hugged each woman in turn.

"Thank you. Now all I have to do is get out there and research without embarrassing any of you or giving Professor Clifton any reason to pull the plug on my thesis."

"She wouldn't, would she?" Sharon thumped the table.

"She could, but not if I conduct my research with all of the sensitivity you've taught me."

Robbie dribbled the last of her tea from her pot, raised her teacup, and saluted. "To success."

The other three women clinked cups. "Success."

The hot air furnace billowed the white lace window curtains. The cedar potpourri filled the air. Robbie lifted the torso from her bed. *I will be successful. I will.* She wiped the inside of the body cavity with a special cleaner to kill body odor germs. It felt as if the brainstorming, wig purchase, contact fittings, and glasses happened yesterday, but the transformation had taken two very full and busy weeks. So if Sherlock Holmes Jake didn't report her to the care home security, she could continue her research, which Margaret, Sharon, and Mavis dubbed 'FLM'.

She hung the torso and leggings in the closet, then flipped a pair of jeans from the hanger and chose a T-shirt from the drawer. She had thirty minutes to shower, change, and drive to the university for her conference with Dr. Clifton, her thesis advisor.

If only she had a sympathetic advisor who would accept her need to research disguised as Robin Smyth, but Critical Clifton was suspicious of any anecdotal and field research.

After her shower, Robbie dressed in her jeans and periwinkle blue fleece jacket, applied lip gloss, and tipped her lashes with mascara. *Get a move on or Clifton will be tapping her red pen all over my papers.* This professor hated to be kept waiting.

Robbie slung her backpack over one shoulder, twisted her key in the deadbolt, pressed the button on the remote opening the garage door, jumped in her Ford Focus and backed out of the garage. The traffic was sparse around University Park Drive, and Mavis's karma was on her side when every traffic light was green. She waited for another student to reverse out of a parking spot close to the building. Robbie swung her backpack onto her shoulder and marched toward the Humanities offices.

Even though the sun streamed into Frank's window, Jake tucked a blanket around his grandfather's shoulders. In the corner was the brown corduroy recliner that had been in their family living room for as long as Jake could remember. On the bulletin board was a collage of family photos. Pictures of Jake bent over a birthday cake blowing out various numbers of flames on candles and his grandma always beaming with pride. Jake tearing Christmas wrap off of a parcel. Jake leaning into his grandmother's shoulder while watching TV on the cabbage-rose upholstered sofa. Jake dressed in his graduation gown holding onto his degree. Jake posed with the elders of the !Kung San people in the Kalahari Desert. Fastened in the corner of the frame, Jake wrapped in a blanket in his mother's arms. He peered closely at his mother's photo. He had her brown eyes and dark complexion. She had died before he had taken his first steps and the man, not a father but the sperm donor, either didn't know or didn't care. Jake's grandparents were the only parents he knew.

On the bedside table was a photograph of his grandparents with their arms around each other. He knew they were proud of his education and career, but his grandmother had wanted to see him settled into family life before she died two years ago. He had disappointed her.

He took one last look at Frank's closed eyes, walked down the corridor and out of Care Manor past the smokers sitting around the ashtray in front of the building. The air stung his nostrils as he breathed. The frozen pavement had occasional patches of frost when he crossed the street to his vintage Mustang convertible. It had been his mother's before she died and this car was his only tangible evidence of his childhood and teenage years. As soon as he grasped the door handle, his hand tingled, just like it used to when his grandfather drove the car out of the garage. Washing off the accumulated dust and rubbing cloths slick with turtle wax along the paint until he could comb his hair in the mirrored hood had made him feel he was a part of his mother. He remembered sitting in the dark garage just listening to the radio. After he passed his driving course he had cruised thesis would be defended by then. Until she knew more, she'd be careful and make sure Jake Proctor wasn't around when she went to the park in her disguise.

While she waited, she tried focusing on her possible responses to Dr. Clifton's questions, but Nadine's fingernails clicking on the keyboard seemingly in rhythm to a song on the radio combined with Dr. Clifton's laughter echoing in the hall kept disrupting her concentration. *Focus, focus. Robbie, you have to focus.*

Nadine's keyboarding stopped. She put her chin in her palm and said, "I sure hope he has a lot of questions tomorrow."

"Tomorrow. You're kidding, right?" Robbie groaned.

"What's with you? A new face is always a pleasure, especially one with that rugged shadow. Yum." Nadine winked. Her white teeth contrasted against her coffee-toned lip gloss.

"Nothing's wrong. I'm just surprised. Do you suppose he shaves like that or does his beard really grow that quickly?"

"I don't care, just so long as I see it often," Nadine said, plucking the phone from its cradle.

Until Robbie came up with a better solution, she would fly under his radar at the university, too.

The outer door swung open. Dr. Clifton leaned on Nadine's desk. "Jake will check in tomorrow. If there's anything he needs, I've told him I'm available." From behind her notebook, Robbie watched Dr. Clifton scan the room. "You can come in now."

Robbie closed her notebook and picked up her backpack. She knew Clifton's previous laughter wasn't going to change her professor's attitude toward their interview.

In the office, Clifton sat in her chair rolled up to the desk, which held an aquarium with a bright blue-patterned Betta fish and a box of tissue ready for any tearful, stressed student. Robbie felt as if a starting-pistol fired when her advisor picked up the top file from a stack of a half dozen, then opened the buff folder.

From her guest chair, Robbie saw red pen scrawls in the margins of her thesis manuscript. If only she could read upside down. At any rate, the signs weren't promising. Just a week earlier, Robbie had endured a mini-lecture from her professor about her need for attention undermining her academic credibility, or so the professor said. Robbie was running the risk of misappropriating the identity of heavy women and could, therefore, jeopardize the respect that Clifton had built for the department. And now she suspected the lecture continued.

"If you insist on parading around in this so-called get-up you've described here, you could end up in trouble," Dr. Clifton said. "Big trouble."

"What exactly are you suggesting?"

"We've had students expelled from programs or, at the very least, given a conditional pass with major revisions. Are you prepared for those consequences?"

Robbie pressed her spine against the contoured back of the chair and counted to ten before answering. She had spent eight months listening to women, and she was not going to be thrown off track now. Many had urged Robbie to learn more about the issues facing women who were large.

"This has nothing to do with getting attention," Robbie said. "The women in my group want me to walk a mile in their shoes."

"Cliché."

"Historically, women padded and corseted themselves to conform to the ideal shape of their time. I'm changing my body to experience what society suggests is a disgrace when a woman can't control her body size." Robbie pressed her notes onto her knees to quiet the rustling of papers caused by her trembling hands.

had accused her of trying to fleece an old man just because she had dirt on her body and her wig was askew.

As she continued walking, she felt like she was in the main street at high noon, and was sure Clifton's eyes were boring a hole in her back. She shivered slightly before finally turning the corner, holding the tissue to her cheek. Who was she kidding, a lowly student? She stuffed the tissue into a side pouch of her backpack. Besides, Jake could make trouble for her if he found out she was the same person he'd encountered in the park this morning; the rules were professors hung out with other professors.

She kept her MP3 player in her pocket until she was hidden behind the bookshelves in the library. *What a roaring mess I can make, not once but twice within the same day. First, I'm accused of being a female predator; the next I'm a bumbling student staring awestruck at his five o'clock shadow on his strong jaw. The universe is reminding me to have a social life. But not today. I've got work to do.*

Chapter 3

At 8:30 a.m. on Saturday morning, Robbie set her coffee cup on top of her vanity, which rested in front of a bedroom mirror with a bright makeup light above. Her hazel eyes were the first frontier in her face. She placed a chestnut brown contact on her index finger and positioned it in her left eye and then repeated the procedure for the right. The deep color brought a protective, stable gaze to her reflection. Her eyes were her window to feelings. She needed to protect this project from prying eyes. On the side of the mirror she had taped a sketch that looked like a paint-by-number drawing, the precise transformation instructions for her face. She dotted and then blended concealer under her eyes. By using different shades, Monique, the makeup maven, had taught her how to create illusions of shadow, depth, and definition to specific areas. Instead of highlighting her cheekbones with a contour brush, she applied makeup to the top portion of her cheeks making them appear round and full with a light, flesh-toned pressed powder. Robbie accentuated her nose by lightening the areas around her nostrils and brushed light-tone makeup along the lower half, emphasizing the shape of her jaw. Her natural bone structure was her guide. Pressing the softened wax along her gum line plumped up her mouth. The lighter shade applied outside her natural lip line created the illusion of a fuller face. She leaned closer to the mirror, then applied the foundation onto a foam sponge and blended with the facial contours. The effect was a natural veil, allowing the shadows and highlights to show through.

Robbie parked her car at a mall entrance. She turned her body and stretched her legs so her feet were touching pavement and then grabbed onto the door and swiveled her body on the seat, extracting herself from her previous familiar space. Compact cars were made for compact people. She smacked her forehead, no wonder Margaret, Sharon, or Mavis didn't want to ride in her car. The big mall doors opened smoothly and she sauntered down the hall toward The Better Half. Nadine was right. The store sign advertised sizes for full-figured women, for women who had dimples in more places than just around a smile. This was the place for her. The store was well lit with plenty of space for maneuvering around the clothing racks. There were emerald greens, royal blues, and deep pinks—so many choices besides black. A middle-aged sales clerk approached her. "Can I help you find something?"

"I can't believe I haven't been in your store before. I'd like to purchase some fall clothes."

"What do you have in mind?"

"I'm looking for a business suit for an interview with a corporation, something stylish for a high school reunion, and some casual outfits."

"You've come to the right place. Here are the corduroy pants and light sweater tops. Our formal wear is in the back left, and the business attire is on the right. By the way, there are sizing charts on the pillars around the store."

"Thank you so much. I'll browse."

"When you're ready, you can take your selections to the fitting area over there." The clerk pointed with her perfectly manicured index finger.

The dressing rooms were spacious, furnished with a chair, and the full-sized door went from way past the top of Robbie's head to the floor. There wasn't any chance of anyone seeing things they shouldn't. It was a luxury to sit and pull on slacks rather than trying to balance on one foot.

Robbie had picked out a gray skirt and jacket for the interview, some matching tights, and a crisp white blouse, as well as a couple of pantsuits.

The other shoppers were busy carrying armloads of clothes into the fitting rooms. No one paid attention to her.

She twirled in front of the mirror. Normally, her clothes were purchased to accentuate her modest figure, but this fabric clung to her bust, complimenting the voluptuous curves. This was going to be easier than she thought. Sitting, she started tugging on the tights. She reached her mid calf when sweat beaded on her forehead. Talk about one inch forward, two back. She would wear pantsuits for the interview as well as the high school reunion.

"Would you like any help?"

Robbie's breaths came in quick, agitated puffs. Her voice was high and squeaky. She couldn't risk anyone seeing her in this get-up, but getting in and out of these clothes was proving a chore. "Could I have a size twenty-two in these?" Standing behind the door, and out of sight of the mirror behind her, Robbie handed the salesclerk the lavender embroidered, beaded jacket, and five-pocket blue jeans.

After several more exchanges, Robbie felt she'd done the best she could with what she had, and it wouldn't use all of her godmother's money, either.

With two shopping bags full of new clothes, Robbie strolled toward the door when the salesclerk motioned to her. "Now you come back when you need more clothes. We'll be getting in a whole new Christmas line next week. You'd look good in a deep, sexy red."

"Thanks. Sexy red could be interesting." Robbie waved, then with her shopping bags in hand she meandered through the mall. At a trendy boutique, she saw a red dress. *Do I dare spend money on a red dress?* A sales clerk met her just inside the door and said, "Sorry, we don't have anything in your size."

Jake felt as if he'd been sucker-punched in the gut. Could the rumors about padding his expense account have followed him? Was it general news? No, it couldn't be. He'd upset her again. He'd obviously touched on a sensitive issue.

He watched Robin's generous hips sway while she labored around the sofas toward the doors. He wondered whether she had been ill and there was a reason for the wig. He witnessed her humiliation due to some designer's idea of convenience to weld seats to tables so they what? Couldn't be stolen, or so that the cleaners could mop under them in record time? The Bushmen, with whom he had lived for three months, believed all people were part of the world. Why hadn't his society gotten it right?

He followed other shoppers through the mall door, jamming his hands into his jacket pockets as he headed for his car. He had meant to purchase gloves but Robin, with her dignity and generous nature, made him forget this practical need. She reminded him that he wanted to care about and handle essential matters, first. Right now the only thing he wanted to do was to be with his granddad as often as he could be.

The Mustang wanted to surge past the speed limit as he gripped the steering wheel and pressed his foot hard on the accelerator. He couldn't be late for his appointment with his grandfather's doctor. The reason must be important for the doctor to see him on the weekend.

Chapter 4

Robbie drove home and levered herself out of her car, then gathered her parcels and struggled up the walk to the front stairs, her purse and shopping bags dangling off her arm like charms on a bracelet. Mavis's bangles had nothing on her now. Coffee, what was she thinking? She needed to go to the bathroom. The costume designer *had* suggested she minimize her fluid intake.

She kicked off her loafers, dropped everything, and hurried up the stairs while she grappled with her coat. When she reached the bathroom, she slid down the slacks and quickly undid the crotch snaps, pulled up her belly, and slid down the leggings. *Whew!*

When she put herself back together, her shopping bags were tipped and spilled in her front entrance, just where she'd dropped them. She examined the emerald green long sleeve T-shirt. It was just the thing for her to wear for her first visit to see Frank in his environment. Even though Jake would think she's doing a job, she wanted to go for Frank because at the end of his life, she reminded him of happier days. *Robbie, be honest, these visits will help your research as well.*

She stripped off the sweatshirt, cut the tags from her new shirt, and slid the plus-sized garment over her head. She felt better already as she wound her scarf tight and put on her gloves. Her wig kept her head warm. Her coat was lightweight but with the extra padding over her body, she really didn't need anything warmer.

As she locked her door, she saw Mrs. Mitchell's curtain flip again. *I have to remember to phone her when I get back.* She gave a little wave and turned down the street to the entrance to the park, then down the paved walkway alongside the lake toward Care Manor. She and all of the residents in the Care Manor were neighbors. If she weren't involved in this research, how long would it have taken her to come to this simple realization and drop in for a visit?

Every parking space was taken. Of course. Saturday afternoon, visiting hours. She looked around. *So any of you belong to Big Spender Jake? He probably drives an oversized pick-up truck to haul his load of assumptions with him.* She didn't want to see him any time soon because she might just swing her satchel at him. It would have been easier if Frank had been outside, but he wasn't. She checked her wig and makeup in the reflection on the glass front door. The thought of running naked in the snow kept resurfacing while rivulets of perspiration settled around her belly. The costume's cleaning instructions were precise; she should wipe the inside down and then every other day rinse the body suit gently and hang to dry. Tonight was definitely a hang-to-dry evening.

Robbie signed the visitor book and with Frank's room number on a piece of paper crushed in her palm, she plodded down the hall. The Candy Striper stopped her juice cart. "Are you all right, Miss? I can get you a wheelchair if it would make visiting easier. You're looking very warm."

Robbie pictured herself seated and with her arms stretched to the sides trying to roll the wheels and stay in a straight line. "Thank you for the offer, but I'm fine." She directed every last bit of energy to her feet. If she'd stayed home with her feet up, she wouldn't look as if she'd just completed a track run rather than a walk across the park. She'd have to sit while she visited with Frank.

When she reached his room, she tapped on the partially open door, then nudged it with her hip. The door swung open to Jake sitting in a lazy chair. The sweet greeting slipped back behind her lips and she felt every ounce of cotton and latex pulling at her muscles. Jake put a finger to his lips and pointed to the bed. She stood half in and half out of the room.

As if sensing her presence, Frank sat up and rubbed his eyes. "Don't anyone ever let me sleep through company."

Robbie focused on Frank, noting the lavender crescents settling under each puffy lower lid and the pale draped folds of skin stretched into a smile. She stepped forward and reached for Frank's hand. "Hi. The geese send their greetings." She smiled. *Fake it until you make it*. She leaned on the bed with gratitude, because the only visible chair had Jake with his half-baked ideas sitting in it.

"Hang your coat on the hook behind the door and sit yourself right up here beside me. It's been a while since I've had a woman in my bed," Frank chortled.

Exhaustion hung around her lips before she collected herself. She slipped out of her coat and hung it up. Then she hoisted her bottom toward the center of the bed and let her loafers fall to the floor. "Don't mind if I do. It's been awhile since I've crawled into a man's bed while company looked on."

Frank let out a huge laugh. "Jakey's used to seeing me and his grandma in bed together."

"Granddad, you know this is different," Jake said as he leaned forward in the lazy chair. "Robin isn't Grandma." There was a hint of puzzlement under his words.

"Jackass." Frank supported himself up on his elbows. "Wipe those lines from your forehead, boy. Of course I know that Robin isn't your Grandma. I'm not senile, just dying."

Robbie felt her grin widen. Poor Jake. Chump. Jackass. He'd been downgraded on the insult chain.

She drew a parcel from her oversized purple satchel. "Here, Frank. I thought you could do with some meat on your bones. People are always giving me chocolates. I've got pounds to spare."

"Thanks. Turtles. My favorite. Want one, Jake?" Frank held the box with fragile fingers.

"My favorite, too." He strolled over to the bed. "Push over, you two."

"Snuggle in beside me, boy," Frank said.

Robbie's heart thumped like an uneven load of laundry in a spin cycle. She gripped the lowered bed rail. She could see herself rolling onto the floor with no way of getting up. "I'll take the chair if you're giving it up."

"Haven't you shared a bed with two men before?" Jake asked, eyebrow raised.

Two can play at whatever game he was into now. "Every day for a whole summer," she said.

His mouth tightened at her response.

She smoothed her green T-shirt across her ample chest. "You don't believe me."

His thighs nudged the mattress. "It must have been a king-size bed."

"No, just a double." Her smile slipped its smirk when she watched the muscles in his thighs strain against the fabric of his pants when he placed one knee onto the mattress.

"No, wait. I was five and my cousins were three and four."

"Okay, you two, remember there's an old man who's dying here. I take it back, Jake, there's not enough room for all of us in this bed. One of you has got to go."

Jake watched her for a few more seconds, then he reached into the box of chocolates and popped a turtle into his mouth before he sauntered back to the chair. After he settled back into it, she found herself mesmerized as he licked the tip of his thumb and index finger and winked. She crossed one ankle over the other and concentrated on the fringe of her scarf. *Naked in the snow bank, naked in the snow bank.* Was he flirting with her? Or had her heated body and perspiration shorted out some wires in her emotional circuits? She shrugged and hoped she didn't look as confused as she felt.

She'd read books suggesting that when a woman wanted a man to notice her, she should mimic his movements. Her fingers wound around the bedspread to keep them away from her lips. *Did she really want him to notice her as a woman? Of course she did. In or out of disguise, she was a woman and he was a handsome man.* She lowered her eyelids and she brought her fingertip to her mouth and her tongue flicked over the tip.

"Robin, are you in there?"

When she turned back, Frank seemed to have been poking her arm, but it was difficult to feel through the cotton layers. She stared at the spot. "Ouch. Of course I'm here, where'd you think I was?" Though foreign to her true body, she reached over and rubbed her forearm.

If Frank hadn't said something to her, she would have forgotten where she was and done something to blow her cover.

"Frank, when we met in the park, you said you were Frank by name and nature. Would you share some of your life stories with me?" she asked. "I'd like to visit more often and hear them."

"Why'd you want to spend time with an old man when there are plenty of young men around?" He looked directly at Jake.

"I took a sociology course a few years back and the professor said we should know our elders, and it'll help us understand who we are. My grandparents passed on before I asked them about their lives, so I thought I'd ask you." She reached for his hand.

"Sure, girlie, you come around when you want to, and if I'm not visiting with the queen, I'd be glad to have a chat with you." Then he looked over at Jake. "Guess I still have some usefulness left."

"Of course you do, Granddad." Jake leaned forward. "I came back so we can spend time with each other, too."

"Robin, you know Jake here is a doctor. Doctor Proctor. Sure has a funny ring to it. Good thing you're not a proctologist." Frank gave another raucous laugh.

Jake grimaced. "You always enjoy a good word association, Granddad."

"What kind of doctor are you?" Robbie asked, knowing full well, but having to keep up the guise.

Frank wiped his eyes and turned to her. "My boy here studies people."

"A psychologist?" Robbie watched Jake.

"No, an anthropologist," Frank said. "He goes away and writes about groups of people and their roots. Guess it will do me good to remember the past and maybe good for both of you to hear." Frank sank back into his pillows with a sigh.

"As much as these two girls"—she patted her thighs—"enjoyed our little rest, we've got to get going. We've got things to do and people to see." She levered her elbows into the hard plastic-covered mattress and managed to twist with a minimum of decorum, dangling her legs over the side of the bed.

Jake was at the bedside in a flash. "You're wearing your new shoes." He picked up her shoes and placed them on each foot. "I used to do this for Grandma when I was around. Remember, Granddad?"

"Said it made her feel like a princess, but she was really our queen."

Robbie saw Frank's throat muscles tighten as he swallowed hard.

She clasped Frank's hand and kissed his cheek before sliding off the bed.

"See you guys," she said as she folded her coat over her arm and then stepped into the cool corridor.

Jake took Robin's place on the bed and draped his arm around Frank's shoulders. "Granddad, do I have to sign any papers allowing Robin to visit whenever she can?"

"Ask at the information desk. It'd be nice if she came around. There's something different about her."

"You really miss Grandma."

Frank sighed. "We were together a long time."

"Are you strong enough to talk for a few minute?" Jake asked.

Frank snuggled against Jake's arm. "Depends. No, I don't need any."

"Always the jokester." Jake tapped Frank's shoulder.

"Ouch."

Jake jumped away.

"Just kidding." A grin spread across Frank's lips.

"What do you know about your leukemia?" Sometimes asking straightforward questions was the best way.

"So you've spoken with Dr. Alley," Frank said softly. "I'm glad."

"Thanks for having him call and giving permission for me to meet with him."

"Thought it was easier if the news came from the doctor." Frank closed his eyes and spoke. "My leukemia is acute. Didn't know I had it. Thought I had the flu but when the blood work came back, the results said something else. Talked with the specialist and because I'm old . . ." He stopped and took a couple of deep breaths.

Jake waited, knowing what the doctor had told him, but

also wanting to know how his grandfather interpreted the information.

"The chemotherapy doesn't work well on us old guys as it does on the young. Besides, that toxic stuff is hard on the body. Doc said it wouldn't give me much more time anyway. That what he told you?" Frank turned toward him.

Jake nodded. "Said you could have a year."

Frank reached for Jake's hand. "Or less. I asked for the palliative care route, where they take care of the pain and keep me comfortable."

"I'll be here making sure your wishes are met," Jake said with conviction.

"Thanks, son. Now enough about me, tell me about your latest research." Frank had a bluish tinge around his lips.

"I see you have the photo of me while I lived with !Kung San in the Kalahari Desert on your bulletin board, thanks. They're an ancient culture of hunters and gatherers. Their language is hard to translate because it has a series of clicks and pops. It's like listening to someone snapping their gum and talking."

Frank's eyes closed, but Jake continued, knowing he was listening. "They share any little food they have with everyone around, including strangers."

"Grandma always served the best she could to company."

"She sure did." Jake remembered fresh buns at least once a week, homemade soups for lunch, and when company came, the table glowed like a buffet line.

Soon Frank's mouth fell open and spittle settled in the corners of his lips. He was sound asleep. Jake leaned over and kissed his grandfather's cheek. Frank and Mabel had always kissed each other before they left and kissed again on their return. Grandma always kissed him, too. His heart slowed. He hadn't been kissed with such accepting love in a very long time.

Jake closed the door quietly and stopped at the administration office. He changed the first contact number to his cell, then the university, lastly the hotel. He reviewed all of the forms the doctor suggested and he wrote Robin's name on the special visitor's list.

When the front door slid open, Jake looked across to the park he saw the geese along the shore but the bench was empty. He hoped Robin Smyth would visit Frank often because he just couldn't be there all the time. The doctor had been kind but firm that a year without treatment was optimistic. He'd pay whatever Robin wanted to be sure Frank didn't spend too much time alone.

Monday morning, Nadine seemed lost in thought when Robbie asked her to put the revised thesis pages into the professor's mailbox.

"She's not in right now," Nadine explained. "She took tall, dark, Jake to lunch."

"Oh." Robbie leaned against the desk. *Thank you, Jake Proctor.*

"Have you seen him on campus? He's easy on the eyes."

Nadine was wearing gold dangling earrings that slipped below her styled hair. She tugged on them while she swooned over Jake.

"Nadine, are you drooling over a man just because he has a great body while you work in the heart of the women's studies programs?"

"So you agree!"

"I have noticed, but there has to be more to him than a broad back and a dark shadow over his strong jawline and you know it. I've been treated like an object, I understand what you're doing to him."

"Objectification may be better than not being noticed at all. Besides you know that a strong jaw says the man eats healthy and exercises." Nadine sighed.

"What's up with you? You work here, you've seen the studies about self-esteem torn to shreds because of someone noticing or not. We're supposed to know better."

"I have, honey, and I do know better, but right now this is personal. I'm trying to find a way to make Ken understand I'm worth seeing."

"Who's Ken?" Robbie studied Nadine's round face, soft eyes, and wistful smile.

"He's a real sweetie. I met him at the sociology social on Saturday."

"You're so lucky. You meet men. I've been so busy, the only guy who sees me regularly is one very sweet gentleman who feeds the birds. I run past him and wave and he waves back, if he isn't focused on the geese." Robbie hesitated. "Hmm"—she leaned over the counter—"he knows me in the body suit. I've been visiting him as Robin. He's old and dying and I remind him of happier days. He has a grandson, too, who I see occasionally."

"So, you're using them as part of your case study?"

"Yes." Robbie leaned away from Nadine as if even a small distance might improve the necessary deception.

"And they don't know who you really are?" Nadine asked.

"No, I'm considering this part of my field research."

"Your suit must be something. Remember, you're going to show me one day real soon?"

Robbie stroked her chin. "I have more outings planned before I put the suit away, but I'm being cautious. I can't have any complaints or draw negative attention to this research. I will try."

"I understand. Just let me know if and when it will work. I want you to finish your degree and graduate this semester, too." Nadine gave Robbie's hand a gentle squeeze.

Robbie swallowed her fears and changed the subject. "I do have a small social life. I'm seeing Brad on Friday."

"What fancy event is he taking you to this time?"

"Brad skimped on the fundraiser details. He promised a good dinner and networking possibilities for the pleasure of my company. Besides remember, he has a partner."

Robbie leaned closer and concentrated on the candy bowl on Nadine's desk. "If this Ken can't see what a wonderful woman you are—drop him now." Then she popped a candy in her mouth and opened the door to the corridor.

Nadine's laughter rose and fell as Robbie closed the door behind her.

During the week, Robbie became Robin with more and more confidence. Her jewelry and vibrant blue or green shirts accentuated her style. She walked faster and didn't bump into nearly as many doorframes or chairs.

Her chest tightened as she thought of her last visit with Frank. He was dying, but he seemed ready. She'd been visiting him every day while Jake taught or met with students at the university. They spoke of the weather and how he wouldn't miss the minus double-digit weather. He wondered if the geese would miss him. He knew they wouldn't, but he would miss not seeing them again. Usually one of the other residents popped in to see how Frank was doing and then he'd ask them about their day and the conversations would shift away from the coming end and focus on the present. She felt a knot lodge in her throat. Frank had become such a part of her life she couldn't imagine a world without him.

Friday evening, from her front room window, Robbie watched the light fade in the late afternoon sky. The bare poplars were silhouetted against the pinks and oranges of the sunset. Where was Brad? She tapped the foot of her high heel. He was supposed to have picked her up fifteen minutes ago. She blew out a breath of frustration and hugged the chiffon jacket closer to her chest.

If Brad weren't a childhood friend, she'd have begged off tonight. Lights from an approaching car lit up the street. The black Celica stopped against the curve. She watched Brad swing open the door and jog up her stairs. After she answered the door to his familiar knock, he embraced her, feathering her cheek with a kiss without disturbing her makeup. Holding her at arm's length, he turned his head to one side and analyzed her appearance. "I'm in the running with you on my arm tonight."

Robbie's stomach quivered. "Is my appearance really all that important?"

"Of course. You're my best business function date." His shoulders slumped. He reached for her hand.

In her two-inch heels they were eye-to-eye. Every black hair on his head was in exactly the right place. His beard was a slight blue shadow against his dark skin. He could be a poster man for *GQ* in his tuxedo.

"The big boss wants to see the choices we've made in all aspects of our lives."

"Brad, what choice is your boss going to assume tonight? I've accompanied you on a half dozen occasions."

He met her eyes. "Robbie, this is a big career move. When the time is right, I'll break the news gently." He brought a jeweler's box from his pocket and flipped it open. "If you wear this, he'll assume even more."

Robbie glanced down at the solitaire diamond. "No, Brad."

"You don't have to acknowledge anything. Just wear it. Guys never ask or gush over a ring. They just see it and take for granted something permanent may be in the future."

"What about Sam?" Her life was getting very complicated. She'd forget who Robbie was if she wasn't careful.

"He suggested it. This was his mother's ring. When I'm stable, he and I can be an open couple."

"Sorry, Brad. It's one thing to be your date and it's another altogether to pretend we're planning a future."

He shrugged. "Sam loses twenty bucks. I didn't think you'd go for it." He straightened his bow tie in the mirror and winked. "We're a very impressive couple anyway. Ready?"

She enjoyed her dates with Brad where she networked and met some of the influential business people in the city. The conversations with regard to new taxations and new community ventures were enlightening. The last dinner she'd attended she heard about an inner city project where piano teachers volunteered their time to teach at-risk youth living in disadvantaged situations. The students were allowed to practice on donated pianos at the schools.

"I always learn something new about our city or Province when I go out with you. I wonder what it will be tonight," she said as she locked the door.

He guided her toward his glossy black sports car idling at the curb, held her arm until she was settled on the warm leather seat, and then drove confidently down the street.

She turned toward him. "Any idea about the main speaker tonight?"

"I haven't a clue. It was supposed to be the boss's favorite cause but that someone got sick and cancelled, so there is a substitute guest speaker."

When they approached the hotel door, a valet greeted them. Brad looped his arm through hers as they walked along the carpeted hallway to the Regency Ballroom. Inside, the chandelier glowed with miniature lights, reminding

Robbie of the way Frank's eyes twinkled when he talked about his wife, Mabel. Tearing herself from her thoughts, Robbie clung to her chiffon jacket as Brad helped her out of her coat. The president, Mr. Lawson, of Lawson Supply Management, called to Brad. Robbie stayed by his side for a few minutes, smiling and waving at familiar faces and hearing snippets of conversation about the new customer Mr. Lawson wanted Brad to begin designing a complex computer network proposal immediately, if not sooner.

The sequins and tuxedoes parted and allowed someone seemingly important to enter the ballroom. Her hand flew to her lips. The distinguished couple consisted of Jake, looking ever so handsome in a stunning black tuxedo and Jean Clifton, the rail-thin body dressed in white practically glued to Jake's side.

Robbie swallowed her disbelief. Of course, they were colleagues and old friends. Heat raced up her neck and she pretended intense interest in the conversation but glanced at the banners looking for a clue to the occasion. The speaker's topic was the African Zhun/twasi, '*the real people*' culture.

What was her problem? Jake wouldn't recognize her after one little collision in a university corridor. Jean Clifton hadn't seen her in the body suit. Therefore no one would be any wiser. Her secret identity was safe.

Robbie excused herself to the powder room for a quiet moment.

When she came out of the cubicle, Dr. Clifton was leaning close to the mirror straightening her white pencil dress over her thighs.

"Dr. Clifton, you look sensational." Robbie turned on the tap.

Clifton's eyes met hers in the mirror. "Hello, Robbie. Thank you." Clifton stepped back on her clear acrylic high-heeled shoes.

Robbie stood motionless as Clifton scrutinized her from the top of her styled black hair, past her simple gold hoop earrings, and then over her simple shift and jacket and stopped at her gold sandals.

Clifton raised her eyebrow. "You look nice. I haven't seen you dressed up before. I forget that my students have lives outside of their research and exams." Her tone suggested they shouldn't.

Biting her tongue, Robbie held the door for the woman in control of her destiny and allowed her to make a spectacular entrance into the ballroom before she followed. The band was playing a swing tune. Brad came toward her with a grin that showed his irresistible confidence.

"There you are." He bowed and offered his hand for a dance.

"I'd love to." She immediately felt the magic in his lead. He kept the tension in his hold and rock-stepped to the beat.

"You're happy tonight," she said when the music stopped.

"I am. I have a good feeling about this evening's event. You're beautiful. And I'm lucky." Brad placed his arm around her waist as a camera flashed.

"You're fortunate that Sam likes me or he might be jealous," she said.

"He knows we're doing this for the two of us," Brad whispered in her ear as the bandleader announced dinner.

Brad put his hand on the small of her back and guided her to the front and center, near the head table.

Robbie silently thanked the universe because the seats facing the speaker's podium were taken and she couldn't see Dr. Jean Clifton or Dr. Jake Proctor without turning her chair.

Chapter 5

Jake enjoyed the Saskatchewan pickerel with wild rice and the baked apple in puff pastry with warm spiced cream. So far the evening had been full of pleasant surprises. Because Jean studied and worked in Regina, she knew many people. He'd been reintroduced to men who were on his midget hockey and high school baseball teams. He thought he recognized some of the women, but he couldn't be sure. High school was such a long time ago.

When Jean had asked him if he would replace the scheduled speaker, he'd accepted. Introducing his research to sated dinner guests was a great way to get his cultural project out in the public, and prairie people were known for their generosity. After the introduction, he stood and walked to the podium. He placed his notes where they could be accessed should he lose his way. After a sip of water, he glanced at the faces in the audience. The overflow light from the stage illuminated a familiar face. No, it couldn't be the student who had crashed her nose into his chest. This was a pricey dinner to raise money for charities. She turned her chair and tilted her head to watch and listen. The movement felt strikingly familiar, as if he'd seen this often. But he had a presentation to give. He cleared his mind and he looked down at Jean Clifton. His colleague gave him thumbs up and he began.

Robbie shifted her chair slightly and peered between the other guests watching Jake straighten his notes and take a sip of water from a glass. She felt as if Jake had looked straight at her for the first few seconds, but that had to have been wishful thinking. She'd looked so different in her jeans and fleece jacket. Now, she carried an evening bag instead of a backpack. As he addressed the audience, Jake's voice grew strong and full of conviction.

She felt safe watching him now that he was absorbed. The thought that had skidded across her brain that maybe, just maybe, he remembered her from one little collision in a busy hallway had sent her heart fluttering. In a small corner of her mind, she hoped he felt confused and recognized something about her that reminded him of his association with Robin. After all, he studied people so why hadn't he noticed her disguise? Whenever they met at Frank's, he was considerate. Or had he accepted her as she presented herself to him? The research side of her brain turned off and she put her hand on her heart. Now that would be the type of man that would be a keeper for her future.

She tore herself from her wayward thoughts and forced herself to focus on the presentation. Jake's passionate voice described the ancient San in the Kalahari Desert. They continued their traditional hunter-gatherer lifestyle even though their hunting areas were invaded by commerce. Food was shared among the whole group. The !Kung San believed it was wrong to eat in front of someone who did not have food, even if he was a big, visiting stranger.

The audience laughed.

While he spoke about the clicks and pops in their language, Robbie felt cocooned in the anonymity of the crowd. She could indulge a fantasy that Mr. Broad-shouldered, dark-blond professor with a passion for his work was speaking to her and her alone. She discerned that they shared common interests. While Jake tried to understand whole cultures, she tried to understand the influences a negative body image had on a woman's life.

Her attention was yanked back into the present when she heard Jake mention "appetite suppressant."

". . . The Bushmen ate the pulp of succulent Hoodia Gordonii for thousands of years during long hunting trips because it controlled their need for water and food. This plant is part of their ancient knowledge and is now under clinical development by a licensed drug company to find a cure for obesity. The San need assistance to protect the plants' environment and their own lifestyle."

Robbie knew about suppressants. Her group had confirmed her research about experiencing rapid heartbeats, mood swings, and expense. Maybe there was a new medical bullet on the horizon. But what did the suppressant do for the crunch of food, the brilliance of a plate of green vegetables and red strawberries, or the social activity of eating? *Didn't anyone else see the irony in an appetite suppressant after a wonder meal?*

Jake spoke about the changes brought to the community by those from outside, with examples of permanent housing and individual wages earned for individual work. He speculated for a moment about how changes seemed to move from the outside toward the inside of a community. He knew that every time he visited with another culture he left something behind and brought something forward to his own life.

Even Brad's attention was held. Usually a few minutes into a presentation he was nudging her to call attention back to himself. Though Sam was the love of Brad's life, Brad felt he couldn't share that fact with the business world yet. But if Brad continued on the fast track, it wouldn't be long before Mr. Lawson would find him indispensable and Brad and Sam could attend these functions together.

The serving staff unobtrusively slipped between the tables with refills of coffee, tea, and ice water.

For now, Robbie felt safe in stealing a long look at Jake's full, open face. His broad smile, his white teeth, his deep brown eyes seemed to look directly at her. The room was decorated for the season where gifts were given and received.

"You okay?" Brad's arm cushioned her back from the chair.

She leaned into him with a wispy smile on her lips.

"Close your mouth. You're drooling." Brad's breath tickled her ear.

"But he's handsome and a Ph.D. and I'm swooning and wishing that the universe will look after my love life for a few minutes. Indulge me."

He leaned closer, then kissed her cheek. "Consider yourself indulged."

"Thanks. I'm done now. I have a big life ahead of me after I get my degree. I'm not looking for love in all the wrong places." She was a student and Jake was a faculty member and never the twain shall meet. She leaned her head on Brad's shoulder before she filled her mind with more clichés, then watched the end of the formalities as Jake accepted his small token of appreciation with practiced grace.

As the overhead lights brightened, people stood, stretched, and chatted. Robbie saw the Master of Ceremony lead Jake and Jean Clifton straight to Brad and Robbie's table.

Brad's boss, Mr. Lawson, pumped Jake's hand heartily and turned his attention to Brad. "This is the man who should be working with you, Dr. Proctor. If anyone can set up your cause in a wide network, it's Brad Mason."

"Glad to meet you, Mr. Mason." Jake stretched his hand to Brad.

Robbie watched as the two men seemed to reach an understanding during the firm handshake. "I'd like to have the opportunity to draft some ideas and discuss them with you, Dr. Proctor."

"Sounds good." Brad turned to Robbie. "I'd like to introduce Robbie Smith."

Jake nodded and extended his hand. "It's nice to see you again."

Robbie smiled and felt her hand secured in his. He remembered her. She sobered when the white-clad Clifton moved toward her.

Robbie stepped back. "I've learned my lesson. I stop and set up my MP3 player before I rush through the halls." Her hand reached up to her nose. She recalled the scent of his leather jacket and his subtle cologne.

"Glad to see there wasn't any permanent damage. I haven't seen you at the university."

Clifton stepped forward. "Robbie's almost done. As you know, grad students work on their own, some more than others and then they defend their material and they're off to a new life."

"Thank you, Dr. Clifton. From your lips to the committee's ears. You've been my role model." *If Clifton's sights are set on Jake maybe she'll be too occupied and forget about her thesis. Sure, and elephants can hide in a pile of Smarties Candy.* After Jake and Clifton moved on to the next table, Robbie reached up and kissed Brad and swung him around. "The universe is a great place. Did you hear Dr. Clifton? She's positive about my thesis. If I hadn't come here tonight with you, I wouldn't have met her in a social situation."

"Looks to me like she's got your man," Brad said.

"I told you I was swooning for a few minutes. Those minutes are up," Robbie whispered. "The most important issue is that for some reason Dr. Clifton seems to really be interested in Dr. Proctor and maybe, just maybe, she might be too busy to hassle me about my project."

"Can I bring you another glass of wine to celebrate?" Brad asked.

She covered her mouth as a yawn exploded. "To be honest, I'd like to go home. I need sleep."

"If you can wait a few more minutes, I'll drive you. If you think you'll fall asleep on your feet, I'll call a cab."

"I'll stay if you're sure you'll be ready to leave in half an hour."

"Deal." He paused as his gaze swept the room. "They do make an elegant pair, but it looks as if the prince's neck is on a swivel. He's checking us out again." Brad tilted his head to the left and wriggled his eyebrows.

She reached for her handbag and looked in the direction Brad was indicating. "Maybe he's checking you out. After all, you could be working with him," she whispered.

"He can check all he likes. His life will never be the same if he gives me a chance and I set up a system to help the San with their concerns about the environment and traditional medicines."

The lights dimmed and the band began to play. Brad and Robbie circled the room extending their holiday greetings. While Brad helped Robbie with her coat, they both turned at the now familiar voice. "Mason, I've written down my cell phone number. Call me when you've had time to think of an approach for the !Kung San or if you need more information. I know the leaders would appreciate the assistance."

"Yes, sir."

While Brad and Jake exchanged a few more words, Clifton and Mr. Lawrence danced. Robbie felt Clifton's stare. She stepped away from the men and was tempted to put her arms in the air as the general signal for surrender.

At the end of the evening, Robbie gratefully settled back into the heated leather seat in Brad's car.

Brad put his arm around her shoulder and turned her toward him. "Thanks."

"You're welcome. I had a great time. We danced, and I ate a meal that I didn't have to cook or pay for, and I mingled with men dressed in fine suits and women in their seasonal glory. And Professor Clifton suggested I'd be starting a new life soon."

"And don't forget the swoon." Brad nudged her.

"Oh yes, swooning is such good exercise for the heart."

When they stopped at her house, Brad came around and opened the door for her and held onto her arm while they climbed the stairs to the front door.

"You're such a gentleman. It's a lost art."

He gave her shoulders a squeeze. "It's easy to be a gentleman to a lady."

After the door was unlocked and the hall light was on, he kissed her cheek.

She took off her gloves. "Say hello to Sam for me."

He yawned. "I will. Sleep tight."

Robbie hung her coat next to the oversized coat she wore when she was in disguise. Her life was complicated right now but in a few weeks it would be all over.

She yawned while she undressed, then washed her face and brushed her teeth. It had been a long week. As she lay in bed, she thumped her pillow and scrunched further under her comforter. A fuzzy warmth settled over her as she remembered Frank's comfort at having her next to him in bed and Jake's gentle motion of pushing the loafer over her toes and heels. It felt like she was wrapped in a hug where all was right with the world just being there for Frank and Jake, even if she was in a costume. Just because she didn't look like herself didn't mean that she was different.

Saturday whizzed by, filled with chores and studying. Sunday morning arrived, crisp and bright, no reports of road closures, no storm warnings, nothing to keep her from attending her high school reunion. After her first cup of coffee, she checked her thesis agenda. Her personal field research was supposed to help her understand how difficult it was for larger women to fit into their physical environment as well as any positive and negative reactions from those around her. Other than Jake thinking she was a danger to his grandfather and not asking her to visit but hiring her, she couldn't report any personal negative reaction of other people to her as a woman of size. She must be doing something wrong. Could Dr. Clifton be right and she couldn't walk in someone's shoes? No, she did have those sales clerks who refused to help her and there was the matter of the chairs that were too small.

She was on the right path. Size had different meanings depending on the silhouette a person reflected in everyday life. When she was dressed as Robin, she left behind her comfortable world. For the purposes of her research and if because of her project corners of hidden discrimination and prejudices were illuminated and changed, then discomfort was worth experiencing.

Jake fumbled for the receiver. "Jake Proctor." His heartbeat slowed when the mechanical voice announced his wake-up call. He scrubbed his hand over his face and through his hair. The twisted blankets were evidence of his restless sleep and now it was morning. With the pillows stacked to support his head, in that magic place between dreams and wakefulness, he wished that he had the power of the San healers. The San believed that spirits shot misfortune, sickness, and death at a person with invisible arrows. The healers focused on stopping or removing the arrows while they danced around a fire until they were in a trance. In that state, they healed everyone around the fire. He pictured Frank, Robin, and himself around the flames while the clapping and singing women from the community added power to the healers. What was he thinking? Frank was ready to leave this world, and Robin didn't appear sick. Perhaps she just had a bad hairstyle and he wasn't guilty of misappropriating money. His lawyer was investigating the allegations, possibly at this very minute. He stretched. Everything would fall into place.

After listening to the local news and weather, he showered and then stood with a towel around his hips lathering his face for a shave. When the telephone rang again, he jerked and the razor slipped and blood pooled on his chin. *Get a grip. Not every phone call is the care home telling you to rush over because his grandfather's drawing his last breath.*

"Morning. You still coming to see me today?"

Jake heard his grandfather's gravelly voice over top of labored breathing.

"Of course."

"Good. I feel like company this morning."

Jake glanced at his watch. "I'll be there around eleven."

"Wear your gloves. It's cold out."

"Will do." Jake understood that it didn't matter that he was thirty-five years old, to Frank he would always be a kid.

Robbie, disguised as Robin, found a parking place across the street from the home. The city's street decorations of giant snowflakes fastened to the streetlights, wrenched against the fasteners, as if they were asking to be set free to float on the winter wind. While driving the short distance to the Care Manor, she'd argued with herself. *Just tell Frank that I'm researching people's reaction to a woman of size. No, wait until he calls me on it? Am I using a dying man? Do I really want to be a comfort to him?* She hadn't reached any firm conclusion when she tapped on the partially opened door and listened. She heard, "Come in. You're on the outside."

"Hi, Frank." She glanced around the compact room.

Frank's fragile, decaying body seemed marooned in the brown landscape of the recliner. His wedding band nestled into the skin folds on his finger. Robbie reached for his hand and held his palm in hers.

"You're a sight for sore eyes." He attempted a whistle. "Are you all gussied up for me or something special?"

Robbie hung her coat on a hook on the wall. "You first, and then some place special."

"I'm glad I'm first. You look better than you've ever looked." He pursed his lips and once again attempted a wolf whistle of appreciation.

"Thank you." She hesitated, her fear of exposure dampened down. "I'm going to my high school reunion and I want to look my best." Each time she met Frank, she waited for him to call her on her disguise. She wondered if he just accepted her or if he wanted so much to be reminded of Mabel that he overlooked any disproportion in her appearance.

Frank gripped the arms of the lazy chair.

"No, stay where you are. I'll sit on the bed," she said.

"Look behind the door. I had the staff bring in a folding chair since sometimes you and Jake come around at the same time."

Robbie moved aside the imitation pine garland festooned with red poinsettia bows that stretched from his window to his door, then unfolded the chair and placed it in front of Frank and sat down.

"Don't mind if I do," she said.

"Didn't sleep that well last night." He scrubbed his thin hand across his forehead.

"Would you like to sit quietly or would you like tell me about your life with Mabel?" She concentrated on his face. She'd half expected his agreement to be ready and quick.

With a sigh, he leaned back. His hands moved along the

arms of the chair, trying to settle. "You don't want to hear about me. My story's an old one."

She took a few precious seconds weighing the pros and cons of his response. "I do. I want to know that there's a chance for me to find the kind of love you and Mabel shared."

His reaction was slow. "There's always hope."

Her hands couldn't remain still and they bunched the polyester of her wide legged slacks, pleating the azure folds before smoothing out the creases. "If it's not too much for you, I'd like to hear a bit. I'm going to my high school reunion where the majority of my classmates will be married with children and I don't even have a boyfriend in the wings. I could use a little moral support." She hadn't realized that was what she was seeking until it was out in the open. Rolling onto one hip, she rested her arms on her belly and waited.

"When I met Mabel, we were older than most of the singles. She was happy as a secretary, playing the organ, and singing in a band part time. I had to chase her and convince her that she was the woman for me. She put up a fight." He was looking at some faraway spot on the ceiling. "We got used to the idea it might be just the two of us no matter how many times we tried. But after we'd been married for five years, Mabel became nauseated in the mornings. We thought it might have been a stomach bug but the doctor told us otherwise. Mabel was beautiful while she carried our child. We didn't care if it was a boy or a girl, we were just so happy. Karen was born like she was meant to be, all smiles and rosy cheeked. Mabel stayed home and cared for Karen and me. She put both of us first. Karen and I went swimming, bike riding, ice-skating. Our Karen had the same independent streak as her mother. She didn't want to sit in an office or teach kids, she wanted to explore the world. She became a flight attendant as they call them now. She saw a lot of the world. She loved her job, the travel, the excitement. Then one day she rang our front door with her suitcase in hand. She asked if she could have her old room back because she was pregnant. This was the time just before women could work late into their pregnancy. We were with her when Jake was born." His eyes closed.

Robbie imagined a cozy scene of a mother and newborn supported by loving grandparents. The fantasy made easy by the slow, familiar words of a well-told story.

The groves around Frank's mouth seemed to deepen. "Karen caught a flu, a simple flu, that somehow took her away from us before Jake's first birthday."

"Oh, Frank. I'm so sorry." Tears pricked the back of her eyes. *This is where your curiosity brings you, Robbie.* She reached over and covered his hand with her hand.

He didn't seem to hear or feel her. "A part of us died too, but we had Jake to care for."

He paused, then withdrew a tissue from his sleeve. "Jake was a good boy. Never gave us much trouble. Smart. Always had his nose in a book or fingers on a computer keyboard."

Robbie considered his comment. No doubt being raised by grandparents had something to do with his independence.

"That's probably why he loves to travel a lot," Frank said. "I think he got that from his mother. Mabel and I didn't roam too far from home."

"It probably has more to do with you and Mabel. You raised a confident man," Robbie said.

Frank cleared his throat. "He took a lot of ribbing about Mabel's size and our age." Frank's shoulders sagged. "Today, I see grandparents out and about with their grandkids, but thirty some years ago it was a different story."

An odd sensation stirred in her heart when his voice filled with sadness and regret.

"We did what we could and hoped for the best." His voice was almost a whisper.

"Jake's an intelligent and well-traveled man. He's probably resolved all of his childhood issues." A nervous bravado crept into her voice.

Frank shifted in his chair. "If he hasn't, it's a bit late. He's thirty-five and still no true love in his life."

Robbie understood all about parents' expectations and goals for their children. She was an only child, too. Even though her parents didn't hint at grandbabies, she saw her mother slowing down when they passed children's wear in the mall, all the while vehemently stating that she and her father were too young and busy to be grandparents like some of their friends.

"He'll find someone. He's good looking now and will be as he gets older because I can see a lot of you in him," Robbie said. She knew Frank just wanted his grandson to be happy.

"Thanks. Mabel was glad when both Karen and Jake took after me physically but they were all her in spirit. He'll most likely marry later, like Mabel and me, or maybe not at all, like his mom. Nowadays you don't need the ring and paper to prove love."

Robbie glanced at the clock. There was a dusty blue tinge around Frank's mouth. He'd talked too much. "I'm sorry, Frank. You're tired. I shouldn't have asked you to talk so much."

"I'll close my eyes for a minute. Jake should be here soon."

"Thanks for sharing your memories. You rest. I've got to go anyway. Take care. I'll drop by again soon," she whispered as she leaned in and kissed his forehead. There wasn't a way to explain the closeness she felt for this special man. She heard a small snore escape his lips.

Robbie tried to swallow past the huge lump in her throat. Was research really worth all this? She was essentially betraying the trust of a dying man.

Chapter 6

Frank's door swung into the room and Jake, with red cheeks, scarlet ears, and a bright green band-aid on his chin, stepped in. "Good Morning."

Robbie jumped away from Frank's chair, heart pounding, dry mouth, and a trickle of perspiration slipping out of her navel. She and Jake had been in the same room just the night before last. He'd been within inches of her. He couldn't fail to recognize her, be fooled by her appearance now. But he seemed to have eyes for one person, the man in the chair.

Robbie stepped away from Frank and folded her chair. It was time for her to leave, but her heart slowed and her concerns seemed to dissolve in a room where Jake leaned into Frank and kissed his cheek.

Frank's eyes fluttered open. "Oh, you made it."

"I came as soon as I could, but I see I didn't have to hurry. You have company." Jake's thoughts bounded and bumped over each other. Mentally he started to list the things he'd bungled rushing here—the most important, he'd brushed off Jean Clifton when she called while he rushed out the door. At least he'd agreed to drive her to wherever she needed to go this afternoon. He felt indebted to her. After all, she recommended him for his job and presented him with an opportunity as the main speaker for the fund raising event. Second, he had to cover his chin with a neon bandage, a leftover from his emergency supplies for children he met during his travels. At this moment none of it mattered. He desired time with the man who had raised him.

At least Frank hadn't been alone. He filled his chest with air and mentally pounded himself on the back. Hiring this woman, Robin, no matter how strange she looked was the right thing.

Jake shrugged out of his coat and hung it on a hook and turned toward his grandfather. Frank seemed swallowed by the chair. For as long as Jake remembered, his grandfather had always had his own special chair in which he relaxed, read the paper, and mulled over problems. When Jake was young, disturbing his grandfather in his armchair was like approaching a king on a throne, even when he just called him to dinner.

Robin stood tentatively beside the closed door smoothing some filmy material over her hips. The material clung to her breasts, cantaloupes that would flood over his palm. How did you test the ripeness of melons? Tapping or smelling the place where the fruit had been attached to the vine? *No way. What's he doing?* His hands were cupped as if he was testing their weight right this minute. He shoved them under his armpits, as if they had been cold. His total focus was supposed to be on taking care of his grandfather. Stealing another look at Robin's chest, he wondered if remembering the warmth of his grandmother's hugs had reawakened an unconscious breast fixation. *No. Stress, that's it. Stress does many things to a man's thoughts.*

Robin moved toward her coat. Jake removed his hands from their hiding place and lifted her coat from the hook and held it open for her. When she turned her back on him, he breathed in a sweet ripeness. Shaking his head, he laid the coat along her shoulders. He'd been focusing on work and the problems associated with funding for too long. He needed to unwind. He would be with Jean later. Reminiscing would help him relax for a while.

Robin spun on the balls of her feet and she looked as if she could spread her arms and fly. The image brought a smile to his face. She watched him with a brown-eyed gaze for what felt like several seconds.

"Thank you." She flipped her thick, black scarf over her shoulder. "See you, Frank, and thanks for the encouragement. Bye, Jake."

Frank stroked his chin with his age-spotted hand while he nodded his head.

"What was that all about?" Jake asked.

His grandfather wriggled himself out of his chair. "Not much. She just got me thinking, that's all. Are we going for a drive or what?"

Jake moved to his grandfather's side, then put his arm around his shoulder. Grandfather felt like a Bushman child's rope doll. They were made of thin rope under the colorful material used to fashion the doll's dress and headscarf. He hadn't understood how this type of doll could be any comfort, unlike the plush animals he had hugged as a child, when he was frightened, or lonely, or even happy.

"Glad you're home, boy." Frank gripped Jake's hand.

"We'll drive around and go for an early lunch somewhere."

His grandfather's familiar thin lips stretched into a full denture smile.

Jake's breath caught and he coughed. He should have kept the whole day open. But Jean was responsible for his being here so he could work and be with his grandfather and so he couldn't shrug her off entirely. "I hate to tell you but I've got another appointment at one-thirty."

Frank's smile faltered. "Don't worry. I usually sleep in the afternoon anyway. There's a scarf in the closet. Get it, will you?"

Jake slipped his hand from Frank's shoulder and stretched his arm into the darkness of the closet and retrieved a red wool scarf. "I remember this scarf."

Settling his glasses on his nose, Frank glanced at him and then away. “Mabel gave it to me to celebrate when the adoption finalized and you officially became ours. Can we go and visit her?”

“Absolutely.”

Sunday traffic was sparse and Jake drove into the cemetery parking lot several minutes later. He held onto Frank’s arm as they wandered to their destination.

Frank stopped at a headstone. “Remember Len. He died shoveling snow.” A little further on, Frank stopped again. “George didn’t last long after Emma died.” When they reached the familiar headstone, Frank bowed his head and ran his palm along the smooth, polished marble.

“I miss her arms around me,” Frank said.

“You were always there for each other.”

“We almost made it to our sixtieth anniversary.” Frank scattered pebbles with his feet.

“I remember that you always kissed each other before you left each other and when you returned.”

“Glad you learned something to take with you to your relationship.”

Frank seemed to have shrunk in just the past few days.

“Grandma was a caring and lovely woman. She always did what she could to make my life a happy place to be,” Jake said.

The trees, the equipment shed, and the frozen mound of earth, drew Jake’s attention. He scanned them rather than continue looking at the gray marble stone with his mother’s name or the identical marker with his grandmother’s date of birth, followed by a dash and the date she died. His grandfather’s name was chiseled into the marble with his birth date followed by a dash and a blank space that would be filled in. Jake should have been glad of Frank’s foresight but he wasn’t.

Frank leaned in and put his lips to the cold marble of his wife's headstone and straightened. "Just wanted to see one more time where my remains will be. I'll be with the two women I loved most in my whole life." With his index finger, he poked at his glasses again. "You come back every now and again just to make sure they haven't moved us."

That did it. Struggling against the wave of emotion that threatened to overwhelm him, Jake put his arms around Frank and held on tight.

The prairie wind blew harder. Jake felt sure it would blow Frank over if he didn't hold onto him.

Jake clamped his free hand over one ear. "Forgot how cold a November wind can be."

Frank dragged a knitted hat from his pocket and handed it to Jake. "That Eastern weather's making you soft. What're you going to do without me?"

"I don't want to find out for a long time. I've got to make up for lost years."

Frank's gloved hand squeezed Jake's sleeve. "You know that isn't going to happen."

"At least we'll be together one last Christmas."

"We'll see."

A flock of sparrows flew across the sky and settled in the branches of the evergreen trees lining the roadway.

Jake cinched the seat belt across Frank's waist. "Where would you like to have lunch?"

"All I really want is a milkshake. Old-fashioned, like me. Thick." Frank smacked his pale lips.

"Any particular flavor?"

"Everybody knows chocolate is the only respectable milkshake."

While the car idled to warm up the interior, Jake glanced at the clock on the dash. "We could get lunch to go and spin around the old neighborhood."

The cold leather creaked when Frank settled. "Sounds good. Just turn up the heat in this sweetheart and I'll be happy."

They drove to a fast-food drive-in and ordered their lunch. The restaurant was on the same property where Frank had worked as a machinist for forty years.

"I came to this address through rain, snow, hail, or sunshine. Jobs were a lot like women back then. You got a good one and you stuck it out," Frank said between slurps of his milkshake.

Jake ate his burger with one hand and drove with the other. They passed Central Collegiate, Thomson Elementary, rounded Wascana Lake, and Grace United Church.

When Jake parked in front of the Care Manor doors, Frank's eyelids kept fluttering closed. "You're tired," Jake said.

"If I wasn't proud, I'd ask you to carry me to my bedroom like a blushing bride," Frank wheezed.

"Stay there. I'll get a wheelchair."

"No. Your arm is enough."

The automatic doors swished open, and they plodded down the corridor. Frank touched the hand of a man in a wheelchair, nodded to another pushing his walker, but he straightened when a nurse came into view.

Once in Frank's room, Jake closed the door. He led his grandfather to the bed and held his coat until Frank's arms were out of the sleeves, then steadied him when he sat on the side of his bed. Jake was about to lift Frank's feet onto the mattress.

"Stop. My boots. Can't dirty the blanket," Frank growled.

Jake was once again on his knees removing footwear. He swung Frank's legs onto the bed, tucked the blanket under his arms, then passed him Mabel's picture and turned out the light. "I'll tell the staff that you're back and ask them to check in on you."

Frank lifted his fingers off the bed and waved. "Thanks, son."

"You're welcome." His grandfather's cheek was cool against his lips when he kissed him goodbye.

"I'll come back later."

"That would be nice." Frank mumbled through sleep-relaxed lips.

The parking lot at Lumsden High School was full of new sports cars, SUVs, vans, and half-ton trucks. These were similar styles to the cars the students drove but without the dents and rust pocks. Robbie checked her reflection in the sun visor mirror. Her wig was in place. Her hand shook slightly when she touched up her lips then adjusted her glasses. She'd read that it took only small changes for people not to recognize someone familiar to them. She wanted her old friends and acquaintances to be aware of and accept the changes in her body. Her cell phone gave the familiar sound of a received text message from her parents: her father wrote 'good luck' and her mother sent 'break a leg'. Robbie laughed. She had discussed this field research with her mother and her father. Her father in his professional doctor voice had said, "You be very careful. It's easy to cloud your research and forget to maintain your critical stance toward others' reactions to women of size."

She held onto the door and heaved her body off the seat, stood, and locked the door. When she straightened her coat, she leaned her cheek into the collar where Jake had held it for her and felt comfort. She felt a smile slide across her mouth because knowing that Jake began accepting her for who she was both inside and outside the suit was an accomplishment. He just didn't know it. In so very many ways it showed his depth of character and lifted him from nincompoop and just another pretty face. While she walked toward the welcome banner vibrating in the wind outside the high school gym she felt the old familiar sensations she had when she'd played these grounds before. As a kid, she'd stuck her tongue to the metal pole in the winter just over there at the elementary school. She remembered her long gangly junior high self as a silver ribbon high jumper, and finally as the senior who led the petition against smoking in the schoolyard. All of these memories made up who she was today. Her reflection in the plate glass door told her she looked different than she did so long ago. She shook her weighted arms loose at her sides and opened her mind to every possible experience in the next few hours.

Her first stop was the registration desk. The table had signs that indicated the homeroom teachers. Robbie headed straight for Mr. Roberts' class. Before she gave the woman her name, she heard a screech and realized it came from her own mouth. She had left screeching behind in grade ten, hadn't she? She spotted a familiar face. OMG, Nancy Harris had not changed. She stood next to the registration desk organizing the organizers. She still tossed her straight cut, shoulder-length blond hair for emphasis. Robbie beamed. Nancy's body was as toned and tanned as it had been on the cheerleading team. "Nancy Harris. Wow, you look just the same."

Nancy's hand fluttered in front of her face. "Robbie?" Her former classmate's eyes darted across her chest, down her belly, and back to her face.

"Hey, Hey, are you ready?" She clapped twice. "If you score one, we'll score two." Robbie sang and jumped just a little in the air. She was glad she'd come. "Yes, it's me. Are the rest of the team here?"

"Yes, we're almost all here," Nancy replied as she patted her blond straight hair and ran her finger down the list.

"We thought we'd perform again. As chair of the committee I was so excited when we received your reply, but . . ." 'The word hung in the air.

Robbie took a deep breath. "I can do some of the routines, but I don't think I'd make the top of the pyramid this year," she said.

"Meg, Steph, Kim, Kenda, Christie, and I are changing into our cheerleading costumes later," Nancy said, while fixating on Robin's thighs. "That is, if my ex-sister-in-law gets mine here on time. I just knew I shouldn't have lent it. It's irreplaceable." Nancy stomped her high heel, then leaned closer to Robbie. "Did someone tell you to bring your outfit?"

"No, I didn't get that message." Robbie remembered checking her phone messages yesterday. "It wouldn't have mattered anyway because I sent mine to the Goodwill a long time ago or you could have used it. We used to be about the same size."

"Robbie Smith." She said, turning and smiling at the check-in woman who peered down the list.

"Thank you." She scooped up her nametag and event schedule. "See you on stage," she said to Nancy, then strode, head held high down the hall to the girls' washroom, checked the stalls, and leaned against the sink. Under the fresh scent of expensive cologne she sniffed at those lingering odors of gym socks, tampons, and cheap hair spray, but it was still a refuge from the hallways as it has been for girls throughout their school years.

Nancy hadn't changed. She'd upstaged her again. *So what if I can't get into my cheerleading costume today. Those days are gone but strangely not forgotten by everyone.*

The door swung open and a woman who looked as if she was ready to deliver right there on the floor flung herself into a cubicle.

"Sorry to rush by you. But when you gotta go . . ."

"You gotta go." Robbie straightened her long-sleeve top. Not everyone at the reunion could fit into the sizes they wore back in high school. Yes, it was time to meet her friends and acquaintances from the past. She held her arms out from her side and twirled. The filmy material rose behind her like a protective cape.

Chapter 7

Jake caught a glimpse of himself in his rearview mirror. The neon plaster was still stuck to his jaw. *Thank you, Granddad. You could have at least said something, pointed to it.* Jake knew the obvious little things about appearances weren't of much interest to Frank. He paid attention to how a person lived their life. His grandmother had tried to stay in Jake's life with her care packages. White sport socks, season-themed underwear, and chocolate chip cookies.

Various roommates over the years had laughed and teased him, especially women, that his grandmother still bought him underwear. He tried to suggest that she stop but she had said, "It's the least I can do for you, Jake. A man can always use spare underwear and socks." After a couple of years, he gave in and sent her his right size, medium, and the brand and brief style. He'd forgotten how much he missed her care packages. Even though she didn't give birth to him, she had a mother's intuition where he was concerned. Maybe he should have taught at the university here. Maybe he could have encouraged her to think about what was best for her. Maybe she'd still be here.

Jake checked the needle on the round speedometer. It was easy to drive without care and attention and lately he had so many thoughts vying for attention.

And maybe the University of Ottawa wouldn't be investigating his integrity. He would never misappropriate research funds. The anthropology department head and the President of the University believed him, but the money seemed to be gone and they had a responsibility to the government and to the taxpayers to conduct an investigation. It had to be a technical error, but until his name was cleared he felt as if he was guilty. His lawyer, Harold Richmond, came well recommended for his experience in these types of allegations and was working hard reviewing the evidence and had even hired a private investigator to scout around the department.

Driving North on Albert Street, Jake wondered why Jean had decided to contact him after at least fifteen years. She hadn't hinted at specific reasons while they were in each other's company at the university, nor Friday evening when she had picked him up from his hotel. They'd had the same homeroom teacher in their final year in high school but hadn't been in touch since graduation. He suspected that Jean had emailed him more by design than coincidence just when he needed to be close to his grandfather. She suggested that he compile his research notes at the University of Regina. She must have her finger on the pulse of Regina because she knew that the Chamber of Commerce needed a replacement guest speaker for a fund-raiser.

She lived in one of the downtown office towers that had been converted into condominiums. The concierge telephoned her, then escorted him into an elevator and swiped the security card.

When the elevator door opened to hallway with plush carpet and polished porcelain tile, Jean stood in her doorway and with her arm extended. "Jake, come in."

The open-concept apartment had huge windows that drew his eyes to the horizon. He could see for miles. Only in a city like Regina could he be on the fourteenth floor of a building and see forever.

"Great view."

"Isn't it just," Jean said.

He heard the closet door close.

"You don't mind if we hurry, do you?"

"No, of course not. I'll drive you to where you need to be and get you there on time."

When she handed him her coat, he felt the difference between the bulk of another coat he'd held not too many hours ago and the cashmere he held for Jean. What was wrong with him? Jean Clifton was a beautiful woman who'd provided him with an office and a teaching position. His anthropological experience taught him to pay attention to the person he was with. They always knew if he was not fully engaged. Robin Smyth probably reminded him of a future without the two people who had loved him unconditionally, and that was that.

Jean hooked her arm through his and they closed the door on the magnificent view of blue sky and farmland stretching to the horizon.

After locking the door, Jean said, "I'm glad we'll have this time together. There doesn't seem to be enough hours in a day to catch up on all the years that have passed."

The elevator doors swished open and they stepped inside.

"I'm all yours until three forty-five. I promised Frank that I would join him for dinner."

He thought her lips pouted for just a second.

"Frank?" she inquired, brows drawn together.

"My grandfather, Frank Proctor."

"Oh yes, one of the reasons we could tempt you to our university."

With her back to him, he watched her shoulders straighten before she turned to him with a look of concern on her face. She laid her hand on his sleeve. "He raised you, didn't he?"

"Yes, he and my grandmother." Jake's gut clenched. Soon he would be the last branch of the Proctor family tree.

"I met him at our high school graduation. I almost fell into his lap," she said. "He was so sweet."

"He's a charmer when he wants to be." Jake remembered his grandmother calling Frank a lady's man. Of course Jake could never see it.

"How is he?"

"Not well. That's why I want to be with him whenever I can."

The prairie wind whipped at Jean's coat. She held the collar tighter.

"It's like a wind tunnel downtown with the tall buildings," Jean said.

Jake opened the passenger door and helped her in. When he settled into the familiar leather seat and started the ignition, the heat blasted on the high setting that Frank needed. He fumbled with the dials. "Sorry about that. Granddad wanted heat." He turned to Jean. "I haven't had the chance to thank you for contacting me when you did."

"Works for you and for us. It's a feather in our cap, having a young, famous researcher at our university, teaching our students. I know the Vice-Chancellor was pleased when I told him you agreed to come on board and fill the temporary position." Her eyes sparkled and she swayed toward him.

Uh, oh, time to move. He checked over his shoulder and turned the signal indicator on. "So where are we going?"

"Not far. Just down Highway 11 to the Town of Lumsden. It's only about twenty minutes. We'll be back before you know it."

"I remember Lumsden. It was place to go for an ice cream on a hot day." He turned toward her.

"Oh, I never did that." She blew out a sigh of frustration. "I borrowed a cheerleading costume for a Halloween party from my brother's ex and it seems that she needs it right this minute for a school reunion or something. She was the captain of the squad and their idea of fun is to perform some old cheers. I just haven't had a minute until today and then my car wouldn't start."

After they were settled in their seats with the belts securely fastened, Jean looked around at the dash. "What a great car. This couldn't be the same car I envied during high school?"

"One and the same. It was my mother's."

Her blue eyes flashed. "I'll bet it cost a pretty penny to store for all those years?"

"Yes. But it is important to my grandfather that it's here. He bought it for her after she passed her driver's test. I drove it until I left for the University of Ottawa and when I came home for visits." He felt her fingers brush his hand on the top of the gear shifter. He gripped the knob tighter to keep from pulling away from the contact.

"That's sweet."

"Do you keep up with our old class?"

"I never left the city, except to travel, of course, so I tend to hear about most of us."

He accelerated along the straight highway. "I've been away for so long, I think I recognize people on the street but I'm not one hundred percent sure. Friday night was great catching up with some of the guys. Thank you again."

"You're welcome, but remember we both benefited." She turned her body in the seat and spoke to the side of his face while he watched the road. "You're probably wondering why I contacted you when I did."

He turned quickly and glanced at her before he looked back to the road. "Yes, I have. Don't get me wrong, it's great but it does seem more than coincidental."

"Sorry, it isn't a coincidence at all. I heard from a friend of a friend that your grandfather was ill, and the circumstances at your own university might be right for you to return home for awhile."

With an economy of motion, he held the car on the road. For a moment, he stared at the horizon. Who would have told her? Only a handful of people knew that he was under investigation.

He glanced when he felt pressure on his arm and saw her red nails lay against his black leather sleeve.

"Don't be upset, Jake. There wasn't any direct information about the university's investigation. I made some discreet inquires. I wanted to put your name forward for our university but I also needed to protect my back."

He sat deeper in the seat, loosened his grip on the wheel. "There isn't basis for these allegations. I promise you." He met her watchful eyes.

"I believe you. I convinced the Dean that there must be some mistake. He believes me." She responded readily enough. She shifted in her seat, turning to watch the hills and leafless trees rush by. Finally she said, "Let's enjoy the drive. Get to know each other again. Tell me more about Africa."

He relaxed his left foot on the floorboards. "As you know, I lived with the !Kung San in the Kalahari Desert. They were the people portrayed in the film *The Gods Must Be Crazy*."

"I saw that movie. You lived with them for *three* months?"

"Yes."

"But why them if they've been studied so often?"

"I studied the changes in their life since the movie. Drought and overgrazing have impacted the wildlife they hunted and they've also been exposed to the role models from the outside world. Some of the members of the community have permanent houses and cultivated gardens, instead of packing up their material possessions and abandoning their temporary grass houses to hunt and gather food."

"Everything changes."

He enjoyed talking about his research. Downshifting, Jake eased up on the accelerator while he turned into the town. Judging by the traffic, something big was happening.

"Just down Main Street then left on Sixth Street to the high school. I'll only be a minute. I want to hear more about what you discovered," she said.

When he approached the school, the parking lot was full. He stopped in the loading zone and stood beside his car as men and women climbed out of half-ton trucks, vans, compacts, and SUVs. They were in dresses, suits, and jeans. He nodded to those who greeted him as if he might be a former classmate and said "hello." Jake released his breath in a half laugh when he saw Robin's vehicle. Her vanity license plate, 'Almost There', gave her away. Wonder where 'there' is she wants to be? He'd paid attention to the license plate one day when he arrived as she drove away. He could not have missed the mass of curls in the driver's seat. *So this is the reason she was dressed up.*

The canvas welcome sign ruffled above the entrance doors. It looked as if someone had played fox and goose in the skiff of snow on the grass. *Can't take the kid out of us.* He'd run his fair share of winter tag. Shifting his body off the car, he followed another couple into the foyer. Class photographs lined the hall. He wandered through them, seeing mullet cuts, big wind-blown hair, pixie cuts, and eyes filled with hope.

Muffled laughter filtered through the closed gymnasium door. He slipped inside, then leaned against the pillar and observed. The basketball hoops were folded up to the rafters. The stage was set up for a band. The all-too-familiar bleachers were tucked against the wall. It looked as if Jean had found the woman she needed to see and was handing over her package. They'd be driving back to the city again soon. His attention was caught the moment Robin turned away from a group of women. He'd been waiting to see her. Her face was flushed but beaming. She listened attentively, laughed openly, and hugged freely.

When she looked in his direction, Jake raised his hand and grinned, but she didn't see him. A short, bald guy was guiding her into a seat beside him and she focused all of her attention on the man who spoke to her with an old familiarity.

The emcee announced Sue Brown, the class of '95 star jazz singer, would sing and those who wanted to dance should because they were older now and they'd better get their dancing in before they had to go home to kids and bed. Most of the members of the crowd laughed, some booed, but couples began to reach for each other and move toward the dance floor.

Jake moved away from the wall and ambled toward Robin. She shook her head in disbelief, looked into his eyes, then her brow furrowed. He offered her his hand and led her to the dance floor that was quickly filling up.

"Jake, what are you doing here?"

"Dancing with you." He moved to place one hand onto her back. She grasped both his hands and kept him at arms' length. "You know what I mean. I know that you didn't attend this school."

"No, I didn't. We could say I happened to be looking for a dance." They moved to the music in sort of a high school version of a waltz.

The mellow notes soothed Jake and he felt Robin's hands relax for a moment. His thumb of its own volition massaged her palm.

"Seriously, how come you're here?" she asked.

"Coincidence. I drove a colleague here. She's standing over there next to the stage returning a cheerleading uniform."

Robin dropped her hands free from his grasp. "I'm sorry, I promised to meet a friend." She wove around the dancing couples.

He felt his mouth drop open, before he clamped it tight. He'd never been abandoned on the dance floor before. While he watched Robin slip away from him, Jean touched his arm. "I'm glad you came in. Nancy can talk the leg off a table. I see you recognized someone."

"Grandfather's friend."

"Oh." Jean smoothed her hands along her hips. "Dance?"

Jake raised his arms once again and this time the woman willingly stepped into his arms. His palm rested against the sinew beneath Jean's shoulder blade, so different from the arms' length Robin kept him at a few minutes earlier. Jean's hand slipped behind his back and she leaned her head on his shoulder. Strange, though he held a beautiful, successful, woman in his arms, his thoughts kept drifting toward Robin, wondering where she'd gone to and why she'd left him so quickly.

In the restroom, Robbie ran her wrists under cold water and then let the hand dryer roar. She needed to gather her courage and go back into the gym and hang around and see if Dr. Clifton recognized her. If she didn't, then she scored points. Dr. Clifton assumed that people would recognize the suit and they would not have the same reactions as if she was a true woman-of-size. It would falsify the data and throw Robbie's other research into jeopardy. If Dr. Clifton recognized her, she could deck her. Seriously, she didn't want her friends to know that she was in a sense lying to them because she hadn't changed as much as she appeared. Some of her friends, like Nancy, had been surprised, but for the most part they had accepted the changes and continued to laugh and kid around with her. And who else was she concerned about? An old man at the end of his life, and yes, even a grandson who was going to be grieving very soon.

She glanced around at the tiled floor and the corners where years of grunge had accumulated. Actually this might be the best place to be discovered if she had to be. No not the bathroom but this event. The friends would laugh at her pretense. Or at least some of them would, but what about the women who had really gained excess weight or those who were larger throughout high school, would they understand it was part of her research or think it was an insult?

When she reached up to fluff her wig, her sleeves billowed in the mirror. She appeared formidable. She took up space. She looked good. It was time for Robbie to live in the moment.

Robbie moved toward Dr. Clifton's watchful eyes and prepared herself for any sign of recognition. What she saw instead were Clifton's eyes sliding right past her without even a slight pause while she gave Jake her undivided attention. Clifton played with her hair, laughed at something Jake said, and put her hand on his sleeve. Robbie felt relief that Dr. Clifton's attention was focused on Jake. Jake didn't seem to notice her either. She was just one of the many people milling around the edges of the dance floor.

The emcee's announcement of a fifteen-minute break before the next entertainment was scheduled came none too soon. Robbie turned away from the dance floor where Dr. Clifton and Jake stood and she meandered toward a group that gathered around a table at the back. Soon her classmates brought up the time the lab caught fire and class was cancelled for a week. Her grade eleven lab partner stood and bowed. Finally, after many years, he could accept credit for the extended holiday.

Robbie scanned the crowd for Jake and Clifton but she couldn't find them. She relaxed and laughed at more remembered antics.

Jake drove expertly weaving his Mustang around slow-moving traffic, completing the trip in less than twenty minutes, despite the fact that there seemed to be every Sunday driver out on the road on this sunny fall day.

He thought while he carried on a conversation about his research. He enjoyed an attentive presence, so why was he rushing away from Jean instead of responding to her obvious signals?

He stopped next to her building, turned off the ignition, and unclipped his seatbelt. Jean Clifton seemed lost in thought. He opened her door and extended his hand to help her out of the low-slung seat.

She smiled at him. "Time for a drink?"

He checked his watch. "Maybe next time." He stood still rather than moving back toward the car.

She linked her arm through his while he escorted her to the building.

With her hand on the glass door, she turned. "I enjoyed myself today. You're an asset to our students and the staff is pleased to have your expertise in our department as well. I'll see you at work tomorrow."

"I'll be there." Jake kept his voice professional.

When the door swung closed, he slid behind the wheel and accelerated away from the high rise.

While traffic flowed past him and the lights turned green he thought about Jean Clifton. She was a beautiful, intelligent woman. Why didn't he want to spend more time with her? Could she be attracted to him or did she have other motives? The Jean he remembered was always focused on a goal, whether it was being first in class or the school president, she worked very hard to be successful. She seemed genuinely interested in his research. Where else was he going to meet a future partner if not a colleague? But he also saw what happened when work romances went south.

It was never good. But there were some examples of happy couples too. He drove toward Care Manor. He had bigger issues to think about than romance.

Robbie knew the ability to compartmentalize her thoughts was the foundation for her honors status and the opportunity for a small amount of social life. But even though she laughed and added to the memories of teachers and pranks, she was preoccupied. Her thoughts- scurried around two pairs of eyes, one pair whose life was about to end and the other whose life would dramatically change. Both men loved and were loved by a woman who wore dress sizes in the double digits.

Stacy waved a hand in front of Robbie's eyes. "Hello, are you in there? I've been tapping your arm and no response."

Robbie stared at her arm. Unless the person put pressure behind the poke, she didn't feel the light taps through the inches of batting. She lifted her eyebrows. "Lost in memories."

"Wake up. They're calling the cheerleading squad up to the front. Get up there." Stacy nudged her chair.

"I don't have my uniform."

"So what. You can't let a little thing like that stop you. Your pantsuit will work out just fine. Let's see your feet."

Robbie showed off her bronze loafers.

"You'll be safe in those shoes. Go on."

Robbie felt a surge of pride through her veins when Steve and his wife, Jane and her husband, as well as Stacy, stood and cheered when she wove through the tables across the floor and up the stairs. The next thing she heard was Nancy saying, "Move over, Fat Lady coming through."

Robbie squeezed in beside Nancy, gave a polite smile and said, "I'm fat, but you're mean." Robbie performed the first cheer and bent and swayed. She avoided the high jumps and splits, but her voice was strong. The squad members were still building moral at their school, just like the old days.

The crowd clapped and whistled. Nancy glared at Robbie when they trudged off the stage, while a couple of the other women gave her the ‘thumbs-up’ sign.

Her scalp was wet. Exercising in the body suit was like a steam bath. In the restroom, before the other women exited the stalls, she sponged her face with wet tissues. Her mascara streaked down her cheeks and the wax along her gum line had shifted. She was beyond a quick repair. There was nothing she could do but leave. *I know how Cinderella felt*. While the participants lined up for the buffet, she gathered her coat and purse and opened the double doors to the outside cool air.

As she drove, she played with the smooth material of her slacks. Why did she have to be stubborn? Familiar landmarks on the highway whirled by as fast as her thoughts were chasing each other. She set the cruise control. She didn’t need a patrol car stopping her in this condition. She should’ve moved her research to another city where no one knew her. She’d been lucky that no one called her on her disguise. Dr. Clifton’s accusation about her need for attention spiraled into her confused and exhausted thoughts. Could that mean that she was more like the Nancy Harris’ of the world than she thought?

Robbie remembered when Sharon, in her usual white v-neck T-shirt and jean Capri pants, gave her a lesson about walking with dignity. They were in the meeting area of the church. The torso had arrived but the leggings were still at the designers. Robbie had arrived disguised in her wig, glasses, contact lenses, and the large body with a blouse and pants.

“Wow, look at you.” Mavis waved, her bangles clanged with the vigorous gesture. “Get over here and let’s have a look.”

Robbie moved forward.

"Stop right there." Sharon jumped up.

Robbie had looked around sure she was about to step into something unpleasant. "What is it?"

"Are you trying to imitate Frankenstein or something?"

"No. I'm just walking," Robbie said, miffed.

"You're moving like you have a rod up your back and your arms are hinged at the shoulders and elbows. Watch me."

Sharon glided down the aisle and around the tables over the playschool carpet with her chin perpendicular to the floor. Her arms swayed easily at her side. "There. You try it."

Margaret plucked tissues from her burnt orange purse and wiped tears from her eyes as she called, "Take smaller steps."

Sharon put her hands on Robbie's hips and helped her feel the natural shift from hip-to-hip. Soon, Mavis and Margaret had joined them in an impromptu "Bunny Hop Dance." "Right kick, left kick, hop, hop, hop," Sharon called.

They collapsed into a heap onto the couch and chairs giggling like teenagers in dance class.

"How am I going to learn how to be in this disguise? You have had years to learn." Robbie yanked her wig from her head and scratched her soaked scalp.

"Practice. Practice. Practice." Sharon blew down the V of her shirt.

Margaret kicked off her burnt orange shoes. "At least you're trying. You'll get there. But I don't know if I'm ready for the conga line dance any time soon."

"Hey, we can keep practicing and we can enter the talent show as cancan dancers," Mavis jumped from her chair and began singing the tune and kicking her legs.

"As my tap dance teacher said, 'If you want to learn anything, set it to music and add some steps and it will stay with you for a long time,'" Sharon said.

Mavis gasped for air. "I know just what you mean, every time I'm in a mall and hear the music from one of my exercise videos, my arms want to fling out to the side or I have a sudden urge to bend and twist."

Robbie laughed at that memory while she applied the brake and slowed her speed along the merging ramp. *I'm okay. Sure I look a little rough right now, but I'll only get better. Mavis, Margaret, and Sharon believe in me. I can do this.*

As she parked on the street in front of her house, all she could think about was a shower washing away the perspiration from her body. The cool air felt delicious on her skin. She waved when the curtain across the street twitched open. Mrs. Mitchell was on front door watch. While her sleeve billowed like a windsock, Robbie was momentarily glad her neighbor's distant vision was compromised. *Oh man, I still haven't made that phone call to Mrs. Mitchell. As soon as I get in, I have to call Mrs. Mitchell.*

The warm air and vanilla aroma greeted her in her entryway. *No, I'll do it after I clean up. Mrs. Mitchell loves to talk.*

She hung her coat in the closet and climbed the stairs to her bedroom. She slipped out of her filmy pantsuit and placed it on the chair. She would take it to her drycleaner. When she pulled her arms from the torso, freed her breasts and stomach area and finally her legs, she felt the cool air wash over her skin.

It would be great to take the body suit to the cleaners as well but there wasn't time. Instead she followed the directions and sponge rinsed the inside of the torso, paying special attention to the armpits and belly. She turned the leggings inside out and ran the sponge with disinfectant over and into every dimple in the fabric. Now it was her turn to clean up. She glanced at the clock. *Wow!* She needed to hurry if she was going to meet with Margaret, Sharon, and Mavis at Atlantis on time. Robbie's original plan was to go directly to coffee from the reunion. Instead, she'd used up precious time cleaning the body suit.

Robbie waved at the window just in case Mrs. Mitchell wasn't enthralled in her TV programs. She adjusted her seat and hoped for green lights down Broad Street.

When Robbie arrived, she found Mavis doctoring her coffee at the coffee bar, Margaret sitting with her back to the door. Sharon waved when she burst through the coffee house doors.

"Oh, I hoped you'd come straight from the reunion. I wanted to see you all dressed up," Margaret said. "I am just dying to see you in that beautiful pantsuit. Maybe I'll get one just like it."

Mavis balanced her cappuccino in one hand and a muffin on a plate in her other. "Give her a chance to talk, will you?" She tucked her hair behind her ears.

"I wanted to, I thought I could, but when I tell you what happened, you'll understand." Robbie took her wallet from her purse. "Sorry, I have to eat something. I'll be right back." She scanned the display case. "I'll have a Caesar salad and a tall decaf with room for milk, please."

After her order came up, she popped a crouton into her mouth and added her milk to her coffee, then chose a plastic fork before she sat in the empty chair at the table. "Thank you for coming out on a Sunday evening."

"I'm dying to hear how your day went," Mavis said while she sliced her muffin into slivers.

"Is that all you're eating?" Sharon pointed at Robbie's salad, and twisted her braid hanging over her left shoulder. "I could have brought you some fresh sausage rolls. I took them out of the oven just before I came."

"Thanks, Sharon. I know your pastry is light. This will tide me over until I can make something more substantial. I didn't stay for the buffet because I discovered that I cannot do strenuous exercise in the suit without looking as if I am melting from the inside out."

"Exercise, at a high school reunion?" Sharon placed her teabag onto a napkin.

"I was on the cheerleading team all through high school. The message that the squad was performing some of our routines must have been lost in cyberspace because I didn't get it."

"So did you watch?" Margaret asked.

"I was prepared to but some of my friends encouraged me to go on stage and do my best. We were the school morale builders after all. It was a blast, but when it was all over, I couldn't repair my makeup in a high school bathroom. So I ducked out the door without eating."

"I thought the suit had pockets for cool packs." Mavis placed one slice of the muffin into her mouth.

"It does, but with my anxiety about possible discovery as well as all the laughter, hugs, and then the routines, they were long past their cooling ability." Robbie forked a helping of salad into her mouth.

"Mavis, what are you doing? You don't play with your food, you bake all day." Sharon swatted stray crumbs onto the floor.

"If you must know, I read about a new study on the Internet today that said that if children eat slowly they have a less chance of becoming obese."

"You're not a kid anymore," Margaret said, stating the obvious.

"I know, but I thought I'd try to savor bites. Anything is worth a try." Mavis slipped the fork under another piece. The three women watched the slow arc from plate to lips while the rock music played in the background and conversation ebbed and flowed from the other patrons.

After the crumbs dropped into Mavis' mouth, Margaret broke the spell. "I suppose if you have all day to eat, it could be successful, but when I have a thirty-minute lunch break and have to walk the length of the building to get to the cafeteria and back as well as use the facilities, I'm not so sure a person would have enough strength to finish their shift with a few morsels of muffin."

"Another part of the study showed that kids who have a choice between playing with friends and eating choose friends. I look forward to our meetings and the topics we discuss." Mavis reached and held hands with Sharon and Margaret. "I, for one, am glad that I saw your advertisement on *Used Regina*."

"Thank you, Mavis."

"Enough of what the Internet says, let's have reality. How did the reunion go? Anyone catch on?" Sharon leaned her elbows on the table.

"Yes, one of my friends asked me what was up but when I tried to explain it she wasn't really interested. She wanted to connect with friends, so it wasn't an issue. But Dr. Clifton was also there for a few minutes and she didn't recognize me. So I am pumped about that." She gave each of the women a big smile. "We did it."

"Really?" Sharon trudged her chair. "Are you going to tell us that everyone just accepted the changes?"

"Pretty much." Robbie chewed the inside of her cheek.

"So what else happened?" Mavis reached over and patted Robbie's hand.

"When I came into the registration area, one of my classmates didn't hide her surprise but she didn't come out and ask me anything, just assumed that I wouldn't be able to join the rest of the cheerleaders on stage and then when I did go up on stage, she said 'Move over, Fat Lady coming' or some such thing."

"Did you give her a hip check?" Sharon growled.

Laughter bounced from the table next to them.

"No, but I wasn't mature either. I said, 'I may be fat, but you're mean.' Then of course I had to participate in as many of the moves as possible. Sadly exiting as fast as possible was necessary." She drank a big gulp of cool coffee.

"What about the other women?" Mavis shoved the remainder of her muffin to the center of the table and covered it with a napkin. "Another trick. If I don't see it, I probably won't eat it."

"Good one," Robbie said, "I'll have to try it."

"How did the other women act?" Margaret asked.

"They were fine and gave high fives all around because of course some of us couldn't talk for a few minutes." Robbie tapped her fork against her empty salad container. "I know that I had the usual trepidations before I went, wondering if I would be the only one without children or a significant other in my life. But school friends are friends again."

"What about your experience of being with your old friends in a different body shape?" Margaret pressed on.

"Maybe it's true about the eyes. I know I overheard concerns about a woman from an earlier class and people were worried about her. Because she was very thin, they assumed an illness. Then there were women who were pregnant and guys who were balding. Yes, there were women and men who looked fine, too, but in a lot of ways we were the same crowd just older and wiser until we slipped back into our high school selves for a few hours."

"Hmm, I don't know, I think you had a different experience than we would have had. I don't think I could have looked at some of my classmates who used to call me frumpy and dumpy," Margaret said.

"I'll record today in detail and after I've had other experiences, I'll include your feedback in my notes."

Mavis looked at her watch. "I have to go. Susie needs a 'show and share' tomorrow and it's her turn to bring snack."

"I need to go home as well." Robbie yawned. "I'm beat. Thank you again for coming out on a Sunday evening."

"Yeah, what's with a reunion on a Sunday anyway?" Mavis tucked her used napkin into her cup.

"Never thought about it. The organizers must have had their reasons. I'll email tomorrow after my interview," Robbie promised and followed her friends out of the coffee house. The wind had picked up and she bent into it, slogging her way to her car.

Chapter 8

Jake drove his Mustang along Wascana Parkway and saw a woman with a yellow lab jogging in the weak dusk. The dog reminded him of Custard. As a young boy, he and his dog had been inseparable. They explored the creek together for golf balls, played Frisbee on the lawn, and ran in the early morning. One day, during Jake's final year at Central Collegiate, Custard didn't wake up. He didn't tell his basketball teammates or anyone else why he couldn't focus on the city championship practice for days afterward. His grandparents understood. They rationalized that it was for the best because Custard would've been heartbroken when Jake left for the university that fall. Jake would have given up his scholarship to the University of Ottawa if staying would have brought Custard back.

He missed his routine jogs. Running into a wind helped him clear his mind. He would run again tomorrow. When he arrived at the nursing home, he went directly to Frank's room. "Hi, Grandpa." Frank's blue-tinged eyelids flickered open.

Jake gave a quick pat to Frank's bony shoulder under the comforter before he settled his body into the contours of the brown recliner. His fingers played with the worn fabric on the armrests.

"What did you ever do with the new chair I bought you last year?" he finally asked Frank.

"Common Room." Frank sat up. "Tried to but I couldn't part with this one. When I sit in it, I feel as if Mabel's going to walk through that door and bring me a coffee, or tell me what she heard on the news, or read me one of your letters."

While he was away studying, teaching, or traveling, Jake had scrounged for news he could tell the two old people he'd left behind. "I know the letters were boring, but I couldn't tell you about the keg parties or the weekend barbeques."

"Not our Jake." Frank's brown eyes watered with mischief.

"You read between the lines," Jake said.

Frank's feet dangled on the side of the bed. "We were young once, too."

"It took me a few years to figure that out."

"So are we staying here for supper or going out?" Frank slid into his slippers.

"If you're up to it, let's go out." Jake wasn't sure if Frank had lost his appetite, which was another symptom of the disease. He'd enjoyed his milkshake earlier today and perhaps he needed a change from the dining room menu.

"I'll be ready in a couple of minutes." Frank's breaths were uneven.

"Do you need any help?" Jake offered.

"No. I can still do this on my own." Frank closed the bathroom door.

Jake settled his body further into the chair upholstery and closed his eyes. A tiny tap seemed to feather his cheek just like his grandmother did before she would bend and kiss him and tell him that she loved him.

The rushing of water from the bathroom tap and the glare of fluorescent light tried to pluck away his feelings of well-being. He heard Frank open the bathroom door, slide his feet along the floor, and open the closet. Jake watched his granddad fumble with his parka, pull on his gloves, then tug down the flaps of his cap over his ears. "Ready when you are."

While Jake retrieved his coat from the hook and took the knit cap from his pocket, Frank nodded. "You're learning, boy. It's cold out there." He used the long shoehorn easing his foot into his boot. "Don't forget your gloves."

"I need to find a heavy pair of boots as well. I saw all those people today who were prepared to survive in this cold."

"Thanks for reminding me." Frank reached into his breast pocket. "Here, I have a handicap decal we can hang from your mirror and you can get me close to the doors." Frank waited beside the front doors of the manor until Jake brought the Mustang around. Jake lent his arm as added support to Frank's cane.

A group of women in red capes edged with fur waited for them to pass through the doors.

"Sorry, ladies, I'm going to miss your carols this year, my son is treating me to dinner." Frank nodded toward Jake.

"We'll be back to sing for your Christmas dinner, Frank," one woman replied and shook the gold bell in her hand.

"Then we'll plan to be there," Jake replied.

After Jake clicked Frank's seat belt into position, he asked, "You really okay with missing this performance?"

"You bet. Change helps a man appreciate what he has."

They drove to a mom-and-pop diner and over tomato soup and grilled cheese sandwiches, Frank asked, "How'd the drive go?"

"Fine, I think. It's hard to tell with colleagues. She seemed to enjoy my company." He swept his fingers through his hair. *If I didn't blow it because I ducked away from her advances.*

Frank leaned forward. "Where'd you go?"

"We drove to Lumsden."

"That's a pretty town. I'll bet it's a lot bigger now than when I saw it last."

"It was bustling. Dr. Clifton needed to deliver a package to a friend at a school reunion. Strangest thing though, Robin was there, too." He tapped his spoon on the edge of the saucer.

"Ah, Robin Bird. She didn't name the school but she told me about her reunion. She was anxious about going. Was she having a good time?"

The server filled their water glasses and asked about dessert. They ordered pecan pie for Jake and apple pie with cheddar cheese for Frank.

Jake continued. "She was laughing and kidding around. We even had a bit of a dance."

Frank spooned the ice cream into his mouth. "She's pretty in a strange way."

"You noticed, too."

"I'm almost dead, not dead, son." Frank laughed and his fingers drummed on the tabletop.

"She laughs a lot. She's intelligent. She seems to have an inner core of strength."

"So you used your observation skills."

"That's what I do, I watch people."

Country music played in the background, and a skirt covered with an apron swished by to pour coffee at the next booth.

"I saw a woman attend her high school reunion and have a good time," Jake added.

Frank set his fork beside his empty plate, then gathered his gloves and hat and grasped the table edge and stood.

Jake picked up the bill.

"Glad to hear. Robin's a good woman." Frank fumbled in his pocket and put a couple of dollars under his saucer for the server.

"Maybe Robin and I can be friends," Jake said as he supported Frank to the car. "She acts more comfortable around you than me."

Frank leaned against the seat. “Can’t ever have too many friends but some need more care than others. Just remember that. You did accuse her of trying to steal my few dollars. Besides some women just fancy the more mature man.”

“Is that a smirk?” His grandfather’s upper lip twitched.

“It is what it is. I like her.”

His grandfather’s eyes were closed when they reached Care Manor. Jake parked the car and retrieved a wheelchair from the lobby. Frank didn’t object when Jake helped him to sit and then wheeled him down the hall lined with paper cut snowflakes.

Frank allowed Jake to unzip his jacket and help him with his pajamas. Frank wasn’t far away from Robin’s initial fear about assisted bathroom duty. Jake kept his ear on the sounds coming out of the door, the flush of the toilet, the tap running. Frank shuffled to his bed and leaned his rear against the side until he hoisted himself up, dropped his slippers, and sank back against the pillow. “I tell you I feel as if I have worked a twelve-hour shift without a break.”

Standing and watching Frank’s chest rise and fall, Jake leaned in and kissed his grandfather’s cheek. He ran his hand over the back of the recliner, then checked one last time on Frank covered up to his chin in blankets. Jake wished that he hadn’t stayed away so long. His grandmother’s voice echoed in his mind. *Enjoy what you have, not what you wish for, son.* She’d said it often around the time he wanted to sell his mother’s car for a motorcycle.

Even though he should return to either the hotel or the university and work on his research notes, he needed to drive. He liked engaging the clutch and manually shifting the transmission as he headed out on the highway. He increased the pressure on the gas pedal, his hands relaxed on the wheel. In the darkness, as his headlights shone back and forth across skiffs of snow, he thought of hips swaying close to him and then away. He steered the car into the merging lane. He turned onto the overpass and slowed to reenter the city limits, passing through a new subdivision with a billboard advertising two-car garages, three-bedroom houses with family room. There were snow racers on one driveway and a failed attempt at a snowman in another yard. Wasn't this what he'd always thought his future would be, when he'd considered that kind of future? But when was the future going to happen? He wasn't getting any younger. Is this why he'd stayed away? He had known there was an exciting world away from home. He had thought he'd had so much more to offer the world than to stay around exclusively for the two people who loved him most. Maybe he wasn't capable of loving in that way. Maybe he was like his biological father who didn't love Jake's mother as his special woman or Jake as his kid. Jake slowed the Mustang and pulled over to the curb. The engine idled, pushing warm air through the interior. Jake focused on the streetlight ahead of him. His mother died. His grandmother became his mother. He hadn't even been there when she died. He'd been abandoned by his father and now the man who took his place and had loved Jake with all his heart was dying. How was he going to make it without breaking down? A half-ton truck drove up beside him. The driver honked and rolled down the window.

Jake rolled down his window.

"You lost, buddy?" the guy called.

More than you'll ever know. "No. Thanks anyway."

"Are you stalking someone?" The voice was gruffer.

"No, I'm leaving." Jake pressed on the clutch and slipped into first gear.

"Have a good night." The truck slowly drove forward.

"You, too." Jake suspected the guy had Jake's headlights in his rearview mirror making sure Jake drove away like he said he was going to do.

At the stop sign, the truck went straight ahead and Jake turned left toward the hotel.

Robbie stacked her dinner dishes in the sink. She switched the desk lamp next to her computer. The blank computer monitor was like a bottomless hole waiting to be filled with her experiences. *Maybe he'd call.*

Where did that come from? Of course he couldn't call if he didn't even know where she lived or her phone number. Remember this is part of the plan. I am not some schoolgirl waiting for the boy at the dance to call me.

Robbie forced herself to gather her scattered thoughts. She had kept her promise to the women who had shared their high school memories of shame and exile. Robbie, as a woman of substantial size, attended and had fun. Yes, she'd rather not have had Nancy stare at her and call her fat or leave without saying goodbye to friends but there were moments in her everyday life she'd rather not deal with. Especially those challenging times involving critical Dr. Clifton questioning her field study. A little feeling wormed its way through Robbie's determination. *Just because I dress up, can I experience what it's like to be seen as fat as other than ideal? No, I won't stop now.*

When she sank beneath her eyelet comforter, she allowed herself to sink into the memory of brown eyes, tiny bits of his beard growing on a straight jaw, palms pressed and fingers wrapped around her hands. Jake circled his thumb across the fleshy erogenous mounts beneath her thumb. Her abdominal muscles tightened remembering those moments of closeness. Jake had danced with her.

She sat bolt upright. Jake was supposed to be observant. He didn't even raise an eyebrow when they danced. She was good but not that good. Monica had come right out and asked her what she was up to, so she had asked her to follow Robbie to the back corner of the gym for privacy and gave her a thumbnail sketch about her *Fat Like Me* field research. Robbie cut her explanation short when Monica's eyes glazed over. Monica just shrugged and said 'whatever' and went back to the party.

Oh, that truckload of assumptions, he didn't really see her. When she thought about it, other than Monica, her classmate, who really saw her? This time she punched her pillows and slammed her head into them and yanked the comforter up to her chin.

Chapter 9

Robbie woke to Monday morning coffee aroma. Many times just before bed she almost neglected setting the timer on the coffee maker, but in the morning she was always glad she stayed up a few minutes longer. Who needed a partner when there was an electronic device that met most of her needs? She yawned and during tidying her kitchen and living room, she reviewed the company prospectus on Heavenly Treats and the qualifications for the position of assistant to the Human Resources Officer. Robbie had received confirmation that both applications, one as Robbie Smith and one as Robin Smyth, had received interview appointments.

Robin Smyth received the first interview and was scheduled for one o'clock and Robbie Smith the following day. Part of Robbie's field study was to present herself to one company with her identical qualifications on a résumé, but for one appointment she would present herself in the bodysuit as Robin Smyth and the other as herself. *Hmmm, did Robin Smyth draw the first appointment interview because her name sounds more professional than Robbie Smith?*

After she applied her makeup, Robbie slid her feet through the padded leggings, fitted the specially designed frozen gel packs into small pouches along the abdomen of the suit and zipped up the torso. She wanted to look cool and professional inside the suit. The faux fat neck roll fit securely into position. She finished with her wig and glasses. Then she dressed in her pressed gray wool suit and crisp white blouse. She chose a gray and red silk oblong scarf and knotted it around her neck. Her shoes shone. With a perfect résumé in her briefcase, Robin Smyth was ready. She didn't know what would happen when she appeared as a woman of size. She wanted to substantiate that not all managers disqualified candidates on body size, but they made their selection based on education and work experience.

Robbie parked and put in coins for two hours. This would give her time to arrive unhurried and not worry about the meter running out and receiving a ticket. The air soothed her scurrying thoughts while she strolled beside other office staff on their lunch hour.

She focused on the clicking of her heels on the tile to calm her mind. At the bank of elevators, she saw Jake's familiar face. He noticed her at the same time. He waved and walked toward her.

"Hi, Jake."

"Hey, Robin. We sure meet in unusual places." He was smiling.

"You're right. This isn't a big city but I can go weeks without seeing some of my friends." His skin glistened in the bright lights. "You look pleased with yourself."

"That I am. When I was up early reading the apartments for rent, I found one close to the university and I called immediately. It's mine on January first. I can move out of the hotel in a few weeks." He waved an envelope. "And you? You're looking very professional this morning."

"Thanks. I have an interview for a position in human resources."

"Good luck, Robin. You're good with people." He cupped her shoulder with his hand. His long fingers pointed toward her breast. She had on a coat and layers of foam and padding, so she could not feel his warmth. It was impossible. But memories of his thumb massage slipped into her minutes-ago calmness. She realized he was expecting a reply. "Thanks. I believe we'll see each other around town."

He chuckled. "You have that right."

He leaned forward, and her heart banged against her ribs. *Was he going to kiss her? So much for a calm mind. She couldn't let that happen. Not now.* She took a step away and gave him a salute. "Say hello to Frank."

His eyebrows drew together for a split second. "Will do."

She looked at the clock on the wall. "I've got to run."

She turned and stepped into an elevator. After the door closed, she drew in a calming breath. That was close. She would not have been able to go through with this interview if he would have noticed and commented on her makeup. When the door opened, she gripped her briefcase and with her head held high she strode up to the receptionist's desk. "Good afternoon. I have a one o'clock appointment with Mrs. Jones."

The woman glanced at her appointment book, nodded, and indicated a green chair situated by the wall. "Please have a seat." Instead of picking up the telephone to announce Robbie, the receptionist walked down the hall. Robbie admired the woman's straight-cut black suit with matching pumps. Margaret would be impressed with the receptionist's style. *I'll have to remember every detail for her.*

Robbie folded her coat over her arm, fluffed her scarf, and smoothed her pleated slacks. She hoped that not wearing a skirt and heels in the twenty-first century wouldn't be the deciding factor between a job and no job offer.

"Miss Smyth."

Robbie jumped in her chair. The thick carpet must have muffled any sound of approaching footsteps.

"Miss Smyth, would you follow me please?" Ms. Receptionist held open another door down the hall.

Robbie stood and resisted the urge to tug at her jacket. She was led into a room with a computer monitor and keyboard on a desk.

"I'm logging into preliminary keyboard timed tests."

When the receptionist bent to retrieve some paper for the printer, a ripple of envy crept through Robbie at the way the material in the skirt altered and the skirt clung to accentuate her assets in a subtle shift. If she were without the fat suit, she'd look like that. Robbie gave herself a mental kick in the backside. *Wait a minute. I'm doing exactly what Mavis, Sharon, and Margaret talked about and I complain about. I'm objectifying this woman because of the way her body looks.*

Robbie sat up straight and waited for instructions.

The woman spoke. "Please call me when you've completed the prompts that the computer gives to you."

"Excuse me. If I'm to call you, may I have your name, please?"

The woman extended a hand with a diamond glittering on her finger and French-manicured nails. "Eve Winston."

Robbie extended her hand with her flashy costume-jeweled finger and clear, polished nails. "I'm pleased to meet you, Ms. Winston. How long does this usually take?"

"There isn't a set time. Just complete it at your own speed. It's all powered up and ready to go."

Eve walked out of the room and closed the door before Robbie turned the chair and adjusted it for her height and breadth toward the computer. She seemed to be all thumbs and her speed was slow. The computer gave her three attempts to improve. The next prompt led her to a multiple-choice personality test. The questions seemed to change before she had time to contemplate her answers. An hour later, the computer thanked her and told her that the interview was over. Her previously pressed slacks were creased across her thighs and her blouse bunched at her waist. Her scarf, a gray and red puddle on the floor. She was hot and thirsty.

When she stood, she noticed the accordion creases in her jacket where she'd sat on it. She tugged at the cloth and wished she'd had the foresight to hang it up instead of peeling it off and letting it slip behind her. Someone knocked on the door.

"Have you completed the little quizzes yet?"

"Just finished." There must be a signal somewhere when the program shuts down or someone had telepathy. *Yet. What did Ms. Winston mean by 'yet?' Was I that slow?*

"Great. Mrs. Jones will see you now." Ms. Winston held the door wide for her to go through.

As she walked into the plush office Robbie reviewed the ways to create a positive impression. She had her answers ready if she was asked where she'd see herself in five years: management. What were her greatest strengths and weaknesses? Creative determination and purposeful inventiveness were both strengths and weaknesses depending on the situations.

Mrs. Jones stood and extended her hand over the desk. Robbie was forced to lean and her thighs bumped the edge and caused a framed photograph to clatter onto the desktop. "I'm sorry."

"Ms. Smyth, please take a seat."

Robbie stepped away and sat in a chair and when she looked at her lap, her thighs seemed to ooze out from under the armrests. She did her best to smile and respond to the questions with thoughtful answers, but she felt like a hamster on a wheel. Mrs. Jones asked her if she considered herself successful.

"Yes. I set goals and have met some and I am on track to achieve others." She watched Mrs. Jones mark a sheet. Again Robbie wished she could read upside down.

"What motivates you to do your best job?"

"I enjoy challenges and achieving goals. I appreciate recognition for a job done well, too," Robbie replied.

"Have you tasted our double chocolate marble brownie with walnuts?"

Mrs. Jones produced a thin white china plate with two brownie bits. She tilted her head to the side and a smile played at the corner of her lips when she walked around her desk and extended the plate.

"No. I've sampled many of your products. The Strawberry Tulips, Pecan Mousse, and of course the Cherry Cheesecake are to die for." Robbie licked her lips in anticipation. "These look decadent." She took a tiny bite and allowed the flavors to settle around her taste buds. "Wow, they really pop."

"It's a new product line. I'm glad you're enjoying it. Take the second piece, please."

"No, thank you."

"Are you sure? The sample pieces are so small." Mrs. Jones offered again.

Robbie shook her head. "When will these be available to the general public?"

"Our media campaign begins next week. Last chance, are you sure I can't tempt you?"

"Thank you, but no."

Mrs. Jones returned to her desk. She tapped her pencil against the desk and looked up at Robbie. "How would you know if you were successful in this job?"

"I would set high standards for myself and when I meet them, I could consider that a success. Also, when my outcomes to different projects are successful and when my supervisors and team members tell me."

"Thank you." Mrs. Jones wrote a note. "Do you have any final questions?"

"How soon would I be able to be productive at Heavenly Treats?"

"We like to make everyone feel welcome. The new employee shadows the present human resource assistant for two weeks and then gradually assumes the duties and by the end of the third month we would evaluate your progress."

"Thank you, Mrs. Jones. The timeframe sounds generous." Robbie maneuvered herself out of the chair. She glanced over her shoulder making certain there wasn't some mystery Velcro that had held her in place. She grasped Mrs. Jones extended hand and shook it firmly. "Thank you for your time. Your web page didn't suggest that the skills and personality test would be part of the interview. Did I miss the detail?"

"We try to surprise our candidates. It allows us to observe how they react when something new is given to them. We know that our successful candidates will have researched our company and tried our products. We would appreciate if you'd keep this to yourself if you know other candidates. It'll make the screening process fair." Mrs. Jones looked over Robbie's head as she said these last statements.

Robbie nodded. "Could you tell me the next step in the employee search and who I should contact?"

"Ms. Winston will provide you with that information. We're all part of a team at Heavenly Treats." Mrs. Jones smiled and walked behind her desk. Ms. Winston opened the office door.

Robbie wondered if there was a button that Mrs. Jones pressed or if Ms. Winston was indeed intuitive.

Ms. Winston gave Robbie a business card and assured her that she would hear by the end of the week if she were to be included in the second round of interviews.

Robbie stopped with her hand on the door. "May I ask where you purchased your suit? You look as fresh as you did when I arrived."

Ms. Winston raised one eyebrow. "It's a little boutique on Hamilton Street that caters to professional women."

"Thank you. I'll stop by one day," Robbie said.

"I wouldn't bother." Ms. Winston's nose wrinkled.

"I wouldn't copy you. The boutiques where I've

shopped keep records of purchases made by women in the same offices."

"You wouldn't have to worry on that account. They don't carry plus sizes."

"Oh. I see." Robbie bit her cheek and took a deep breath. Why did she seem to run into nastier women than men around the issue of body fat? Perhaps she was more sensitive when she was with women. She'd have to note this in her field journal. It wasn't Ms. Winston's fault that the store didn't carry women's sizes. The store could just be another example of preferential marketing in the women's clothing industry. But Ms. Winston did have control over her offensive tone. Robbie remained calm. This was a possible employment opportunity.

"Thank you for telling me. I will visit the shop when I'm downtown and then I'll know what to look for in my size." Robbie slipped into her coat. "I'll look forward to your call on Friday. I have voice mail if I happen to be out and I will return your call as soon as possible."

Ms. Winston raised her head to a neutral position just before turning back to her computer monitor. *That wasn't encouraging. Hold on, perhaps it is company policy that staff do not confirm expectations and Mrs. Jones makes all of the decisions.*

The wind gusted and tugged at her coat and threatened to freeze her ears. She had to find a hat that she could wear or ear warmers at least. She tucked her head into her collar. She'd reached the hood of her car when the parking commissionaire approached. *Whew*. She'd been spared a parking ticket. Pedestrians hurried across the streets, while people huddled into bus shelters. Winter was definitely on the way.

After Robbie drove into the garage at home, she released the seat belt and lifted one leg over the car frame and then the other. The armrest on the door was her lever to exit the small interior space. Robbie didn't feel professional next to the crisp Ms. Winston and Mrs. Jones. She didn't have the skills to act as a dignified woman of substance. A picture of the proficient Nadine in Jean Clifton's office flashed in her mind. Nadine knew where to shop and how to dress because she was at home in her body.

Who was *she* fooling? She could never truly experience circumstances the same as women who have always been larger just by wearing a fake body. She slapped the foam and watched it vibrate.

Stop right now. This is research. I need to stay focused. Inside, she hung her coat, kicked off her shoes, and focused on each stair. Her job now was to get undressed and clean up and record her data. She removed the melted gel packs and placed moisture-soaking packages into the legs and arms and torso of the suit, so the suit would be dry and fresh when she went out in it again.

Robbie sank into the tub. Why was she suddenly feeling as if she should just accept Clifton's assessment and get the thesis over and done with and move on? Her parents would welcome her into their business. Her father was a general practitioner doctor in the town of Lumsden and her mother was the counselor. She wouldn't have to put up with the 'one word to describe yourself' questions. Her parents were very familiar with her creative determination on good days and stubbornness on others.

With her back against the hard surface, the bubbles dissipated across the swell of her breasts, which were tiny in comparison to those of her interview persona. Her tension eased. She was prepared for the sessions today and she would be prepared tomorrow, too. She had inside information about the proficiency and psychological tests. The position at Heavenly Treats would be great for the successful candidate. The web site showed opportunities for movement in the company, as well as a great medical plan. She would probably have to turn down the position if it was offered to her as either Robin or Robbie because of her research, unless Mrs. Jones accepted Robbie's explanations and would see her creativity as an asset to the company.

Her treadmill stood idle in the corner. Even though it was only six in the evening, it was dark and she craved the crisp air on her face. The calendar showed a three-quarter moon. She would run in the familiar safety of the park where she could avoid cars and curbs. She dressed in her reflective vest and tugged on her knit hat fitted with a head light. A quick call to her parents fulfilled a promise. They only needed a voice mail or text message before she began and when she returned if she ran alone after dark.

She set an easy pace and followed the yellow line down the middle of the path, past leafless deciduous branches and outstretched evergreen limbs. Running in the dark required a trust in her own abilities that she wouldn't stumble where the path wasn't even. The only sounds were her steady breathing, her feet striking the pavement, and the wind. She saw a shape on Frank's bench. It was too late and too cold for the person to be Frank. Her eyes strained at the faceless shape hunched on the bench. Her light beam outlined the edge of the opposite side of the path. She gripped her pepper spray, another promise to her parents, but her feet slowed their pace on their own volition. When she glanced over, she recognized Jake's leather jacket. Her headlamp outlined his profile. She stopped. "Professor Proctor?"

The figure looked up.

She sat down beside him. He wouldn't see the similarities between her and Robin tonight, not with her hat pulled down over her ears covering her hair and dressed in her running gear. She turned off her light when he held up his hand to block out the glare. "Robbie Smith," she said. "We met at the university and at the fundraising dinner last week. Are you okay?"

He lowered his hand from his eyes and he straightened. "Hello."

She dropped her spray back to the bottom of her pocket, then hunkered down in front of him. "Have you been here long?"

"I was thinking of leaving." His voice was husky and lacked conviction.

Maybe something had happened to Frank but she couldn't ask. As Robbie she wasn't supposed to know that Jake had an ill grandfather. Her body was cooling down and she shivered, but Jake looked chilled to the bone. "Listen, I live through those gates. Why don't you come with me? I'll make some coffee. I have a fireplace."

"No, thank you. I can't. I appreciate that you mean well but . . . I'm faculty at your university and you're a grad student."

"Come on, it's freezing out here." She clutched his gloved hand, and she stood. When she turned, he followed. She hurried along the path and he trailed in a daze just behind, their clouds of exhaled breath mingling and blowing away. She unlocked the door and guided him into the vestibule. He stepped out of his loafers and was drawn toward the fire, while she unlaced her runners and tossed her coat and hat into the closet. She needed the warmth of the fire, too.

He stared into the embers. She bent and placed logs on the grate and closed the protective screen, then tipped the photographs that lined the mantle facedown.

The phone rang and she picked it up on the second ring. "Yes, home safe and sound. Talk to you tomorrow. Love you. Goodnight."

The conversation didn't break his concentration on the flames licking the logs. While coffee brewed, she looked around for visible reminders of her project. The coat was in the front closet and the rest of the disguise in the bedroom. If she kept the closet doors closed, her alter ego would be safe. She made his coffee sweet and black.

Jake sat on the ottoman with his shoulders rounded and his head in his hands. His jacket lay on the floor. *At least he's warm.* "Professor Proctor." He looked up. She put the mug of coffee into his palm and he circled it with both hands and brought the mug to his lips. She watched him swallow the steaming liquid.

"Thank you."

"What happened?"

"The doctor told me tonight that my grandfather won't live until Christmas." He didn't look at her but at the wavering flames in the grate.

She touched his arm and felt his sorrow radiating from him like heat from the fire. "I'm so sorry. Please, sit on the sofa." He looked forlorn perched on the stool, staring into the fire.

She thought of Frank's small body, asleep, marooned in the white landscape of his bed. Robbie hadn't expected his death to be imminent. She wished she had the power to become Robin without leaving his side, so then she could ask the questions that ran through her head. Instead, she stood until he sat. She wanted to sit next to him and draw his body close to hers, stroke his back, hold him and bring him into her warmth. Instead she sat in the chair across the room. She couldn't have him recognize her or have him feel compromised because of her student position. "Is there anything I can do? Something to help?" Her voice sounded flat.

He set his coffee cup down. He seemed to look through her. Frank's impending death loomed between them. Drawing a deep breath, Jake shook his head. "I feel as if you know my grandfather. Your voice sounds familiar. I'm sorry."

"My voice changes in the cold weather." *Robbie, be careful.*

He stood and gathered his jacket, took one last look at the sparks in the fireplace. “Thanks for the coffee but I’d better go. I didn’t think the reality would hit me like this.”

Robbie followed him to the front door and watched him slip into his shoes. “Can I drive you somewhere?”

With his hand on the handle, he turned. “No thanks. My car’s across the park. Thank you for everything.”

“You’re welcome.” She broke eye contact before she told him that she knew Frank. Now was not the time to burden him with her deception.

As soon as he was out of the door, she turned the lock and watched out the window until he disappeared into the park. She knew his car was at Care Manor. Before she washed his mug, she circled her hands around the width and held it. If only she could have offered him something more. She dropped the mug into the soapy water. What had she expected, a lingering warmth? She couldn’t indulge in this kind of fantasy. Her degree was at stake. Frank was dying and Jake was hurting.

She woke through the night to tree branches banging against her eaves and the sound of frozen pellets hitting the windowpanes. *First thing in the morning, I’ll call. Before I have coffee. I need to know. I want to be who Frank needs me to be.*

When her alarm went off at seven o’clock, she knew she would have to wait. She didn’t want to frighten him. She drank a pot of coffee. Paced. Could she dress up as Robin and visit Frank and then come home and get ready for her interview as Robbie? What was she prepared to do? What was her plan? The radio announcer called the top of the hour. It was nine. Heart pounding, she pressed the speed dial. “Good morning, Frank.”

“Hello, Robin. Are you coming to see me this morning?”

“Sorry. I have a job interview this afternoon and I need

to be all shiny and squeaky clean. That's why I'm calling to tell you I'll drop in later."

"Guess I can wait. Not much happening anyway. If it warms up and I can convince the staff, maybe I'll be outside."

"Make sure you wear your scarf and mittens. You take care until I see you again." She didn't even know if Frank knew what little time was left. Jake said before Christmas. That was a month, four short weeks.

"Don't feel as if you have to come and see an old man."

"I want to, so don't go suggesting I have a little guilt trip. Save that for your grandson."

"No, not him either. He's been pretty steady since he's come home."

"Good for him. Take care. I have to run."

She jogged in the park, trying to stay focused on the second interview at Heavenly Treats. Just before lunch, she dressed for the one o'clock appointment in a pantsuit similar to the one she'd worn as Robin. Her black hair was curled and she wore blush, foundation, eye shadow, mascara, and lipstick. She didn't wear the scarf today. She carried her résumé in the same portfolio as she had as Robin yesterday.

Another parking meter, another two hours paid for. Today, she'd appreciate running into Jake and receiving his good wishes but that would really be too much synchronicity. Robbie was a masters' student. She was qualified to apply for this position. With her shoulders back and head held high, she approached Ms. Winston and introduced herself.

"Good afternoon. Robbie Smith for a one o'clock appointment."

"One moment." Ms. Winston closed the file she worked on, then rounded her desk and said, "Follow me."

Ms. Winston wore a suit similar to yesterday but today

it was a deep shade of caramel, with matching shoes. This woman knew how to dress for success.

Robbie was led directly into Mrs. Jones' office. Today she slid into the chair with ease. Mrs. Jones asked the same questions. Robbie tried to give the same responses as she had when she was dressed as Robin Smyth.

"Robbie, do you understand the importance of image in the food industry?"

This was new. Robbie looked directly at Mrs. Jones and replied, "Of course, image is always important in any business."

Mrs. Jones fingered her smooth hairstyle and flicked an imaginary speck from her tailored blouse. Then she said, "Because we're in the food industry our staff is required to maintain good physical shape. We can't give our customers even the slightest hint that eating our food may cause weight gain."

"But all food, if eaten in large quantities with little exercise, can cause a weight gain."

"That's true. Do you have self control?"

"I eat a healthy diet and you'll see in my résumé that I have a membership in a health club and that I walk or run almost daily," Robbie said.

"What about your parents?"

"What do they have to do with this?" Robbie leaned forward.

"Genetics."

"From the family photographs, we seem to be above average in height with a medium body frame."

"Excellent. Your credentials are very promising. Do you have any questions for me?"

"On your website, it states that your company has a health plan. Does it reimburse employees for time to work out and health club costs or nutrition counseling?"

"No. We assume employees would be proud and would manage those areas on their own."

"What happens if an employee puts on weight due to medication?"

"We would find an area that's less visible until the situation is rectified."

"And no one has filed a suit against the company?"

"Not since I've been in charge. We promote hard-working independent women into management." Mrs. Jones swiveled in her chair.

"When will your team make the hiring decision?"

"Eve will telephone the successful candidate at the beginning of next week. I know you'd enjoy working with us at Heavenly Treats."

"Thank you for your time but I disagree. I couldn't work at a company where my dress size and genetics were used as a mark of achievement."

Robbie turned on her heel and marched out of the office. If she had heroic powers, she'd find a closet and change into Robin and go right back in there and flick the fluff off of Mrs. Jones' shoulder and tell her what she could do with her Heavenly Treats.

Today there wasn't a parking attendant ready to write out a ticket because the interview hadn't taken the same amount of time. Robbie wanted to report this incident to human resources immediately. She needed to slow down. This is the type of proof she needed for her thesis. She knew one thing was for certain, she wasn't turning on the ignition until she had herself under control.

Later when she drove past the park, Frank was there in a wheelchair, all bundled up with a blanket around his knees. She parked in a vacant spot and stomped through the park.

"Hi, Frank," she said and plopped down beside him.

He raised his gray brows. "Have we met?"

She'd been so excited seeing him outside and on his bench that she'd forgotten she didn't have her suit until he was confused by her appearance. She considered spilling the beans. But then she thought about his Mabel, and her friends, Mavis, Sharon, and Margaret. "Sorry. I'm Robbie." She extended her hand. "I've waved at you whenever I've run by. Robin, my friend, told me your name and that you feed the geese."

"Your mamas didn't have much of an imagination when they named you girls." He strained against the blanket across his knees.

She decided not to comment on the names. Maybe if she didn't say anything more she'd be able to climb out of the hole she'd dug for herself. "You're wrapped up pretty warm today."

"Between the staff and my grandson they wrapped me up like a mummy. I can't get my bread for the geese."

"The lake's almost frozen. I don't think any will come today."

He turned and looked at her while she spoke. "You sound like Robin. You could be twins, similar shaped eyes, different color though."

"Could we really?" Robbie chewed the inside of her lip.

"You move your hands the same."

She tucked her hands into her pockets.

"You're about the same height but you're smaller," he said.

"True." Robbie couldn't just leave. Frank looked so vulnerable sitting alone beside the frozen lake. "Guess we're not as individual as we think." She'd have to chance that he wouldn't notice other similarities. "Can I push you back home?"

"May as well. Since the geese seem to have left."

She maneuvered the wheelchair across the street. An attendant met them at the door, and Frank called over his shoulder. "If you see Robin before I do, tell her I'm expecting her later."

"I will."

He swiveled in the chair again. "You can come, too, anytime you want."

Robbie hastened back to her car as fast as her interview shoes would take her. She needed to change and visit Frank again, but this time in the shape he recalled with fondness.

Chapter 10

Robbie opened the door to Frank's room an hour later and saw his white knuckles and curled fingers clutching the bed sheet. A small moan escaped from his lips.

"Frank," Robin said.

His eyelids flickered and he turned his head toward her voice. She tiptoed to the bed. The room was dim. The sun set earlier every day. His lips pulled into a tight grimace.

"Are you in pain?" she asked.

He laid his head against the pillow and nodded.

"Have they given you medication?"

He whispered, "Yes."

She reached for the chair, placed it at the bedside, then draped her coat over the back and held his hand through the side rail. Her father, the doctor, had often expounded that silence was good company. He always went on and on about visitors trying hard to fill rooms with the sound of their voices.

Robbie blinked back tears. She didn't want to burden him with her emotions. Her parents were healthy. Unless there was a dreadful accident, she wouldn't be walking in Jake's shoes anytime soon. In the distance, she heard a phone ring and a resident mumbled for attention from the staff. She waited. Frank's breathing deepened.

"The pain's almost gone," he whispered. A few deep breaths later, he said, "Robbie must have phoned you."

"We met on the street. She told me you were out and about. You don't mind, do you?" She put her head against the bed rail.

"No. Jake will be here soon, too." He tried to push up on his elbows and looked at her. "He'll need a friend when this is over."

"We've never talked about what's happening with you. Will you tell me?"

"Short answer. I have an acute leukemia. Mainly hits kids or us old guys."

"But they are discovering better ways of handling cancer every day," she said. She didn't want him to give up hope.

"Good news is they can cure kids, but the cure isn't the same for us." He fell back against the pillow again.

She hadn't thought about later. Her over-the-top compulsion had brought her to this. If only she'd stopped and talked with Frank at other times rather than running past him. It was too late. She couldn't explain to Frank that she was deceiving him and his grandson. It wasn't total deception. Her emotions were true. She respected and liked them both very much but there was the big problem of the disguise, the pretense. "I'll try. He'll have other friends and colleagues."

Frank's eyelids drooped. "If a man has the same number of friends as fingers on both his hands, he is very lucky."

"You should rest before Jake comes. He's the important one, after all."

His head wobbled on his neck. "Help me into my chair. I'm better when I'm up."

Frank controlled the button that lifted the head of the bed. Robin lowered the side rail. He slowly moved his legs to the edge of the bed and then dropped them over the side within inches of the floor. She stood close to him when he slid his feet into his slippers. She cupped his fingers in her palm while he walked to the recliner. She tucked the blanket around his legs, then leaned toward him. "Would you tell me how you met Mabel?"

Frank closed his eyes and a smile played at the corners of his mouth. "I loved to ice skate. The war was over. Someone played the organ in the arena back then. One night after the announcer asked for requests, I wanted to hear a song I heard while I was in Paris. I was full of myself back then. When I went up to the booth, I saw the talented player was a woman. I remember that I almost swooned when she turned and looked at me with deep blue eyes and a full moon face. She apologized to me for not knowing the song just before a big bear of a man pointed the way to the door. For the rest of the night, I'd skid to a stop just under the glass booth and doff my hat to her after every song."

"Did you take her home?"

Frank chuckled. "Not that easy. The bear in the office was her father."

He'd stopped talking, his forehead wrinkled in concentration. She knew he was remembering events from more than half a century ago. With her legs crossed at the ankles, she waited.

"Mabel wasn't there for a few Saturdays in a row, but when my skates hit the ice on New Year's Eve, I knew she was back. The melodies were light and fun." His eyes twinkled. "I skated with every unmarried woman at the rink. Near midnight, I heard my song. I darn near caused a collision when I stopped and tipped my hat at the booth."

"Then he wrestled the bear to the ground," Jake said from the door to the room. "And they lived happily ever after."

Frank leaned forward. "Jake, my boy."

"Hi, Granddad. Robin." Jake bowed from his waist and with a flick of his wrist he swept off his knitted hat in a grand movement.

"Jake, you look like I imagine Frank looked when he courted Mabel. The love is in his voice." Then she sighed and shifted her arms across on her belly. She remembered that she wasn't in the middle of a love story anymore. When she looked at Jake's mouth and remembered the sadness, she wanted just for a second for him to recognize her as Robbie, the woman who had given him a warm place to be and something comforting to drink. But not here, not now. It would hurt Frank to discover that she was pretending to be a woman like Mabel. With her hands gripped on the side of the chair, she stood.

Jake raised his eyebrows. "Stay where you are and listen to the end of the story."

"No, you two visit. You're family. I'll hear it in installments." Robbie couldn't bear to be around Jake for lengths of time. She knew his observation skills were probably recording details subconsciously and when he wasn't worried about Frank, he'd start to ask questions that she didn't want to answer before she defended her thesis research and passed.

"You've done something different to your hair," Frank said.

Robbie glanced in the mirror and patted her wig. "No." She dipped her head. *Darn.* In her hurry, she'd forgotten her colored contacts.

Frank continued staring at her. "Something's different."

Robbie snagged her coat from the back of the chair and hurried toward the door. "I'll be back for more of your love story." She had to leave. "Take care, you two." Tossing her scarf over her shoulder and carrying her coat, she closed the door behind her to keep the noises from the halls away from the serenity of Frank's room.

Jake felt helpless after Robin left the room. His grandfather's death was a sure thing and there was nothing he could do to prevent it. Frank looked peaceful with his head leaning against the side of the chair. Robin might have been insulted when he hired her to spend time with Frank but it was one of the best decisions that Jake had made since he returned home. He would have to ask her for an account of her hours and keep the arrangement as professional as possible. He'd learned a lesson with his funding investigation. His lawyer's information indicated that someone had spent money without approval when they were in Botswana. Since Jake's signature was on the budget, he was responsible. The forensic audit would produce the details. He'd have to be patient.

Jake reviewed the few possessions in the room. Frank's life was captured in photographs, his clothes, his chair, and his stories. It would be comforting for Frank to tell someone his story and he would like Robin to hear it. "Granddad, did Robin mention anything about her job interview?"

"No. I'm sure she'll do well at whatever she tries."

"She must be between jobs now. She seems to visit throughout the day," Jake said.

"She doesn't talk about herself, just like your Grandma," Frank said.

Jake looked for an indentation on the chair Robin had vacated. She'd probably had sedentary jobs like most people these days. He wondered when his insidious prejudice toward size began. It felt as old as he was, but as a little boy, he scrambled into the spot on the sofa after his grandmother left, soaking up the lingering warmth from her body. When he sat on the chair where Robin had been, there wasn't any lingering body warmth. It seemed as if she held her warmth inside. He stretched his legs out and leaned back and watched Frank sleep.

He must have dozed. He dreamt of laughing and talking with Robin but not Robin. He arched his back and straightened when the dinner announcement reverberated through the halls and penetrated the closed door. Frank scrubbed the fatigue from his eyes. "Staying for supper?"

The thought of mushy peas, sloppy mashed potatoes, and ground beef in gravy shuddered through Jake's brain. "Sure. I'll stay."

Frank shifted from side-to-side to the edge of the chair and stood. "Be forewarned. I didn't sign you up. There may not be enough."

A small hope lingered. "I can have coffee and get something later." With his arm around his grandfather, they followed the other residents to the dining room.

"Frank, Jake, nice to see you." An attendant in a colorful smock and tiny red bells dangling from her ears said as she offered Frank his chair.

"My boy here hasn't reserved a spot. Can he just sit beside me?"

"Of course. Grab one of the folding chairs over by the window, Jake."

"Will do. I'll have a coffee and keep these men company." Jake turned to find the chair. While he carried the chair to the table, he tried to remember the names of the men who shared Frank's table. Right, Adam from a small town. Roger, a retired carpenter, the third was an uncommon name, Alphonse? Elmer? He couldn't remember; he'd have to ask.

Frank had everything under control, "Adam, Roger, Julienne, you remember my grandson, Jake."

"How could we forget? You tell us about him all the time." Roger spread his serviette onto his lap.

Frank shrugged.

"The doctor, right?" Julienne fumbled with his utensils.

"A doctor of anthropology, so not helpful to you if you need any pills," Frank said, "But he can tell a lot of stories."

"Didn't fall too far from the tree then." Roger turned his coffee cup up.

Frank did the same and passed it to Jake. "You use mine. I'm not in the mood for coffee, today. Might keep me up."

"That and which pill?" Roger leaned over, providing room for the server.

A trolley squeaked next to their table and a young woman ladled soup into bowls.

Jake glanced around. He saw men and women in wheelchairs. Some clients had a staff member beside them spooning food into their open mouths. Others had bibs covering their chests while they used adapted utensils to remain independent. A general hum of conversation, clattering china, bursts of laughter, and behind all of that the ding of call bells and the mumbling intercom.

On their way back, Frank leaned on Jake for stability more than when they'd walked down. Jake knew he could carry his grandfather back to his room with no effort but he wouldn't do that to Frank's pride. "You're tired."

Frank shuffled and held onto the rail. "Time for my pills."

The nursing staff moved efficiently while they settled Frank back into his bed with his medication. Jake moved from chair to chair staying out of their way.

When Frank was snoring gently and his breathing relaxed, Jake kissed his grandfather's cheek and tucked the blanket under his chin. In that instant, Jake looked forward to becoming a father.

It was only by memory of the walkway and the tree in the yard that he found Robbie's house. He was surprised when she answered the door. Robbie had a towel thrown over her shoulder and was dabbing perspiration from her forehead. Flashes of moist skin flickered in his sight line until she wrapped the towel around her like a shawl. His reaction to flashes of a flat abdomen suggested he should turn on his heels and run.

"I thought you were the pizza delivery man," she said.

He showed empty hands. "Sorry."

Just then a pizza delivery car parked at the curb. She punched her fist in the air. "Yes." Then she seemed to get embarrassed. "I'm starved."

Jake stood aside while she handed over cash and then closed her eyes and breathed in the spicy pizza aroma. His stomach growled.

She glanced from him to the large pizza. "Join me? There's plenty. I order a large pie so I'll have leftovers."

"Are you sure?"

She twisted her head in the direction of the inside. "Come in. I'm getting cold and so is this pizza."

After he'd slipped out of his shoes and coat, he reached for the closet. She jumped in front him and made a grab for his coat.

"Let me," she said. "You take the pizza into the kitchen."

His football memories snapped to attention and a successful pizza pass was made. While he turned toward the small hallway, hangers clattered. From behind him he heard, "On your left." Jake stood in a yellow kitchen. He turned to see her lounging in the doorway and shrugged. "Where would you like me to put this?"

She straightened and shivered. "Just move the vase out of the way. Plates above the sink, flatware in the top drawer. I need a sweater. I'm cooling down," she said and then she was gone.

The stairs echoed with each footfall. He enjoyed rummaging through Robbie's kitchen. He set two placemats with plates and wine glasses. He saw a small but fine wine selection in a rack on her counter.

When she strolled back into the kitchen, he noticed she had fixed her hair, applied lip gloss, and wore a sweatshirt that slipped and showed a white clavicle and toned shoulder muscles.

"Good idea," she said, looking at the wine glasses.

He held up a bottle of merlot.

She tore two sheets of paper towels and folded them and placed them on each placemat. "Great choice. My father brings me wine when he travels."

After he drew the cork from the bottle, he noticed that she had moved the place setting he'd put across the table to the long side of the rectangle away from him and had poured two tall glasses of ice water.

When they were seated, she picked up a slice of pizza and took a huge bite and chewed it slowly, humming with delight and then wiped her mouth with satisfaction. "I'm ravenous. I ran five miles on my treadmill while talking with my mother on the phone."

"I can tell," he said.

She blushed. "Sorry, I should have had a shower. You're company."

"No. I just meant that you're enjoying your food." He bit through the layers of cheese, meat, and tangy tomato sauce.

She lifted her glass. "A toast to pizza," she said.

He lifted his glass and smiled at Robbie and wondered at the coincidence that he'd arrived at her doorstep and she'd provided what he needed. "To pizza and serendipity."

Her face was relaxed and her eyes mischievous as their glasses touched.

"Granddad mentioned that you knew Robin," he said. "I'd like to get in touch with her." He could use a friend right now. "You seem to know what I need. Are you a clairvoyant?" he asked.

"I did play with the Ouija board when I was young." She seemed to like having him here in her kitchen. "Robin lives in the neighborhood. I might have her cell phone number." She rushed on. "We chat when we see each other out and about. I'll check after dinner or I can tell her to call you or Frank when I see her."

"Thanks, I'd appreciate that," he said.

"How's your grandfather?" She needed to be casual. She wanted him to see her as empathetic as Robin, who shouldn't be given all the credit for compassion.

She kept her knife and fork in her hands so she wouldn't reach over and smooth the furrows from his forehead. "Want to talk about it?"

He was quiet while all of his concentration seemed to be focused on destroying the small pieces of hard-baked flour and water. "He's old and he's dying. If I had a father, I'd be looking forward to my father being a grandfather for my kids."

She stopped her wine glass mid-point to her mouth and turned to face him. "You have children?"

He was piercing a soggy green pepper. "No. I'm speaking of the future. It should be my future right now. I should've brought a grandchild home for my grandfather. He was the best father a kid could have."

Robbie sipped her wine. "Why haven't you married, had kids?"

"Short answer, time," he said.

She leaned her elbows on the table and turned toward him. "Long answer?"

"Family didn't seem that important. I was an only child and friends were important while I focused on my career. I didn't think about my grandparents. I thought about them but I just didn't consider their age. My mother was dead before I knew her, my biological father was never in the picture, so I guess I only thought about myself." His shoulders straightened against the back of the chair, his chin tipped upward.

"So you were seduced by fame and adventure. That's not all bad." She watched him over her glass.

He shifted in his chair so he looked directly at her. "You're laughing at me."

She shrugged and bit her lip. "No, I'm not. This is a tough time and the decisions of the past sometimes don't feel great. But they were right when you made them."

She tugged the neck of her sweatshirt, attempting to allow cool air to flow onto to her skin. She exaggerated a sniff at her underarms. "Sorry, I'm earthy right now."

He tipped the last of his wine into his mouth. "Do you run often? You were out running last night, too."

While she gathered up the plates and refrigerated the leftover pizza, she said, "Whenever I can. My dad says I was born running."

Jake brought the wine glasses to the counter. "I run, too. Are there trails you'd recommend?"

"The city provides a great map. I'll find it before you leave or you could just go on the website."

He held up the bottle of wine. "Should we finish this?"

"Sure. Let's finish it in the living room. The fire's probably burned down." Not that she needed heat. In fact, she wanted to take off her sweatshirt but underneath was only a black sports bra. The hot flash must be a reaction to the wine or it could be exhaustion. It wouldn't be his long fingers cradling his wine glass. She flexed her toes in her runners recalling the time he knelt before her and slipped her loafers onto her feet.

She followed him and focused on the back of his head while he led the way into the living room. He placed his glass on the table next to the solitary chair and her glass next to the sofa.

"Should I put more logs in the fire?" he asked.

She felt the chill of separation. "Be my guest." His sweater stretched across his back when he reached and placed logs in the grate.

Jake deliberately chose the chair. He needed a safe distance from her. He felt an intrinsic comfort with her. Even though his brain comprehended, his feet betrayed him when his toes strayed away from the heat of the fireplace and toward her. He shifted his legs and concentrated on the stem of the glass. "Maybe we can run together when I have more time and you're no longer a student, perhaps after Christmas." What was wrong with him? He should be saying *Run with me* tomorrow. Running wasn't a date.

When he saw Robbie's feet curled under her, appearing relaxed, he realized he would have liked her to curl up on his lap. He crossed his legs at his ankles and swallowed the last bit of wine. She was a master's student and he was faculty. His position was precarious until the funding matter was resolved and he was cleared. He couldn't take any chances for himself or Robbie. He wouldn't let anything happen. He had more control and he would use it.

Chapter 11

Robbie watched Jake's feet shift closer to the fire, further away from her. Everything about his body indicated that he created distance between them. Did she send off vibrations that she wanted to hug him and soothe away his worries? The other night, she was only being empathetic when she invited him home and she wanted to know what happened to Frank, didn't she? There wasn't anything between her and Jake, right?

She watched Jake move another inch away and acknowledged that lies and deceit have to create distance. If she could bring herself to be truthful with him about who she really was, then she could truly be a friend. But her research wasn't just about her and this man who was in her home. It was also about the women who'd taken the time to answer her survey, the costume designer, Margaret and her love of clothes, Sharon and her fight for a promotion, Mavis and her need for a mortgage to buy her own bakery.

Robbie reminded herself that this was the same guy who had offered her cab fare when he thought she had taken advantage of an old man in the park and then was paying her good money to sit with his grandfather. This was also the same guy who was cared for and loved by a woman of size. Her relationship with him wasn't personal. He was her research project because he was close to Frank. She couldn't reveal anything. She was too close to her pass, her degree, her goal, her future.

She swallowed to calm her truths surging along her

jangled nerves and cleared the word barricade at the back of her throat. "How's your grandfather tonight?" she asked. The mention of his grandfather reminded her of the limited time she and Jake had with Frank by name and frank by nature. The logs crackled in the fireplace and the disc player changed to the next album. Diana Krall sang Christmas songs in the background. When Jake didn't respond, she added, "Sorry, I shouldn't have asked."

His lips remained closed. A loud pop from a log seemed to open something in him and he started talking. "When I first returned home, I thought I could convince him to have treatments for his cancer. But he'd made up his mind. He's ready to leave and be with the love of his life. He doesn't want to be kept alive after his spirit is gone. I'm the only one he can count on to make sure death happens as he wishes." He ran his fingers over his five o'clock shadow. "I'm not sure I have the strength to let him go. I've wasted so many years by not being around for him."

She wished she knew whether she should invite Jake to sit beside her or if she should move over to his chair. What would happen if she moved to the floor and leaned against his legs? Would he feel the comfort of a friend, place his hand on her head, and talk without her having to ask questions? Or would he continue to stare into the fire? Perhaps talking about good times would make him feel better. "Did you and your grandparents have a good life together?" Jake stared at her for a long moment and then turned to stare back into the fire. "They loved each other and everyone around them. They gave people the benefit of their doubt. I was their gift, they said. Late in their lives when their friends were grandparents they were parents again after my mother died. I was surrounded by an abundance of everything. They saved her life insurance for me and I had the privilege of attending any university that I wanted. I chose to be away."

Robbie watched him, waiting for an opportune time to speak. She ached to join him but she didn't have the right. She was using Frank and Jake as part of her field research, trying to understand the life of a woman of size as a wife and mother.

A small smile flickered across his lips. "I never thought of my life as abundant before."

"What was your life like with a grandmother who was older than your friend's mothers?"

"It was tough. The kids used to call her old big butt. I fought in the playground and on the way home. Then my grandparents made me promise not to fight."

She could imagine a tousled blond-haired boy, feet apart, fists swinging. "Did you keep that promise?"

"Most of the time I did. I read a lot. I graduated early. Left home for Ottawa and didn't come back much. I offered them airplane tickets but they wouldn't come to visit me."

Robbie knew many reasons why they might not have traveled on a plane. Besides a fear of flying, she'd also read case studies and heard about the discrimination toward large people by the airlines, sometimes humiliating them, forcing them to buy an extra seat. "Did you ever ask them why they wouldn't visit?"

He made a tent out of his fingers. "No. I assumed they didn't come because they were old. I was busy studying, being successful, and time just moved so quickly. But lately, I've come to understand that Grandma missed me. I was her connection to her daughter, I see that now."

"Studying and being successful isn't always bad."

"Yes, it is, if you don't share it with the people who love you," he said.

"I suppose you're right." She felt inexperienced in sorting through these deep feelings of grief. "My grandparents were independent until they passed on, and my parents are alive. My life is easy compared to your experiences."

"It's all part of life. I'm glad that I'm here now." He drained his glass.

Robbie thought about the feelings the women in her research group expressed about loss of dreams, loss of relationships, opportunities, and their descriptions of anger, bewilderment, and bargaining seemed similar to this grief. All that happened to her was being accused of having no idea of how being fat feels. Were losses of dreams and the loss of life similar? How would she feel if her degree was denied? Jake hadn't asked her what her thesis was about. Of course he hadn't. He's living his grief, while she only researched it and empathized with others' disappointments and humiliations. Her experiences were miniscule by comparison. And while she'd experienced some pain while wearing her disguise, it was just that, not real life. Was this experiment callous selfishness when compared to losing someone you love? At least listening to him and not judging him might give him some consolation for a short while. "Is there anything I can do to help?"

"Marry me?" he asked her abruptly.

Her heart slammed against her ribs like a basketball against a backboard. "What?"

"Sorry, I'm brainstorming out loud. Granddad would like to see me married before he dies. The doctor says he won't live until Christmas."

Was he serious? Robbie glanced toward the fireplace mantle, where the photographs of Robbie in her disguise were tipped out of sight. Did his lips just quiver or was it the firelight reflecting on his skin? If he was asking anyone to marry him, it should be Robin. She had spent more time with both him and Frank, even though accumulated hours of being with someone wasn't a reason to marry, but Robin did remind Frank of the love of his life.

Robbie took a deep breath. "From the little you've told

me about their love, he wouldn't want you to marry anyone just to make him happy."

"I know. I was searching for a quick solution." His face was red. "I'm sorry. Besides, you're just starting on your career and then there's Brad."

She could be truthful about her relationship with Brad but she couldn't break Brad's confidence. She didn't want another deception between her and Jake. "Brad and I have been friends for a long time, but we don't love each other that way."

"Grandma always said that the best marriages were between friends."

"My parents put forward that theory as well. But believe me, Brad and I will only be friends."

He rose and approached the sofa. "It's time I went back to the hotel." He put his hands on her shoulders. "Stay where you are. I can let myself out."

She jumped as if someone had given her an electric charge. "I'll get your coat."

In the hall, she reached into the closet and grabbed his coat, sending the hanger ricocheting against the wall when she snapped the door closed.

Jake raised an eyebrow. "Do you have a body in there or something?" As he reached for his coat, their fingers brushed, sending a sliver of heat through her body.

"Or something."

Without thinking, she placed her hand on his, ignoring the increasing warmth flowing through her and settling in places ignored for too long. "I don't know what to say, except I'm here if you need me."

Her eyes widened when she felt him raise her hand to his lips. She swayed toward him while her core flowed with slip-sliding anticipation. His brown eyes held hers while he kissed her fingers. "Thank you. Your eyes are an unusual ratio of green and hazel."

She leaned away from him, even though every skin cell on her body rose like goose flesh, reaching toward his touch.

"One pair of genes didn't win. My father tells me that's why I can be determined."

"Determination is a fine quality when you begin a career. What's your major?"

"Human resources."

"In anthropology, human resources are the key to many communities. We'll talk about that some day."

"Okay."

After she closed the door, Robbie leaned against the cool metal and slid down to the floor with the weight of wanting more of him than he could give when his life was in chaos and she had the little problem of her other persona.

"Enough." She stood and marched herself to her computer chair. Experimenting with a new identity added more depth to her conclusions than she would have imagined. When she was being Robin around Jake, he seemed more relaxed, a genuine friendship was being nurtured. She hoped that it was because his internal borders were down and he didn't need to keep up the professor-student relationship, or perhaps because he associated Robin with a maternal love that had loved him unconditionally and it was easier to be friends.

She stared at the empty space where her final thesis copy used to be. She had dropped it into the office bright and early before many students and professors were roaming the halls. Nadine had date stamped it and carried it through to Professor Clinton's office. Now all she had to do was wait.

The next morning, Robbie posed in front of her magnifying mirror and inserted her brown contacts. When she brushed on a plum eyeshade, she thought, *Robin, you have style.*

Before her next field trip, grocery shopping, she wanted to relax and enjoy a few minutes to herself. So half an hour later she stepped up to the counter at her local Tim Horton's. Her favorite server was behind the counter. She opened her purse. "Morning, Ryan, I'd like my usual, please."

When Ryan didn't move and tugged at his earring, a clear indication that he was stressed, she shrugged her shoulder. "Large coffee with double, double, please."

When her neighborhood server didn't recognize her, she knew the ancient art of illusion was working. She should be proud of her accomplishment rather than allowing Clifton's subjective and nonacademic research remarks battle for room in her brain. She shivered and understood the old saying that someone had just walked over her grave. It was lonely knowing that *she* could disappear so completely.

"Coming right up," Ryan said.

From a chair along the side, Robbie scanned the other clientele.

A little boy pulled at his mother's leg. "Mommy, look at the fat lady!"

The mother in her dress slacks and high-heeled boots and long coat, bent and looked to where the boy was pointing. She smiled at Robbie and then spoke to the boy. "Yes, Owen, and over there is a tall man and over there a senior and right here"—she poked him in the tummy—"is a little boy."

Robbie saluted the young mother and waved at the boy when they left the coffee house.

Robbie buttoned her coat and put on her mittens before she opened the coffee house doors. The parking lot was the only thing that separated her from her field trip to the grocery store. She watched a woman bend into the wind. She could easily wear a size zero. Robbie had an urge to catch up to this woman with red-tinged hair that sat on top of her head like a scrub pad and ask if she was ill. But her petite size could have to do with genetics, or stress, which she knew could affect the human body in many different ways.

Half an hour or so after, Robbie wound through the grocery store aisles, noticing the Christmas-themed plastic storage containers for cookies or cupcakes. Christmas was right around the corner. She hummed along to carols playing on the store's communication system. She continued to shop, ignoring the fruitcake display, which tempted her. Ever since she tasted Mavis's recipe, she'd acquired a taste for the dried-fruit studded Christmas tradition.

She approached the checkout cashier with her normal weekly fare, as well as sales specials that she usually shared with her parents. The clerk, a thin young blonde with an asymmetric hairstyle, scanned the groceries. "Did you find everything you needed?"

"Yes, thanks," Robbie said.

The third box of barbeque potato chips caught the young woman's attention. She stared openly at Robbie's bulky body with a look that seemed to say, *No wonder you're fat.*

Robbie's face burned. "They're for my parents," Robbie said quickly and wiped her moist hands on her coat. She knew they weren't on any food guide for healthy eating but she and her parents enjoyed them every once in a while. The clerk seemed to want to bag the boxes without touching them. "Good call. Have you read the fat content on these?" She swiveled, causing her tight little top to rise, and flashed a tiny navel piercing. The jewel seemed to wink at Robbie under the hard fluorescent lights.

"Sometimes we all need a little fat," Robbie replied.

"Not for me, ever," the clerk said while the total of Robbie's purchases flashed on the cash register.

Robbie swiped her debit card and waited for the receipt.

"Good luck with that no fat thing," Robbie called back to the clerk while steering her cart toward the exit.

Darn, Robbie thought ramming her cart through the snow. She'd fallen into the trap of justifying her potato chip purchase. The clerk had turned into the food police and she'd crumbled. Would she have done that if she weren't dressed as Robin? No, she realized glumly. She'd failed her walk in the mile of someone else's sensible shoes.

Shoes. She remembered how gently Jake had placed her shoes on her feet, like Prince Charming to Cinderella. But dressed as Robin, she was no Cinderella. How did he learn to look past the weight?

She pictured Jake as a little blond-haired boy holding onto his grandmother's hand and hearing and seeing insidious incidents day in and day out. That had to have made an impact on such a young mind. How many women lived through humiliations like this every day? Maybe if there were enough men like Frank and Jake, the prejudices would cease to exist. Until then, she hoped they had a safe place to be themselves with people who loved them.

Mavis related to her how some of her customers had told her to stop sampling so much of her baking. "They just don't understand that a qualified baker knows by texture, aroma, and appearance as well as a tiny taste that a recipe turned out as expected."

Sharon worked part-time at a women's fitness club. She told the Fat Like Me group one day that a woman decided not to join the club because if Sharon was an employee then obviously the weight loss program didn't produce the advertised results. Sharon replied, "I could have told her that I'd already lost fifty pounds and counting on the program but I wouldn't waste my breath."

Jake drove through the parking lot at the local grocery store looking for a place to park. He'd rushed out of the office between appointments because Frank had asked him for a special kind of rice pudding from this particular store. A glimpse of a brown Ford caught his attention followed by the ample black haunches bending into the trunk. He frowned. Their lives kept colliding. He could park on the other side of the store and she'd never know. *What are you thinking? Robin has gone out of her way to spend time with Frank and I want to sneak away without acknowledging her? Remember the !Kung San.*

He honked his horn. Robin looked out and shaded her eyes against the sun. A grin beamed across her flushed face. The wind flapped her coat like a flag.

"Need any help?" he asked.

"No, thanks. On your way to see Frank?"

He nodded. "How'd you guess?"

With her hands on her hips, she said, "Because I know this neighborhood and it's the closest store to Care Manor."

"He craves Mrs. Chandler's rice pudding, no substitutes. I'm between student appointments."

She shifted from one foot to the other. "I know where it is. Want me to show you?"

"Meet me at the front door."

He stood just to the side of the electric eye that swung the doors open and watched her push her cart to the corral.

She parked the cart and swaggered toward him with confidence.

"Going somewhere special?" he asked.

"Not particularly. Why?"

"You're wearing lipstick."

"Dr. Watson, the lady always wears lipstick," she kidded him.

She stood for a moment. "Would you do a favor for me and follow my lead?"

"Sure." Lead? What was she up to? She reached for his

hand. When he clasped her palm, she blushed, then looked down and shrugged. "In for a penny, in for the pound," she said under her breath, then stepped in front of him and strode through the door head held high as he followed.

When she bumped him with her hip, he tugged her arm and she moved closer to his side. When she rounded the end display, she knocked the cereal pyramid and the display wobbled. She gasped and then laughed. Her laughter was contagious and he joined in her hilarity all the way to the refrigeration aisle. He believed that neither of them actually knew what was funny but laughing felt good.

She pointed to the rice pudding. He scooped two containers into the crook of his arm and they hurried toward the express cashier.

Robbie swiftly maneuvered him behind a customer whose cart was overflowing. The clerk chatted as she scanned the order. Jake didn't know what Robin was up to but he'd spare a few minutes to find out.

Although she looked formidable, she seemed vulnerable as well, especially when she chewed the inside of her lip as she was doing now. He placed the containers on the conveyer belt and reached his hand out and tapped her cheek just like his grandmother had done some many years ago. "I'm here."

Robbie swayed toward the checkout counter until the clerk with her bubbly voice called, "Did you find everything you needed?"

He felt Robbie straighten and heard her answer sweetly, "Yes, we have. Thank you."

The pretty young clerk ignored Robin's reply and leaned toward him, her light blue eyes dancing. "And you, sir? Did you find everything you needed?" She batted her lashes.

"Thanks to my friend. She knew just where to find this specialty." He indicated the rice pudding. Robbie placed a fruitcake she picked up from a promotional display onto the belt. “Do you mind? I have a craving for an early taste of Christmas.”

Jake handed the clerk a twenty-dollar bill. “Whatever you need.” He winked at Robin.

The clerk ran her finger down the nutritional value list. “Are these calories for your parent’s, too?” The clerk brushed the long side of her hair away from her face and snorted.

“No, all for me.” A saucy smile slid across her lips.

Ignoring Robin, the clerk slowly counted the change into Jake’s palm focusing a flirty smile on him. “Come back again soon.”

After Jake pocketed the bills and coins, he found Robin’s hand in the fold of her coat and anchored her to him. He knew enough about Robin to realize that this charade must be important to her.

They bent their heads into the wind as they hastened to her brown sedan. He held open the driver’s side door while she settled into her seat. “Want to tell me about it?”

“Miss Flutter Eyelashes and flashing belly button stud turned into a food police when I went through her register earlier. I didn’t like how she made me feel.” Robbie swallowed. “It seemed important but not now. Thanks, anyway. Give me a minute and I’ll pay you for the cake.” She opened her purse.

“The clerk had a belly button stud?”

Robbie swatted his arm with her mitten.

“Honest, I didn’t notice. I was concentrating on you.”

“Come on.”

“No, Scout’s honor. And don’t even think about paying for the cake. It was worth the fun.” He held up the grocery sack. “I’d better deliver this to Granddad. I have a student appointment in thirty minutes.” He glanced at his watch.

She started the engine and held out her hand. “Let

me. I'm going as soon as I take my groceries home." Jake glanced at his watch again then back at her. "Generosity's a compelling trait." He handed her the pudding. "Tell Frank I'll see him at lunch. I'm bringing a colleague to meet him."

Her shoulders sagged and she licked her dry lips. Maybe he'd found someone else who would marry him before Frank passed away. "Should I tell Frank who you're bringing to visit?"

"I told him earlier." He backed away, allowing the door to close but hesitated and leaned forward again. "I need to squeeze in a bit of exercise. Want to work out at the fitness room at the hotel later?"

"Pardon me?" *What was he thinking?*

He chuckled. "Don't worry. There'll be both men and women there."

"No, thank you. I'm not worried. I don't work out in mixed company. It's distracting."

"We could walk in the park instead."

He began to push the door closed.

"Okay, I'll meet you by the gates at nine after visiting hours. No running, just walking, agreed?"

He nodded. "Only walking, I promise. I'll see you there."

She shouldn't do this. When he'd held her hand and laughed with her in the store, her insides quivered and felt all mushy warm. She'd felt protected, cared for, respected, and honored. Just for a moment, she considered giving up everything and explaining her field study. Then they could get married. It would be their secret when she wore the fat suit at the wedding. Frank would witness the marriage and everyone would be happy.

Robbie struggled to hold on to all this while she watched Jake for as long as she could in her rearview mirror.

He didn't turn around. *Don't be silly, I belong to a family, community, student body, and soon to an exciting career.* As she drove home, parked, and bumped bags of groceries to her stairs, she rationalized that it was an approaching end to the familiarity of the university routine and her uncertainty of the future that made her think she was looking for someone special. Her future was going to be wonderful.

Chapter 12

After she unpacked her groceries, Robbie tucked the rice pudding into her purse and drove the short way to Care Manor. Just outside Frank's door she lifted the pudding from her purse and stuck her head and her hand into his room. Dangling the sack, she sang out, "I'm delivering Mrs. Chandler's rice pudding."

Frank waved. "I send my grandson and a bird of paradise returns. How lucky can one old guy get?"

A heart spasm jolted through her chest as if hit by electricity. He was lucky enough to be nearing the end of his life, lucky enough to be moderately pain-free right now, and lucky enough to have a grandson who loves him. "So if you were going to share with Jake, can I, please, have his portion?" she asked. Seemed like justice to her. "I really shouldn't, should I?"

"Sure you can." A twinkle of life sparkled in his eyes when he grinned, as if they were sharing a big conspiracy.

"It does happen to be my favorite, too." She popped the lid off one container and divided it equally. "Should we save the other container for Jake so he can have some too?"

"One helping's enough for me right now. How about you?"

"Me, too, it's so very creamy."

"Jake told me he had meetings. Said he'd be here for lunch. Said he was bringing a friend." He spooned pudding into his mouth.

Even though winter's sunlight flowed through the

window, it didn't provide any patches of warmth. Frank's skin seemed thinner, his lips bluer, and a tinge of dusk hung around his nostrils.

"Mmmmm." She held the spoon below her nose. "Reminds me of my granny's house and how much she loved me. I buy it when I need to be kind to myself."

"Mmm," he said. "Reminds me of Mabel, before we worried about triglycerides, fat grams, and whatever else we were told to worry about."

They ate in silence. "That's enough for me," he said.

Robin scraped every kernel of rice from the bowl and licked her spoon. "Love."

"A poor substitute for sure, but a substitute." His eyes closed.

She settled into her chair. "Would you like to tell me more about your life with Mabel, or would you prefer to be quiet? I can, you know, be quiet."

"I'm going to tell you some of the end." He seemed to be all black-framed glasses on a skull. "Mabel went out of her way to make people happy. They accepted her generosity as part of who she was. Sometimes, though, she'd confess that she was pretty tired of others always assuming she'd be there to fill in, bake, and organize the canvassers." Frank turned his face to the window. "But you know, Robin, at the end, when I could have used some help, all those she had helped kept complaining that they were busy and only dropped in occasionally with a knickknack or flowers for her. And that includes Jake. It made me so angry no one thought I'd like a pot of someone else's cooking once in a while. We came here, to Care Manor, so we could be together and have help. She didn't last too long after the move. She was sure I would be taken care of." He reached forward as she extended her hand. "I want you to know that I appreciate every visit you've given me. You've helped bring back happy memories in these last days."

Robbie squirmed in her chair. "You're more than welcome." She sandwiched his thin cold hand between her warm palms. "You've given me a place to be myself. I get busy and forget there are people in the world who enjoy sharing a hug." She leaned over, careful not to crush him, then embraced his rail-thin body and gave him a wet smack on the cheek.

She was supposed to stay objective and not kiss her subject's cheek. *But immersion's important because it's supposed to help me learn. What exactly am I learning about?* The realization struck her like a slide show bursting on her heart with images of *Love.*

She sank back in the chair, allowing herself to absorb her realization. She'd learned about Frank's unconditional love for his wife, their unconditional love for their daughter, and Jake, and Jake's unconditional love for them both. She was witness to generations of love.

She'd lost track of the time when the familiar racket of staff readying clients for a meal broke into their companionable silence. "Jake will be here shortly," she said, rising unsteadily to her feet.

"Can't you stay, Robin? Jake said he's bringing someone and I don't want to meet someone new in my pajamas."

"Not to worry. You look regal in your dressing gown." She curtsied before him.

"Besides, any friend of Jake's will be glad to meet you." She blew a kiss from the door, then hurried down the hall. When she caught sight of Jake, she ducked into an opened door and hid out of sight. Her chest tightened at the sight of the woman at his side. Jake had brought Jean Clifton to meet Frank.

She gnawed her lip. Robbie knew that if Jake were to propose to Jean, she wouldn't stammer with her mouth open. She counted to one hundred. When she peered down the hall, they were gone.

When they entered the room, Jake leaned in and kissed his grandfather's cheek and felt Frank's jaw tighten. Could Granddad be in pain? Jake felt the weight of dread and guilt on his back threatening to buckle his knees.

Jake straightened and gestured behind him. "Granddad, I'd like you to meet Dr. Jean Clifton. Jean, Frank Proctor, my grandfather."

"Hello," Frank said and sank back into his chair.

Jean extended her hand and patted Frank's shoulder, and then squatted down so that she was at eye level. "I'm pleased to meet you again, Mr. Proctor. We met a long time ago at Jake's graduation."

Jake was impressed with Jean's consideration but he watched his grandfather's face for clues as to what may be happening, pain or pride.

"Sorry," Frank said quietly.

"We met at the Central High School Grade Twelve graduation. You and your wife were sitting on some chairs along the edge of the gym. Some of us were fooling around and I almost fell over you. I wore a pink organza dress and I had a tiara. You said I looked beautiful."

Jake touched Jean's shoulder. "That was a long time ago."

"Not that long." She glanced up at Jake.

Jake helped her stand. While she moved around the room and looked at the family collage, Jake noticed the two bowls and two spoons on the table. "How was your rice pudding?"

"Good. Thanks. Robin angel, bless her heart, kept me company." Frank raised his voice, sending the intended spiral of guilt through Jake. His Granddad was justified. He should have been the one sharing the pudding with his dying grandfather.

Jean came closer. “Robin. Is she a nurse?”

Jake answered. “She’s Granddad’s friend. You saw her at the reunion.”

“Oh, is she the heavyset woman?” Jean leaned toward Frank. “You be careful. I’ve heard about women who befriend seniors and then marry for monetary gain.”

“That’s what I first thought, but I was wrong. Robin’s not like that,” Jake said quickly. Robin had calmed his initial fears, ten-fold.

Frank wiggled his bottom to the back of the chair and stretched to his full height and struggled forward. “I should be so lucky. I’d take her in a minute if I thought she’d consent.” Then he leaned over the armrest. “I was kind of hoping that she’d find Jake a catch.”

“You’re joking.” Jean said, then laughed. “Jake’s handsome.”

“Looks like me in my prime. Jake, bring me that picture from over there.”

Jake glanced at the photograph and recognized the image that he saw every morning in his own mirror. Genetics were visible in the shape of his face, his eyes, and nose.

Frank pointed to the picture. “See, Dr. Clifton, there is a similarity, even though we are his grandparents.”

Jean looked closely. “Yes, I can see a little of you in Jake. Your wife?”

Jake noted the flash of horror in her eyes as she recognized that Jake also resembled his grandmother.

Frank picked up the picture and held it closer to her. “Yes, my Mable, big in body and big in heart. Right, Jake?”

Jake nodded. “Yes.”

Jean pushed up the sleeve of her coat and angled her watch, allowing her to see the correct time. “Uh, I think we should return to the university.”

"Thanks for coming. You'll understand if Jake has to leave suddenly because I'm dying." He clutched his chest. "Oh no. I'm doing that now. Make that almost dead. Toes up."

"Granddad."

"Can't choose the exact moment. But I'll try for an evening or a weekend."

"Of course I would understand," Jean said.

Frank motioned to his thin body. "All this is real, son. You have to get used to the idea."

Jean blanched at Frank's plainspoken pronouncement.

"You're alive now and that's what counts." Jake kissed his grandfather's cheek. "Do you need more pudding?"

Frank shook his head.

Jake struggled past the stomach acid surging into his throat and asked, "Do you want me to ask the nurse to bring you a drink? Do you need to get into your bed?"

"I'm okay, Jake, go back to work." Frank's head wobbled on his neck as if all the fight to sit up and entertain them had left.

"I'll be back," Jake said, leaving Frank's door partially open to the corridor.

"Jean, I'll meet you at the front door," Jake whispered.

He stopped the nurse attendant. "Granddad's exhausted. Would you check in on him?"

"Sure, no problem. I'll check if it's time for his medication first." She moved with precise movements to the desk. "You can go. He's in good hands."

Jake nodded and retreated from Frank's prediction of death toward the front door, where Jean waited for him. She gripped his sleeve while the door to the Manor closed behind them. "I'm sorry, Jake. You poor, poor man."

"I'm fortunate really. Granddad knows he's dying and there are no secrets. He's not worried about the meaning of his life. He's just waiting to be reunited with Grandma." Jake felt some stress leave his shoulders. His legs felt looser when he walked to the car. As he held the car door open for Jean, he saw the sun sparkle diamonds on the snow and he understood that Christmas would come and go every year, whether Frank was here or not.

"And this Robin?" Jean asked when the car exited the parking lot.

"I thought you might meet her. She's usually here. She reminds Frank of my grandmother and their life of love and intimacy."

"Really, at his age."

Jake chuckled. "As he's said often enough, he's dying, not dead."

"And do you see this Robin often?"

"We seem to run into each other around the city or visiting Frank."

Jean cleared her throat. "Do you think she's interested in, you know, either of you?"

He turned in time to see her blush. "She did tell me when I hired her that if Frank asked her to marry him, she'd consider it."

"Oh," she said and seemed to expel a sigh of relief. "You hired her."

"Yes, since I can't be there all the time and besides she's funny, caring, and generous."

"A lot of fat women are. There's a theory that this type of woman is so busy caring for others that they don't take care of themselves."

"And what do you believe?"

"The statistics are compelling."

"If that's the case then I say, thank goodness. But from my experience with different cultures, statistics don't always show the truth."

"Jake?"

"Yes."

"Were either of your parents obese?"

"Not my mother, and I don't know my biological father. Why?"

"Nothing important. Just wondering." When he stopped in front of the Humanities building, she opened the car door.

"You're concerned about genetics." He had thought about it often enough. Whenever a new announcement appeared in the news about a possible DNA link, he had thought that if a test were developed he would line up to take it. But it didn't seem as important anymore.

"The research shows it is very hard to be an overweight child." She held onto the door for a minute. "Thank you for taking me to see your grandfather."

"You're welcome. I wanted you to understand what's happening in my personal life."

"That means a lot to me." She held onto the door as if she wanted to get back into the car.

"I've got to hurry. I have a student appointment in fifteen," he said quickly.

"Next time, then." Jean slammed the door.

"Not if you slam the door on a classic car, there won't be a next time," he muttered as he patted the dash.

Robbie's message light was flashing when she meandered into the kitchen. Dr. Clifton and the committee had approved her thesis and her defense would proceed on Tuesday because the outside examiner had had an emergency. She sighed. So it was either now or in the new year. Just a few more days and it would be all over. The next call was from Nadine, who sounded excited.

Robbie called her right back. "Hi, what's going on?"

"Can you meet me for a coffee at Atlantis?"

"Of course, when?"

"Twenty minutes."

"I'll be there or be square." When Robbie got back into her car, she was still in disguise. It was going to be interesting to hear what Nadine would say.

Robbie parked half a block down, put money in the meter for two hours, and hurried to the coffee house.

Nadine was in the far corner facing the door. Robbie beamed and waved.

Nadine didn't acknowledge her. Robbie paid for a coffee, then she approached Nadine and said, "Is this seat taken?"

Nadine frowned, then leaned closer. "Robbie Smith, is that you?"

Robbie nodded as she draped her coat onto the back of the chair. Her mauve turtleneck T-shirt discreetly formed against the suit while her four-pocket purple jeans hugged her belly and thighs. She raised her eyebrows. "So, how do I look?"

"Great. Really great." Nadine still shook her head.

"I have to thank you. The shops you suggested were great. It's strange but I feel like me on the outside and inside whether I'm in disguise or not."

"What did you do to your voice?"

"It's not so much my voice but the wax that I place on the inside of my mouth next to my gums and then of course this neck apparatus keeps my chin in a slightly different position." Robbie lifted the fold of the turtleneck sweater away from her neck and tipped her chin where a slight gap was noticeable on close inspection.

Nadine leaned forward. "I wouldn't have believed it if I hadn't seen it for myself."

"That's enough about me. Tell me, what is your big news?" Robbie sipped her coffee.

Nadine placed her hand on the table. A princess cut ruby surrounded with tiny diamonds winked at Robbie.

She checked Nadine's left hand. "Oh, Nadine, does this mean what I think it means?"

Nadine grinned. "It does. Ken proposed to me."

Robbie jumped up and hugged her friend. "Congratulations."

Nadine was laughing and snorting back tears. "I wanted you to be one of the first to know because I spoke my wish out loud to you first. You encouraged me to be real in the relationship."

Robbie handed Nadine a serviette. "When's the big day?"

"Next year. Ken will have a sabbatical and we'll go on a Caribbean cruise."

"Wow."

They sipped their coffee in silence. Robbie cleared her throat. Then they giggled.

Nadine talked about Ken and all his fine qualities, where they've been and their future travel plans.

"I'm so happy for you." Robbie glanced at the clock. "I have to go. Clifton booked my defense for Tuesday. I have to study hard. I can't believe it will be so soon, but my external examiner has limited dates available."

"I heard. I appreciate you joining me on such short notice. You'll be fine during your defense, I'm sure of it. Are you going to be a woman of substance during your presentation?"

"I don't think so. I don't want to cheese anyone off, especially Clifton."

"A few weeks ago, I didn't believe you could pull it off, but you do. She should see this, it really works," Nadine said.

"Thanks, you've been one of my role models whenever

I've felt as if I didn't know how to be, as you say, a woman of substance."

"Robbie, you always had substance. It just wasn't as noticeable before." Nadine laughed.

Robbie put on her coat. "Thanks. I'll see you in the office. Tell Ken he loves a wonderful woman."

Robbie drove home and thought about love. Her parents passed their silver anniversary, Frank and Mable had had a long life of love, and Nadine was beginning one. Jake hadn't found anyone yet and she didn't have a special someone in her life. Well, unless she counted Frank, of course.

She parked her car in the garage. No blinking lights on her message manager. Up in her bedroom, she hung the wig on the mannequin, rolled the wax from her gums and threw the wad into the garbage, then slipped the neck that suggested a double chin off and placed it on the holder, followed by the torso and finally her leggings. She no longer felt uncomfortable with the body parts around her bedroom. The foam and padding were a part of her now.

After she hung up the disguise and showered, she sat down with the marked-up print copy of her thesis. A sunbeam came through her window and played across her face. About an hour passed and she felt her eyelids drooping. She jerked herself awake before placing her head down in the middle of her chapter about insurance and obesity statistics. Just five minutes. That's all she needed and then she'd be refreshed and continue her review. All of her answers to the questions the defense committee posed would be delivered with knowledge and confidence. She would convince the committee that she was not denying the reality of obesity but that the cause of the apparent epidemic could not simply be only a lack of willpower and laziness.

A shiver ran over her body. The room was bathed in darkness. She fumbled for her lamp, and saw that now wet drool marks dotted her pages with the coffee cup circles, doodles, and notes in the margins. When she glanced at the clock, she knew her refreshing break had been much more than five minutes.

Tonight she'd be walking with Jake at his request. *Was that a kind of date? No, it's a friend being with a friend in need, thing.* Changing to meet him in the park shouldn't take a lot of time. It would be dark and he wouldn't be able to see her clearly. She felt a warm pull in her core when she thought about the controlled academic professor who was devoted to his grandfather and the man who was also in flux over the rest of his life.

While she guided her arms into the body suit, she imagined Jake strolling through villages and observing the different traditions. He was probably familiar with a pick and shovel, and possibly dug wells and cultivated fields with the residents. He would have sat with the elders and listened to their concerns. She couldn't imagine him identifying too closely with the people he studied and not maintaining his role as the researcher. He was a learned professor who stood at a lectern or podium and shared his passion for his work. He had more experience and wouldn't be accused that his biases affected his research.

She remembered Jake's sensual curve to his mouth when he grinned, and the rumble of his belly laugh at some of Frank's more outrageous remarks, and the way his eyebrows raised briefly and then dropped again when they met. The way his pupils were a bead of a dark lava rock when he was being impersonal or how they turned into dark pools surrounded by warm, inviting liquid chocolate when he was excited, concerned, or aroused. Most of all, she liked the texture and strength of his palm and the light reflecting off the fine hairs on his fingers that enfolded her hand both when she was fat or thin. When their fingers were entwined, he seemed anchored. And whether she was Robbie or Robin, she felt at home with Jake. A flicker of hope settled in her chest. Maybe he'd forgive her deception.

Jake held the door open for his last student appointment of the day. His life was different than he'd planned just months ago. He thought that his days would be filled with presenting concrete data about the habitats of the foragers in the desert. While he reviewed his notes, he read his observations about the young mothers with their babies and the elders more than he did about the hunters. He had become curious about the female role in the communities and families. He wrote about a twinge of emptiness that had surprised him when he returned a newborn boy to his mother's arms, and he wrote that he was reminded of his grandfather, when he sat in the community center listening to the elders. Many subtle little details and accidental similarities of Bushmen's family life had entwined with his memories of home.

Ever since Jean had suggested that Robbie cared more for others than she did for herself, he wondered what she did to sustain herself. *Some anthropologist I am, I haven't even asked.* Tonight, while they walked, perhaps she'd tell him some details of her life, if he showed some real interest. Even though it had been a huge jump from his first impression, he trusted her completely with his grandfather during this precious time. She was candid and fun-loving with Frank but her guard remained up with him.

When she implied by her actions that she needed him to play along with the game to impress the young salesclerk in the grocery store, he'd felt that he offered her something other than money. He'd given her a part of himself as a personal favor. And when they held hands, he'd felt connected to community, to home.

A memory of his grandmother when he was twelve surfaced. His grandparents had received an invitation to attend the symphony with the Prince of Wales. They had danced around the living room like two teenagers with coveted tickets to a concert. Grandmother had had a dress made. Jake had even told her she looked beautiful. His grandfather embarrassed him with some smart remark or other about breasts. Jake couldn't think about his grandma that way. Yuck. Grandma had shushed Frank. Then she had opened her arms to hug Jake but he had run to the garage and hid in the Mustang until the limousine had driven them away.

As Jake drove to Care Manor he wondered if he was still hiding in the Mustang. What did a Mustang mean anyway but a small wild horse? He certainly was not small and he'd never been wild. Tempted, of course, but his grandparents would have been disappointed. He'd grown up instead.

He parked on the street because the parking lot was filled to capacity. The sights and sounds of the home were familiar to him. He greeted the residents who sat in wheelchairs outside their doorways or those walking the halls.

At Frank's bedside, Jake held a flexible straw to his grandfather's lips and watched him try to pull the liquid into his mouth. Frank pushed Jake's hand away. "It's time to go when you can't suck," he said.

Jake couldn't help but smile. That's the way home life had always been, his grandparents' humor interjected into a serious situation. As a child, he'd felt left out. Then when he'd understood some of it, he'd repeat the jokes at school, and then, when he understood more of the nuances, he became embarrassed by it. "At least you can still blow," Jake said, instead of stating the obvious that perhaps the nutritional shake was too thick.

His grandfather chuckled. "I'm glad you're back. We're family. Grandma was wrong." He laid back.

"How's that?"

"Said that's why you didn't come home. Early damage from living with us. Couldn't be a normal kid."

"Normal is an ambiguous value. Love can't damage." Jake placed the glass on the bedside table.

Had it hurt him to grow up faster than his classmates? "I should have been here when Grandmother was dying. You cared for her all alone."

"She missed you. But she understood."

"She shouldn't have. She should have called me on it. Or you could have called me sooner, told me to crawl out of myself because you needed me."

"Woe, boy. We knew you'd come to it in your own time. There are some things you just can't hurry. We old people learned that from experience, you know."

Jake ran his fingers through his hair. "She knew how grateful I've felt all these years that you kept me after mom died. I don't think I ever understood how that must have felt for both of you to lose a child. I was so young and Grandma just stepped in. She was my mother."

"Yes, it was hard watching our daughter fight for life. She had you and she wanted to live. It's hard to understand why certain people die early and then there are those of us who hang around longer than necessary."

"I should have thought about this before now. Maybe I am damaged."

"That's crap, and you know it."

"I do know that I had all the love and support a kid and man could ever want."

"Thanks, son."

Jake swallowed hard and thumbed the corners of his eyes. "Have you got everything you need?"

"I do now," Frank said.

Jake knew by memory the form that Frank had signed. No cardiopulmonary resuscitation. No intensive care unit. No respirator. No feeding tube. No monitors. Oxygen as needed for comfort. It wasn't easy for Jake to kick aside the life support that would have been minimal in most endings. But this wasn't his life or his wishes. Frank's other request was pain medication for comfort.

As Frank took a short nap, Jake felt his head bob while he read his research notes. He closed the file and gave in to sleep.

A nurse tapped him on the shoulder when visiting hours were over. "You can go home now. He's well cared for."

"You have my cell number and the hotel number?"

"Yes, everything is right here on his chart."

He was meeting Robin at nine after visiting hours were over. He laughed to himself when he remembered her relief when the pyramid of cereal didn't topple. His adult brain told him that their silly laughter had probably been stress relief for both of them. He fumbled his knitted hat from his pocket and held onto his gloves like a kid in a hurry to get out the door and play with his best friend.

After checking on Frank one last time, Jake found Robin sitting on Frank's bench. Her eyes seemed to be focused on some far off point across the frozen lake until his feet crunching on the snow caused her to turn in his direction. He settled on the seat beside her and squinted against the light from her flashlight.

The air around her seemed warmer as she inhaled and exhaled. "It must be hard to be you right now," she said.

Were those tears glistening in her eyes? His hand reached for her mittened palm. "Yes, but I'm glad I'm here."

The snow swirled around her feet. "I'm an only child, too. I understand."

The needles on the pine trees rattled.

"Let's walk. The wind's picking up and soon the wind chill will make it seem colder," she said.

He gripped his collar tighter around his neck. "We don't have to do this. We can go for coffee." He put the knit hat on his head. There wasn't any other way to stay warm. No one looked good in a knitted hat.

"Yes, we do. I skipped half of my normal workout because we'd be walking."

"So you do exercise?" He cringed at his surprised tone. Grandma had exercised, too, just not in the conventional sense. She'd made dinner, done the laundry, took care of the house. Her size had just made it difficult to do more.

"I work out almost every day. You seem surprised."

"Well, you have to admit . . ." Nothing he could say at this point would be good.

She stepped in front of him and stopped, her arms on her hips. "What do I have to admit?"

"That you don't look as if you do," he finished, and felt his stomach churn with remorse.

"You don't appear to be a jackass but sometimes you act like one," she said. She moved away from him and picked up the pace.

Jake closed the distance with a few quick strides and nudged her over so that he could walk beside her. "I'm sorry."

She struck a pose with her fists extended toward him. "If Frank wasn't dying, I would deck you here and now."

He swallowed his laugh at her mittened fists. "Listen, I don't know a lot about you."

His boots squeaked on the cold, paved path. He stopped at the gate that led to the street and to Robbie's house. He'd almost turned to go through it before he stopped himself. He wrapped his arm around her waist. "I know that you're generous, kind, an only child, you attended high school in a town that had an ice cream parlor, you like to dance, shop, walk in the park, and you applied for a job." He gulped a big mouthful of air.

"I'd say you know the important things," she said.

"But I don't know what you're giving up to be with Frank."

"Remember, it's a job right now."

"Are you only visiting Frank because it's a job?" His heart imitated a solo bass drummer practicing on a hilltop.

She pulled her hat tighter onto her head. "You both seem to need me and I can be of some assistance. Frank's a good man. He loved Mabel and they were together for a long time through many hardships. I especially like that she was a woman of size when he married her. It's a hope I can share at my Women's Club." One minute she was expounding on life and the next her foot slipped. The flashlight flew into the air and she yelled, "Not again." She landed with a thud.

His heart became a fist punching against his ribs. Fearing that she'd been hurt, Jake knelt and reached toward her.

She shrank away from him. "No, don't touch me. Just let me catch my breath."

He stood. "I'll find the flashlight." He stepped off the path into the snow for better traction.

Robbie saw the stars past the haloes of the city lights through the branches of the park trees. When Jake came back and shone the flashlight over her, she patted the snow. "Come on down."

He stretched out beside her and turned his face to her. "Are you all right?"

"Everything moves. Aren't the stars beautiful?"

She felt as if she was under a feather duvet, the suit provided warmth on a cold night but she heard Jake's teeth chattering next to her ear. His butt must be ice cold by now.

"Are you getting even with me in some sadistic way? I'm freezing to death. Any idea when you'll stop star gazing?" he asked.

"Actually, I was trying to think of a way to get back on my feet without looking like the proverbial beached whale." She hated that her voice sounded small and embarrassed.

"We can do one of two things. We can wait until spring and hope for a flood, or I'll help you. I may be wiry but I'm strong."

"Don't laugh at me." She slapped the snow-cover ground with her hand, sending up a plum of white powder.

"Let me help you, before I freeze to death."

"Okay. I'm ready."

He stood off of the slippery path and planted his feet shoulder width apart, bent at his knees, and extended his hands to her. He provided momentum until she sat upright on the snow.

"On the count of three," she said. Her breath hung in the air like cartoon bubble above her head.

When Jake stood he held tight and brought her to her feet. "You're much lighter than you look."

"Somehow that doesn't feel like a compliment," she said.

"I'm making an observation, not a judgment." He stepped closer with the light beam pointed to the ground. His gloved finger reached for her cheek. She stepped back. She couldn't let him get close enough to touch her face. She hadn't taken as much care with her preparation as she should have.

"You're a mysterious woman."

She watched his eyes search her face. His lips seemed to be inching closer and then they skimmed her wool cap. Then he put his arm around her shoulder and squeezed. "In order for us to be true friends, I have to be able to give things to you, too." When she started to speak, he raised his hand. "This isn't about money. What can I offer you?"

She swallowed and leaned her head against his chest. "You already have. You're being my friend."

Tonight, Jake decided, he would act like any man and accept her assessment of their relationship and not a researcher and analyze it in true research form until it was magnified ten times or one hundred times. "Friends," he agreed.

He felt her slipping away from him. It seemed as if her frame shrank and she stood out of his reach. "How do you do that?"

"Do what?"

"Slide away from me without me feeling that you're ready to move. It's the strangest phenomenon."

"Perhaps I have a superpower I haven't fully developed." She shifted from foot to foot and rubbed her hands together. "It's time I went home. I'm frozen."

Jake didn't want this time to end. It was as if he was cocooned in a bubble of warmth and when it burst he'd be back in the cold again facing the prospect of being alone.

"I'll walk you to your car." Even though it was impossible to feel her warmth through her mitten and his glove, he knew it was there. They held hands through the park and across the street.

He opened the car door for her. She settled herself into the driver's seat and started the ignition. Biting the top of her mitten she freed her hand and ran her finger across the grooves from his nose to the side of his lips, which seemed to grow deeper each day. "Take care, friend."

She watched his eyes as she placed her fingers against her lips and then touched them to his lips. He closed his eyes for a second, before he stepped away from the car.

"See you soon." He closed the door and moved away

and she shifted into drive. She gave the horn a small tap and drove down the street.

After Robbie slid the garage door into place, she stood alone in the darkness. She took a deep breath. She and Jake were friends. As a researcher, that was all she could hope. Frank had said no one could have too many friends. Then why did it feel like she'd won the consolation prize?

Chapter 13

On Friday at her weekly meeting with her research group of women, Robbie looked around the church meeting room as she outlined her plans. "My defense will take place on Tuesday. From now on, I'm only going to go out dressed in the body suit when I visit Frank."

"It's almost over," Sharon said. "I didn't think you could do it, but you have and I'm proud of you."

Robbie nodded. "Thank you, Sharon. If I'm not mistaken, you look like the proverbial cat that licked the cream."

"You caught me. I thought I'd wait until after Tuesday to tell you but I lost another twenty five pounds and the fitness club has offered me a management position." Sharon put her hand up for high fives.

"That's fabulous." Robbie slapped Sharon's palm and Mavis and Margaret called group hug. They all danced around.

"I thought you were shrinking but you must have a closet full of jean capris and white T-shirts," Margaret said.

"I've tried so often to get into shape. I just didn't find the right venue for me. Now I have. And to answer your question, Margaret, yes, I do. But I have donated the sizes I won't return to again."

"Guess we won't be spending as much time here anymore," Robbie said, feeling a sense of loss. "Hope we stay in touch."

"You can join the fitness club, Robbie. Women of all ages, shapes, and sizes are there."

"Maybe I will."

"What time are you on duty, Sharon?" Margaret asked tapping her manicured fingers on the tabletop. "I might come when you're there. You'd show me what to do." Margaret's eyes were bright with tears. "Russ has been on my case about working out and staying strong for our retirement. He's never said anything about me losing weight. He just wants me to be healthy."

"I'll email you my schedule." Sharon wound her arm through Margaret's arm. "I'll help you."

"You're not getting me to come to one of those places after I've been on my feet since four in the morning," Mavis said, waving her arms for emphasis.

"Of course not, but if we're all there you might miss us," Margaret said.

"Just call me for coffee afterwards," Mavis said. "Let's get back to business here." Mavis folded her arms across her chest. "You're probably right, Robbie. Sometimes it is best to quit while you're ahead."

Margaret leaned closer to Robbie. "And you seriously believe that neither Frank nor Jake know who you are?"

"I have to, based on what they tell me. Right after my defense, I'll tell Frank and Jake and then the Robin they know will disappear." Robbie leaned back into her chair.

"Frank and Jake are focused on important life issues right now," Margaret said. "This shows me that people may see me but don't and that's okay because it isn't all about me. Everyone has stuff in their lives that we know nothing about. Thanks for the lesson."

Sharon and Mavis nodded in agreement.

"You're right and that goes for me, too," Robbie agreed.

Robbie shifted in her seat and crossed and uncrossed her legs.

"Do you have to go to the ladies'?" Sharon asked with a smirk.

"No. It's just that I haven't worked out the details on how to break the news to Frank and Jake that I'm a fraud."

Margaret stood up and stared down at Robbie. "Wait a minute. You are not a fraud. The outside that you showed them is different, but on the inside you're the same woman. That kind of thinking gets us all into trouble."

"Thank you, Margaret. My inside has learned a great deal from this experience."

"Don't think you are the only one. We've all learned a few things. You do not get to have all the credit," Sharon said. "Now, we need directions to your thesis defense. We can still come, right? You mentioned it in the beginning of all of this."

"Yes, you can come, Tuesday afternoon. I'll email you directions and time." Robbie's watch beeped. "That's it for this meeting. Thank you all so much."

Margaret, Mavis, and Sharon called "Group hug."

"You got it. Now I need to go home and practice, practice, practice."

On Monday in the late afternoon, Jake waited for Robin to arrive. He'd missed her for the last couple of days. Her routine seemed to vary around his schedule.

"Go," Frank said.

Jake wore a sweatshirt and running pants so that he'd be comfortable while he kept his vigil in the recliner.

"She'll come." Frank was confident.

Jake turned and felt a sense of relief when Robin appeared in the doorway looking flushed and bright-eyed. He reached for her hand. "We've been waiting for you."

"Oh." She looked at him through her ever-present gemstone-framed glasses with those brown eyes.

She swallowed awkwardly. "I'm sorry, did I promise to be here at a specific time? I didn't see your car."

"No, you didn't promise. We hoped. I just don't want him to be alone today," Jake whispered.

She straightened her shoulders. "I'm here now." She walked over to the bedside. "Hi, Frank."

"I told you." Frank's breathing was shallow. He pointed toward Jake. "He needs some fresh air."

"The nurse just gave him his medication so he'll be asleep soon. I'll take a quick run in the park and be back before he wakes up." Jake didn't want to leave.

Robin gazed up at him and nodded her understanding.

"Take the time you need," she said. "I'm here for Frank, and for you."

Jake slumped against the wall, feeling a burden lift from his shoulders. He had a friend sharing this time with them. They'd been strangers just weeks ago. He wasn't alone.

Robin bit her lower lip before she said, "Go. We'll be fine."

Jake stepped toward her and raised her hand to his lips. He liked her. She reminded him in so many ways of his grandmother. Her outer size reflected her inner strength and generosity.

He snagged his jacket from the hook, looked back once to see that Robin had seated herself next to the bed and held Frank's hand. "I'm here, Frank."

After the door closed, Frank turned toward her.

Robbie leaned closer to his lips. "Hang in there, Robbie. He'll come around. He's smart."

"Pardon?" she asked, not wanting to believe she'd heard him correctly.

Frank's eyelids flickered, then closed.

Robbie. He called her Robbie. He knew.

Surprise and hope clogged her throat and she felt a smile form even during this sad time when Frank was close to leaving. She blinked away the tears pooling and sliding down her face. He always told her that he was dying, not dead. She remembered the time she sat beside him in the park without her disguise and had come up with a lame excuse about her friend telling her about him.

He had told her to visit with him as Robbie as well. She wondered how many other times small details had slipped while they talked. She released the bed rail and maneuvered her body up onto the bed with Frank. She told him about her research while he slept.

When Jake reached the halfway point around the lake in a slow jog through the cold, crisp air, he thought of Frank's feet. They looked like marble. He turned back and jogged faster. He slammed through the care home doors and skidded down the hall. Outside Frank's door, he hauled in a deep breath of antiseptic air into his lungs. No intercoms blared. The nurses' deliberate long, silent strides, provided a type of serenity in the midst of his crisis.

He listened to Robin's calming voice and when his breathing settled, he swung the door open to find Robin lying on the bed beside Frank holding his hand against her cheek.

Jake laced his fingers with hers while she swung her legs over the edge of the bed and gained her balance. He didn't look into her eyes or he'd beg her to stay by his side. He didn't know what to say so he said, "Thank you. We'll be fine now."

"I know," she said.

He leaned his head against her head. She stood still. They breathed the same air, their hands gripped tightly to each other. Her energy seemed to flow into him.

When she stepped away, he watched her pull a hat over her curls and stuff her arms into her coat sleeves.

"I'll drop in tomorrow, if that's okay." She was uncertain again.

"Of course." He didn't have the heart to tell her that they probably wouldn't be here.

Robbie swallowed and snuffled until the automatic doors slid closed behind her, then fumbled in her pockets for a tissue and covered her face. Sobs rumbled out of her chest. Her nose dripped; her eyes ran. When her eyes cleared, she saw a parking patrol officer writing her a ticket.

"Wait a minute," she called. "I'm right here." She hurried across the road.

"Too late, lady. If you'd been here two minutes ago, before I put pen to paper, I could have given you a warning."

"I wasn't in there that long. Besides, what are you doing ticketing cars outside a seniors' home? Do you know what goes on in there?" Her voice got louder and louder. "People die, you know." She fought the urge to run at him and slam him against her car.

"Not my problem. I'm just doing my job. You put money in the meter, you come out in time, you don't see me." He handed her the ticket.

She stuffed the insult into her pocket. "Sorry. I was sure I put enough money in the meter."

"Just don't forget to pay it. The fine isn't that much if you get to it right away." He shrugged. "If I could, I'd cancel it but I have rules to follow."

"Don't we all." She opened the door and pressed her body into the seat. She started the car and leaned her forehead against the cold window. The poor parking guy didn't deserve her anger but it felt good to yell at someone.

She needed to be well rested tonight. Tomorrow was her big day. By four o'clock, she would know if it had all been worth it. She'd rehearsed her opening remarks while Frank slept. Tomorrow evening, she'd come back and tell him all about it again when he was awake and then she'd ask his advice about how to tell Jake.

Jake's evening passed with a curious feeling of calm resignation. In a few days, he would prepare a funeral. His grandfather's obituary would be published in the local paper. He'd known that these things would happen almost from the moment he arrived in Regina, but he had not thought about them directly. He'd been preoccupied with his temporary position at the university, his research, the missing funds, his apartment search, reacquainting with old friends, and learning to be in the moment when he was with Frank. The celebration of Frank's life—the culmination of a well-lived life—had been in the future.

It was no longer in the future. It was now. As it did every evening at this time, the intercom announced the end of visiting hours. Family and friends of the other residents gathered in the hallways prepared to resume their lives in their homes away from their loved ones, but not Jake. The staff had made it clear that he could stay with Frank. Soon his last night with the most important man in his life would begin.

All through the night, the semi-darkness was broken when Nurse Sheila turned Granddad from side to back to side, administered his pain medication, and checked his vital signs. Jake lowered the side rail and cradled Frank's body close to his chest. "Granddad, I'm sorry I should've come home sooner." Jake felt a slight change in Frank's posture. The knot in Jake's chest unraveled and he breathed easier. Somewhere in the night Frank's breaths were shallow and rattled with congestion.

Near morning, his breathing slowed and deepened. Jake held Granddad's hand when he took his last breath at four a.m. Jake stared at Granddad's body. Frank had been exactly that. A *grand* dad to Jake, not an old man who was separated by a generation but the best dad a boy and man could have. What the hell was he going to do without him?

Nurse Sheila put her arms around Jake's shoulders, handed him a tissue to blow his nose and then led him from the room. In a daze, he signed the papers to release the body to the funeral home. It didn't look like a new day but the clock said it was. There were still hours before sunrise on the first day when he was alone in this world.

Jake parked close to the hotel's main entrance. He was numb when the water from the shower rushed over his head; he was numb when he crawled under the blankets.

He slept and when the alarm woke him and sunlight trickled through the seams in the curtains, he knew something was different on this Tuesday in December. He was free of the deathwatch. He could follow Frank's wishes for a memorial service, but he'd be driving around the city, running in the park instead of spending time at the Manor with Frank. His eyes blurred. He couldn't get his butt moving, let alone run. He shook his head. Running. Robbie. Robin. He reached for the phone book in the bedside table drawer, but which one? His fingers and thumbs refused to work together fast enough to page through the phone book. How could he not know her number? Wait a minute. He was sure that Robin had given him a cell phone number when she first took on the job of visiting Frank. Or had Robbie given him the number? He tossed the blankets aside and padded barefoot to the desk drawer where he rummaged through his scraps of paper put for safekeeping.

He needed to tell her about Frank's death. He didn't want her going to visit and . . . and see the room empty.

He sat in the chair and thought about what to say. Perhaps he could meet her in the park and tell her in person. He dialed the number and waited until an automated system repeated back the number he'd dialed and asked him to leave a message. He hung up the phone. What was wrong with him? What would he have said anyway? He couldn't have told a voice recording that his grandfather had died early this morning. Why didn't he know where she lived? As the lump formed in his throat, he was glad he didn't have to say out loud that Frank Proctor was dead. That he'd died peacefully this December, Tuesday morning, days before Christmas and before his grandson could present him with a great-grandchild. His grandfather was gone. He hadn't learned the Canadian etiquette for survivors, but he knew it wasn't like some of the cultures where they wailed and beat their chests. No, he suspected that he had to be quiet in his grief.

After coffee, Jake drove back to the manor and walked into Room 214. It was just another room now, the bed stripped and smelling of antiseptic wash. The pictures had been removed from the wall and placed in a box. Frank's clothes were neatly piled on the shelves in the closet and his books lay beside them. Jake's hands trembled as he picked up the suitcase and packed the remainder of a life into it.

At the desk, the clerk said, "We're going to miss him. He was a real gentleman."

The manager of housekeeping said, "We're sorry for your loss." She handed Jake a metal suitcase, which had been kept in storage at Frank's request. Jake remembered seeing it in the back of his grandparents' closet all the years he was growing up. His fingers moved along the scars around the lock, which Jake had created one day in his youth when he had attempted to pick the lock open with the aid of a fingernail file and a flashlight.

He put the suitcases and box into the trunk of the

Mustang. Jake looked around the parking spaces on the street for Robin's sedan. It was past the time that she usually visited Frank. She hadn't missed visiting in the late morning or early afternoon since they met. With one last glance down the street, he drove to the university, hoping she was okay. He couldn't take losing another special person in his life.

Chapter 14

On Monday evening, Robbie's decision was final. She would not appear in her disguise when she defended her thesis and her relief was immediate because she knew when to step out of someone else's oxfords and back into her own loafers.

But she woke up Tuesday morning, with her defense only a few hours away, and knew she had to change her plan. Robbie disguised as Robin needed to be seen when she shared her passionate social commentary and self-revelation. She would honor all of the women and men who had answered her questions and shared their fears and joys. She would also honor Frank and Mabel one last time.

Robbie knew from the thesis defense routine that a ten-minute break was scheduled before the second round of questions. It was not enough time to become Robin but it was enough time to remove the glasses, the contacts, the wig, and the foam body suit. She packed a suitcase that could hold the body suit after she changed from it back into a matching gray business suit and white blouse that she wore during the first half of the defense, a brush for her hair, and some deodorant. Who knew how much she'd perspire during the first round? She was confident in her material but the committee would now be in control of her future.

Robbie buttoned her coat, slung her briefcase over her shoulder, and wheeled the suitcase into the garage. After she got into the car, she moved the seat back to make room for her belly. *This must be like what women who are in the latter stages of pregnancy have to do. No time for those thoughts.*

Stay focused. This time she splurged and filled a parking meter close to the Humanities building. She needed to look fresh and in control.

Just before one o'clock, the examining room was filled with bright blue, winter light. Despite the butterflies in her stomach, she practiced her opening remarks to the empty chairs behind the committee members' table, then sat on one of the chairs placed along the wall for observers and friends. She raised her hand to welcome Brad and Sam, then quickly dropped it before they noticed her. She was pleased that they came together to support her. Sharon, Mavis, and Margaret sat near the exit. Mavis's bracelets jingled when she gave a thumbs-up before poking Sharon and Margaret. Each opened their eyes wide, signaling their obvious approval of Robbie's choice. Another Women's Studies student arrived and claimed the middle seat. No one else recognized her.

The committee took their places. Dr. Parker, the chair, sat in the center of the board table. Dr. Leddy, the external examiner, Dr. Grainger, Dr. Ross, and finally Dr. Clifton arranged their copies of Robbie's manuscript with pages flagged in various colors. They each glanced expectantly at the door and their watches while they chatted. The chair reserved for the student remained empty.

Dr. Parker looked over his glasses at Dr. Clifton. "Ms. Smith is attending, is she not?"

"Yes." Dr. Clifton continued texting a message on her cell phone.

When the second hand on the clock passed the twelve, Robbie stood up. "Good afternoon, Dr. Parker and examination committee members. Although I appear different, I assure you that under this costume, I am Robin Mary Smith, ready to defend my research and conclusions. I have taken the liberty of appearing before this committee in the disguise that I have worn in public for the last few weeks to gain a new perspective for my thesis research. I feel that I have learned in the shape of this body what I could not learn through research alone."

Dr. Parker leaned over the desk and squinted through his glasses. "This is highly unusual. Please take your seat." He turned to Clifton. "Dr. Clifton, you are this student's advisor."

Clifton tucked her cell phone under her papers. "Dr. Parker, I advised this student not to include this subjective research."

"But can you assure us that this is her?"

"Not by appearance." Clifton's lips pursed.

Robbie turned and straightened her shoulders. "I must inform the panel that even though my advisor suggested that my project would be tainted by subjective information, Dr. Clifton continued to assist me with her thorough knowledge of all issues related to women in our society. I continued this experiment without her knowledge. I must beg her pardon."

"What would you suggest?" Dr. Parker looked down the table at the rest of the panel.

Robbie raised her hand. "I'm sorry, I didn't think it would cause an identity question. I see so many similarities when I look in the mirror. May I tell you that at the break I intend to remove the costume and you will recognize me from my university ID card. I can show you my student card now. If that is not sufficient, I would ask permission to break now and change."

"How do we know that the real Robin Smith won't be hiding in the restroom and return to finish the questioning?" Dr. Grainger asked.

"We could have a security guard accompany her to the area and search the bathroom and escort her back," one of the members said.

"Good idea, Dr. Leddy. Let us proceed. We have a very tight schedule," Dr. Parker said.

"Thank you." Robbie let out the breath that she hadn't realized she was holding.

Dr. Parker invited Robbie to present her opening remarks.

"As you have read in my manuscript, there are reports that state that body size does not make a difference in hiring qualified people for positions, or wait lists for surgery, or even life insurance premiums. However, in my research group of women-of-size, I found that these situations do occur."

Robbie felt the air change and heard the door close. She wondered if Brad and Sam had left. Jean straightened her jacket and smiled at the back of the room over Robbie's head.

"What has been your most important discovery, Ms. Smith?"

Robbie stood. "Dr. Leddy, a woman who is not obese has advantages in our world that are not extended to other women if they are viewed as fat. My control group and research indicate that fat women are considered less intelligent upon first impression because it appears as if they can't control their food intake and their energy expenditure. That belief extends to their competency in the rest of their lives. How could they be the accountant, the doctor, the nutritionist, a fitness trainer, and a mother? I tested the employment statistic where I used my identical credentials for an interview in a human resource department with a food company named in my endnotes. When I appeared dressed as I am now"—she gestured to her business suit— "I was given a keyboard proficiency test, a psychological test, and had an interview where my ability to sample only one small brownie was challenged. I was told that I'd be contacted at a future date. I was not. When I appeared the following day without the body suit, I was escorted directly into the human resources manager's office and the first questions were the same. However, I was also commended on my physique and exercise program. I was told that I was a definite candidate and could be trusted to represent their line of sweet treats with probable promotion opportunities."

"What have you learned about women when they are considered fat in our society?" Dr. Grainger asked.

"Women have waged wars on fat. They abolish fat out of their diets, and surgically remove fat from their bodies as they engage in skirmishes against thighs, stomachs, and buttocks. They battle the connection between thin, young, and vivacious while being bombarded with messages that fat is old, sluggish, and irresponsible."

"You can't mean that everyone you met projected this opinion?" Dr. Ross interjected.

Robbie felt a smile form. She nodded while she spoke and used her hands for expression, careful to keep them below her chin, so the committee could see her face clearly. "On one of my excursions, a young boy pointed to me and told his mother that I was a Fat Lady. He was right. But his mother also pointed out other members of our society, the elderly, the thin, and the young. She showed respect for me as a person and passed it on to her son."

The next hour and a half were grueling, but Robbie knew her answers had depth and passion because she had experienced some of the same emotions that women who live with obesity everyday of their lives experienced in their roles as mothers, wives, and employees.

"But you must admit that our population has an obesity crisis. It is all over the news." Dr. Leddy looked out across the small audience.

Robbie shifted her weight and centered her stance. "Yes, and the practice of telling people to lose weight in order to improve their health isn't working."

"What would you suggest?" Dr. Parker asked as he scanned a page of her manuscript.

"Because my study focuses on women, I believe that women will make things happen by examining the reason we are uncomfortable with our weight and reclaim our bodies making them our personal business and not society's business. When we accept a realistic evaluation of our body, we can build an accurate sense of self. We will address the false stereotypes that fat women are ugly, lazy, and stupid, which are now used to oppress and discriminate against them."

Robbie heard Sharon's quiet "yes" from the audience.

"That's idealistic. Perhaps your field study research is anecdotal." Dr. Parker's knee bounced up and down under the table.

"Yes, you may consider my field study as anecdotal because I discovered that I cannot walk in another person's body. I do not have the day-to-day, hour-to-hour challenges that the women in my research group have faced over their lifetime." Robbie put her hand on her heart. "I can share that I met a man who loved his wife, whose body type was considered obese. He loved her everyday of their lives until they were separated by death. I can only hope that one day I will be mature enough to also experience unconditional love and acceptance of who I am. I would not have discovered this man without this research. It has been my most prized experience."

"Thank you, Ms. Smith. We'll take our ten-minute break now," Dr. Parker announced. "I'm sorry, Ms. Smith, but you'll have to be escorted to the restroom that you wish to use to change. Purely for security reasons, we can't have anyone suggesting that this defense was not performed by the qualified student."

"I understand. I'll get my bag." Robbie turned around and was met by a cold, dark, lava-rock stare. She gripped her belly. Jake. He'd been there the whole time. She swallowed past bile in her throat. She breathed deeply, determined to finish what she had started. With her head held high, she licked her dry lips and nodded to him.

"It *was* you." Jean Clifton stood from behind the committee table and peered over her glasses at Robbie and Jake.

Dr. Parker struck his gavel on the table. "Dr. Clifton?"

Robbie held her breath. She stood alone, sweating in the foam body, with all of her years and investment ready to flow down some invisible tunnel never to be retrieved again.

Dr. Clifton sat back into her chair, tapped her pen against her teeth, and a slow, thin, smile slid into place. "Go and change."

Robbie's knees buckled and she reached toward Jake, sitting straight-backed in the chair. The planes of his face filled with deep shadows. He didn't offer assistance. She teetered. Her suitcase provided the support she needed. His hard brown eyes started at the top of her head and traveled down her body and back again to her face. The man who'd accused her of attempted theft on the first day they met was back. She knew she had played a dangerous game when she continued to become friends with Frank and Jake even though only her outer shell had been a lie.

"Jake, I'm sorry. I'll explain later."

He looked past her to the door held open by a familiar security man.

"Don't tell Frank. I'll tell him. I promise." Her wheeled suitcase followed her out the door. Brad gave her a high-five and Sam gripped her hand and kissed her cheek when she passed their seats. Mavis blew her nose into a tissue. Sharon reached out and touched Robbie's hand.

"You did it," Margaret whispered. "I thought you weren't going to antagonize the committee by dressing up."

Robbie shrugged. "It felt right to be here in this shape. But I haven't passed yet. I still had questions to answer."

"Good luck," Margaret said. "We're here for you, no matter what happens."

"I know." Robbie followed the security guard to a staff washroom. He unlocked the door.

The restroom was filled with bright florescent light. She leaned against the wall and balanced up against the sink. While Robbie emerged out from under the foam body, the makeup, the glasses and wig, her thoughts were on Jake and Frank. She felt uneasy even when she argued with herself that Jake researched all of the time so he should be used to the many different approaches to a subject. While her heart jumped from normal to double-time just thinking about him and their fledgling friendship, she knew instinctively that she had to hide those feelings from Clifton if she was going to accomplish her goal and receive her degree.

When she emerged from the restroom, the security guard whistled. She accepted his much-needed boost to her confidence. She knew that she could still be failed and that a pass depended on the committee's ability to accept her demonstration as well as her research.

When she opened the door to the examination room, the committee members nodded. Except Clifton, who seemed preoccupied but stretched her lips into a thin straight line. She averted her gaze from the back of the room. She couldn't risk seeing Jake, allowing any regret to deter her from her goal.

Robbie produced her official student identification with her photograph.

"Excellent. Excellent," Dr. Parker said. "Dr. Clifton?"

"Continue." Jean Clifton tapped her pen and leaned back in her chair.

Robbie felt humbled by the personality that easily emerged. She smiled more readily and she moved with ease. When she was fat Robin, she worked harder to be accepted before she was heard and valued.

During the last minutes of a defense, it was tradition that the advisor would ask a question showcasing the student's intellect and possibly sealing the passing grade.

Jean Clifton cleared her throat. "How do you think your field study has helped you understand society's bias against size diversity when you can so easily remove the very thing that your research concludes that society is prejudiced against?" Jean paused for effect while she turned her focus to the male members of the committee. "Many women will never be the size our grad student, Ms. Smith, is right now."

Robbie straightened and lifted her chin. "Thank you, Dr. Clifton, for asking this question. You said yourself that to walk for a little while in someone's shoes is cliché. But I also found it an enlightening generalization. I've learned that people of size are constantly bruised physically by the small spaces that are all around us from chairs that are welded onto tables in fast-food restaurants, to small cubicles in department store change rooms. And they are bruised mentally and emotionally every time someone polices the food that is eaten or the changes in their bodies caused by medication or comments on the impact of genetics. Without personal insults, I would not have understood life from that perspective. I've also learned how difficult it is to purchase clothing that has style and that when clothing off the rack doesn't fit, how easily it was assumed to be my body's problem rather than the manufacturer's patterns." Robbie paused and looked at each panel member. "But I've also learned that not everyone would want to be my real size. There are men and women who are starting a revolution. It is empowering to take up space, to be noticed, to be loved and recognized for who you are outside and inside. I met enlightened people who respected me in spite of my outward appearance."

Jean Clifton nodded toward the back of the room and seemed to be preoccupied and fidgety. Dr. Parker asked if there were any further questions. The committee members shook their heads.

"In that case, I'll ask Ms. Smith and the guests to leave the room so that the committee can confer," Dr. Parker said.

"Ms. Smith, wait outside please and we'll give you the results." He looked toward the panel. "In thirty minutes?"

By the time she had exited the room, Jake was gone. Brad and Sam both waited and told her that she had done great.

"You really showed them how small-minded some people can be to big people," Brad said.

"You said it, some people. There are others who love equally the inside and the outside of a person." Robbie held onto her knowledge that Frank was his name and nature. A fair man. But Jake. What would he do?

Sam slung his arm around her shoulder and kissed her cheek. "You rocked. I'm guessing an A-plus for sure."

She remembered other friendship kisses and her heart sank. Where was Jake? She was usually visiting Frank right now. If Jake was here, then Frank was alone.

Brad and Sam asked her to text them when she had the results. "You've got it. You're on the list with my parents and these wonderful women."

Mavis called, "Group hug." The four women stood in a circle with their arms around each other. "I'd love to stay but the kids will be home from school soon. I'm the driver today so we all have to leave," Mavis said.

"I'll text you as soon as I have the results. Thank you so much for your constant support." Robbie waved goodbye to the women.

Please hurry. At every thud from a door closing on its frame she gripped the handle of her suitcase tighter, vacillating between exhilaration and dread at the one the door when opened would reveal if she passed or failed. She had promised Frank and Jake that she'd be there and she wasn't. She should have placed her intrinsic honesty before her need for personal experience and told them right in the beginning. She held onto Frank calling her Robbie, hoping that he knew and could advise her on how to make this up to Jake. What could be taking the committee so long?

She dropped onto a hardback chair in the corridor and watched students bustling to classes and to the library studying for final examinations. She hoped that she would no longer be a part of their angst, but she'd miss the opportunity to grow intellectually in a structured environment as well.

The door opened. "You may come in, please," Dr. Grainger said.

Robbie squared her shoulders and lifted her chin as she pulled the wheeled suitcase containing the outer self that had helped her complete her invaluable research. She held her breath until she realized that her personal and intellectual growth fostered by the project would continue whether she had to do revisions or write a whole new paper. Her experiment had been good discipline and training for the real world. Whatever capacity she worked at in the future, she'd help find ways to hire the most qualified person and promote education for health and fitness in the workplace.

"Ms. Smith," Dr. Parker said.

"Yes." She licked her lips and then contracted her facial muscles that should form a smile while she kept her hand on her roller suitcase for support.

"Although your presentation was unconventional, the majority of the committee agrees that your paper is worthy of a pass with a few minor revisions. Please see my secretary for the final suggestions. Congratulations." He stood and rounded the table. Stepping forward, he shook her hand, followed by the other committee members, including Dr. Clifton.

"Thank you. Thank you all and I especially need to thank you, Dr. Clifton. You are the best." Robbie's tension washed away her fake smile and her mouth felt as if it must have taken over her whole face. She palmed away tears that pooled in her eyes. It wasn't easy to skip like a child pulling a roller case behind her, but she managed all the way to her car. This time she put the parking ticket beside the other one on her passenger seat. Tomorrow she'd pay both of them.

She called her mother from her cell phone. "Mail those party invitations."

"Robbie, I'm proud of you. Can I tell your father or do you want to?"

"Is he around?"

"He has appointments this afternoon."

"I'll text him. Thanks, Mom, for your support. You know I couldn't have done this without the two of you. I love you so much."

Cars moved past her. She saw one slowing down and signaling to take her space when she left.

"We know, but it is nice to hear. What are you doing tonight?" Her mother's voice echoed pride, and love filled Robbie's heart.

"Not sure. But I need to visit Frank, the man in the care home and I need to tell my women's group and I need to jump for joy. Got to go, Mom, someone wants my space. I'll text Dad as soon as I get home."

The road was slippery and she held onto the steering wheel and paid close attention to the traffic around her. She didn't want to cause any of the drivers around her undue concern. She could be magnanimous because she passed.

She parked on the street in front of her house, then opened her cell phone and sent messages to her father, Mavis, Sharon, Margaret, then finally Brad and Sam. What a fortunate woman she was. After she lifted the suitcase from the trunk of the car, she turned and waved to Mrs. Mitchell. *I never did call her and tell her about Robin. I wonder if she is okay? I will be a better neighbor.*

When Robbie saw the blinking light on her answering machine, her stomach dropped. The number identified was the University of Regina. Jake had called moments before her defense started. Heart heavy, she pressed 'play'. The sadness in Jake's voice crushed down on her chest. He asked her to call him on his cell phone. He recited the number. She couldn't call him yet. First she wanted to make sure that Frank really did know she was one and the same woman.

She pulled on her runners and grabbed a jacket and ran through the park to the care home, down the hall to Frank's room. The bed and the room were empty. A loud deep "No" spewed from her mouth. She slid down against the doorframe and sobs filled in the spaces between the noisy intercom, a resident's call for help, and "Joy to the World" playing through the sound system.

Frank was gone.

She'd visited and spent time and loved him and hadn't ever had the chance to tell him how much he meant to her. "Oh, Jake."

She approached the nursing station with her red nose and eyes. She just didn't care. "Excuse me," she said to the clerk.

"Yes," the woman in a white lab coat answered.

"Can you tell me when Mr. Frank Proctor passed away?"

She ran her finger down a list on a clipboard. "He died at four o'clock this morning."

"Thank you."

She sat on a chair in the reception area and tried to think through the buzzing in her ears. Dear sweet, funny, loving, Frank was gone. *Why hadn't Jake called me right away?* She knew the answer. In her duplicity, she'd given him her cell phone number as a way to contact Robin Smyth. If he tried to call, she wouldn't know. She'd turned her phone on silent this morning while she reviewed her notes and got ready for this afternoon. It would have gone to her message manager. She dug for her phone in her handbag, clicked through her missed calls. A number without a name was there. Her heart skipped with gratitude that he didn't reach her before she defended her thesis or she may not have been able to go through with it. There she goes again. All about her. *Frank,* she thought, *I'm sorry. I really am. I need to see Jake now, and it won't be easy.*

Did Frank tell him the truth? Is that why Jake had come to her thesis defense? Did he want to see her humiliation? No, he wouldn't do that. He had called her cell, the only number he had for Robin. The message at home was after he knew who she really was. Her phone number was in the university records.

While she walked through the park, the wind whipped through her hair and tore at her coat buttons as she fought her way back home. She was like the spider whose web was ripped apart in the wind. The only way to fix it was to start again.

The winter sun had set twelve hours and fifty-two minutes after Frank had departed this world. Robbie squinted toward the lock on her front door. She'd forgotten to turn on the outside light in her haste to visit Frank. With the flip of a switch the entryway was bathed in warm candescent light. She was going to graduate. She was poised to put her first foot on the career ladder and Frank, who'd accepted her unconditionally, wasn't here to share her success. She lifted the foam suit out of the case and wrapped her arms around it. This form was a friend but she needed to say goodbye to it. She hung it on its hanger. Her heart felt as if it was trying to squeeze into a small pocket in her chest. It didn't want to acknowledge her losses. At least Frank had known the truth before he died. Deep in her heart she knew this to be true. She had to speak with Jake. Extend her deepest sympathy. He must be so alone. But would he even see her or believe her again?

Chapter 15

Jake telephoned Jean when he left the Care Manor for the last time. She wasn't available. He could have waited for her answer instead of coming to the university. His concern had been for his students and that he wanted to find Robin before she went to visit Frank. If Robbie were at the University, she'd help him. And he had to keep moving, keep busy. If he hadn't been so impatient, Nadine wouldn't have told him where to find Jean Clifton and he wouldn't have rushed down the corridors hoping to speak with her before the proceedings began. He was too late. His gut twisted. He'd been used. And not just him, his beloved granddad.

In his office, he paced. He broke pencils in two. He sat in his chair and he got up two minutes later. Now what? The Robin or Robbie that he knew couldn't have used them strictly for research. Frank and he had trusted her. When he'd first met her in the park, all dirty and disheveled, he knew something wasn't aboveboard. He was seldom wrong. He should have followed his gut reaction. She still didn't know that Frank was gone. Jake snorted. At least his grandfather didn't need to be told that he had been deceived.

When Jake's brain found a moment of clarity he called Nadine. She provided Robbie's number and he left a brief message requesting her to call his cell. He stared out of the window. He'd made acquaintances all the time in his line of work so why was he sitting here like a lost puppy? It was so much more than just a woman, if he told himself the truth. It was his budding friendship with Robin that he would miss.

Without realizing it, he'd looked forward to having her in his life for a short time, as she had been in Frank's, at least until the funeral service was over. He shouldn't be here. He should go back to the hotel.

There was a rap on his door. He groaned. He did not need any interruptions. "One moment." He straightened his jacket, sat in his chair behind his desk, and opened a file. "Come in."

He blinked and shook his head. Jean Clifton. Somehow he thought it might be Robin.

"Oh, Jake, I'm so sorry. I received your message just as the committee settled into their chairs. I would have come sooner, but I couldn't leave." Skidding around the desk, she threw her arms around his neck. "I wanted to pass on my sympathies but you know as the student's supervisor I couldn't do anything to jeopardize her presentation, even if she was way out on a limb."

He tried to dislodge himself from her embrace. "Of course not. I didn't want to upset you, but I had student appointments and I needed Nadine to contact students. I wasn't thinking straight. I could have called her. I also wanted you to know that I'll need some time off to arrange things."

"Thank you for finding me personally. It means a lot to me to share this time with you." Jean continued to rub his arm. "Can I get you anything? Nadine has a stash of whiskey for medicinal purposes."

"No, thanks."

"Nadine rescheduled all of your students. So don't worry."

He paged through his mail absently.

"I'm thankful your grandfather didn't know about Robin's research project."

"He must have been weaker than I thought. He was so sharp and observant when he was alive."

"She passed, you know."

"Her defense was inventive on a subject that has been in the headlines for months. I think she raised the bar for defense projects and I wouldn't be surprised if you receive recognition for your support."

"Do you really think so?" She gave his arm a final stroke. "But that's not important, now. I'll have Nadine make you some strong coffee. You look like you can use something." Jean closed the door when she left.

He groaned at another tentative knock at his door. "Come in."

He sank into his chair. "Robbie." He felt as if he were recognizing the pain from a burn as a blister formed.

"He died and I wasn't there," Robbie said brokenly. Tears swam in her gorgeous hazel eyes.

"I was," he said, relieved his voice was calm.

"Can I do anything?" She stood there, almost imploring him to help her.

Everything hardened inside him. "No. Everything is under control. Frank took care of most details."

"Jake, I'm sorry." She stood marooned on his carpet.

He extended a lifeline from his own grief anesthetic. "Congratulations on achieving your goal."

"I passed my defense, yes."

He glanced around the wood paneled office. His framed diplomas hung on the wall. "I understand field research but I didn't expect to be a subject." His gaze caught the photo of the !Kung Village.

Suddenly he needed her to leave. He glanced at the closed door.

"Could you consider forgiving me?" she asked in a hoarse voice.

"I'm not big into forgiving your deliberate deception to me, but even more so, to him."

"I'm sorry for your loss, Jake." She extended her hands toward him, palms upward.

He swiveled his chair toward the window. "You've made your point," he said evenly.

"I'll leave but remember you don't even know me. We could resume our friendship and see where it goes?"

He recognized Robin's voice. He shook his head. He was going crazy.

She appeared at his side with a tentative smile. "Frank also said you can never have too many friends."

"How would you know what he said? You weren't there."

"But I was Jake. I was. I was his friend. I was your friend, too. Both in and out of the disguise."

He remained silent. He didn't know how to respond to her. A part of him wanted to continue to see her, would miss her tentativeness, followed by her strength to be a friend to Frank and to him. He would miss seeing her and assuring him he had done the best he could. *Wait, that was Robbie.* He'd miss her playfulness, her needing him for support when she felt vulnerable. Wait, that was part of her research. The woman standing beside him could never feel vulnerable. But that is exactly what she was, standing beside him, asking for another chance.

Finally he said, "As Frank might say, or might have said, friendship is based on respect and trust."

Somewhere his brain registered his need to project protective indifference. Jake ran his hand over his chin. "Friendship."

"Believe me. I'd like to be your friend. I will be, if you let me, give me time to explain why I did what I did." She paused and her eyes welled up again. She ran a tongue across her lips. "Was-was the end hard for Frank?"

Jake's stomach knotted, remembering that final breath. "No, he went peacefully. Look, I've got final arrangements to make. If you get the newspaper, you'll read the details in his obituary."

"Th-that's good. I'll leave you to your plans. Goodbye, Jake. Please know I'm truly sorry. But I'm glad I got to know him. He was a gentleman." She closed the door silently behind her.

Jake's chest tightened. If Robin came to the memorial service, it would probably be the last time he'd see her. Even though the city was small, it wouldn't be the same. He'd met people and enjoyed their company all of his life and then left them behind. He would do it again.

As he returned to his desk, he spotted a priority post envelope from his old university sitting in his inbox. How did he miss this? He sat, then tore open the end with little enthusiasm. The enclosed letter stated that the auditor had found the missing funds. He put the letter down and put his face in his hands for a moment. Then he picked it up again and read the details. One of his associates had been influenced by the childhood poverty they had witnessed due to AIDS and had handed out cash to starving mothers and children. He'd emptied his pockets that day as well. He recalled the village orphanage, where it seemed as if children looked after babies, because thirty-two percent of children were orphaned as a result of AIDS. Now he knew money was just a stopgap. It didn't bring back the parent they had lost either. He was in their shoes now and he was educated and he didn't know how to take care of his orphaned status. Another tentative rap on the door brought him back to the present.

"Coffee." Nadine stood with a steaming mug in her hands.

"Thank you." And on her heels, Christie, his student from Anthropology 100 approached, stopped, then shifted from foot-to-foot with her paper in her hand.

"What can I do for you, Christie?" Jake asked.

"Professor Proctor, I just need your help with this one detail please. I have to hand this paper in today."

"Let me have a look."

It took all of Jake's will power to focus on his student. His mind wandered like a piece of fluff in the wind.

But one thought became clearer and solidified. His reputation was safe. He was free to return to Ottawa, or anywhere in the world. There wasn't anything holding him here anymore.

Robbie followed the well-worn path through The Regina Cemetery, where they had the rule that every marker was to be placed at ground level. There were no interesting monuments to find her way to the place where Jake and the minister, along with the other mourners, would meet. An employee of the cemetery directed her toward the burial plot on this Friday, the day of the Frank's final resting place. It was as bright and clear as a solitaire diamond, and Robbie felt as cold and alone in the fat suit. She'd put it on with extra care and attention as her tribute to Frank. Although the sun shone, it brought no warmth as they stood around the gaping hole, with the mahogany casket suspended on belts, ready for the last words to be said. Robbie glanced at the marker to see 'Beloved husband, father, and friend' chiseled in the marble for all to see. This was a legacy to be proud of. She wanted to hope that she hadn't lost the right to be a friend and that Frank knew in the end that she hadn't trashed his trust for her own selfish goals. If only he'd lived twelve more hours, she'd have known for sure that he'd heard her explain everything while he slept.

Her eyes filled and the tears fell unrestrained as she watched Jake, proud and tall, with a handful of dirt ready to drop.

"My grandfather was a man who honored people, and accepted them as they were. He listened when they talked about their lives. He always called a spade a spade." A few people chuckled. "He did not worry about what others thought. I wish he had been able to stay around longer to share his wisdom and courage with me." With a shaky breath, he continued. "And now you should all know what advice he gave for this day. He wants us to share good food, a hearty laugh, and a genuine friendship. So, after we leave the cemetery, we'll meet in the recreation hall at Care Manor and we'll enjoy his last wish."

Afterward, Robbie could not bring herself to return to the hall and mingle with those who came to share memories of her friend, Frank. She was not ready to purge her guilt with self-forgiveness. She just wanted to go home to her mother and be her little girl.

With the attention of a robot, Robbie drove the short distance north on Highway 11 and descended into the valley with the bluffs and curves like the backs of giant cows hunkered down to wait out a storm. She sang along with the tunes of the eighties. She thought about the beautiful forest-green empire waist dress she would buy for her graduation day. She had to purchase her father's imported licorice from the nut and candy store for Christmas and she could probably get her mom's special herbal tea blend at the health food store down the street. But what was Jake going to do without Frank and without her? Frank had asked her to take care of Jake.

When she parked in front of the two-story Victorian house, her shoulders lifted out of their slump. Home. She took a moment and squeezed into the rocking chair on the open front porch. With her hands snuggled into her pockets, her nose covered with her scarf, she rhythmically rocked the chair with her feet, creating its age-old comforting motion.

"Hello?" her mother called out of the door. She wore Christmas red even though it clashed with her copper hair, which she had knotted on top of her head.

"Hi, Mom."

"Oh, it's you."

Robbie laughed a little. She had forgotten that she was in disguise. "I need a few minutes."

Her mother stepped carefully in her satin slippers and bent down and kissed Robbie's cheek. "I'll put on the coffee."

"Thanks."

The rhythm seeped into her soul and gradually she became aware of the sparrows flittering amongst the branches of the evergreen trees.

When she went indoors, she found herself surrounded by garlands, colored glass balls, twinkling lights, and porcelain villages. The Christmas tree seemed to reach the top of the second floor with the angel that anchored the gold ribbons hanging down the branches.

Robbie hugged her mom. "It's beautiful."

Her mother stepped back and shook her head at her daughter. "Here, let me hang your coat in the closet. You must be very hot."

"No, not too bad. If I know I'll be indoors for a long time, I can put cold gel packs in little pockets around the abdomen."

"Clever. Are you sure you don't want to change? You've got some workout clothes in your bedroom. I could lend you some lounging pajamas."

Robbie shook her head. "I'm honoring Frank. Today was his celebration of life." She glanced at the plate of festive cookies. "He talked about his wife's favorite recipes during this season. They always baked Jam Jams. She'd roll out the dough and bake the cookie. He was the thimble-hole-cutter man and jam-assembly-line person. His job was spreading the strawberry jam on warm cookies and pasting the cookie with the thimble hole on top. He felt he contributed to their Christmas container that they delivered to their neighbors." She sat at the kitchen table with a glass vase filled with pinecones and Christmas balls. "The year she couldn't do what she loved, they moved and got the assistance they needed."

"Megan, Robbie's car is on the street. Is she in yet?" her father called from the den.

"I'm in the kitchen, Dad." She played with the tassel on the placemat.

"Nice get up," her father said as he entered the kitchen.

"This is the disguise that allowed me to experience so many different emotions." Robbie stood and turned around for her mother and father to see her from all angles. "I drove here from the cemetery. I couldn't go to the hall. Jake still won't talk with me."

"This is the guy whose grandfather you visited almost every day. This is the same guy who you took home from the park like a lost puppy. Come on, he deserves whatever he got if he didn't recognize you." Her father always championed her creativity.

"Dad, look at me. I've changed my eye color, I wear glasses, see my gum line. Lots of people don't recognize me." Robbie stood with her hands on her ample hips.

Her father brought cookies to the table. "I can't imagine a warm-blooded man who would be insulted that his friend put all that she had into something she believed in."

"That's just it, Dad. Don't you get it? Without this padding, we shared some intense moments, but we were mindful that he was a professor and I was a student, but when I was in disguise we were friends."

Her father sat down, his thick salt-and-pepper hair parted and combed. His glasses rested firmly on his straight nose. His clean-shaved chin with a dimple comforted her just as he had all her life. "But you are Robin, so you are his friend."

"Give yourself a break, Robbie." Her mother patted her shoulder. "Drink your coffee. Have one of your father's cookies."

"The examination committee understood. Jake's smart, but he had a lot on his mind." She shook her head. "I don't know what to do."

"Guys always need friends. Right, Megan?" Her father placed a plate of gingersnaps on the table.

Robbie thought about her parents' relationship. They had known each other for thirty years. They were friends and lovers. Mabel and Frank had been friends and lovers, too. Maybe there was hope. "Guess I'd better take my backside back to Regina and be a friend to Jake."

"You may as well stay for dinner, dear, we have a few things to discuss with you," her mother said, refilling her mug with steaming coffee.

Robbie thought about the feelings Jake had shared. He'd wished he had spent more time with the people he loved. "I'd enjoy that."

"It's my turn to make dinner," her mother said.

"Oh, don't fuss. How about using the leftovers from the roast chicken from last night's dinner?" Her father's eyes twinkled.

Ever since she was a child, her father had cooked and baked. He enjoyed it and was good at it. He always worked and cleaned up as he went along. Robbie and her mother did not venture into the realm of exotic meals. The simpler, the better was their motto.

"Great idea, Ron. You don't mind leftovers, Robbie?" Her mother tied an apron around her sweater with Rudolph's red nose flashing on and off.

"I love Dad's leftovers. I'll set the table." Robbie joined in the chorus of "Winter Wonderland." She rolled up the wax that pressed against her gums and tossed it in the garbage, then put her wig into her coat sleeve so she wouldn't forget it.

During dinner, they talked about her parents' upcoming trip to Halifax for a medical convention, Christmas dinner, and their tradition of sharing their commitments they had made the prior Christmas. Robbie helped clear the table. Then she straightened her wig in the hall mirror, put on her coat, scarf, and gloves, and hugged her mom and dad. "Thanks, I needed you."

"You're welcome, Robbie. Be patient. Grief is tough," her mother said.

During the drive back along the highway to Regina, she nibbled on the inside of her cheek. An idea formed in her mind. If Jake were a girlfriend, she'd console and listen, perhaps prepare a meal and share memories. She would pick up some food, a bottle of wine, and go to his hotel room. Instead of going directly home, she swerved into a mall, purchased her supplies, and hurried back to her car.

She felt powerful as she held onto the guest telephone.

"Hello," Jake answered groggily.

Robbie had an image of his features awakening from sleep, his hand brushing through his hair. She had to keep this real to stay grounded. Perhaps he had spittle running down his chin. Better.

"Hi. It's Robbie," she said with a bright voice. "Can I come up?"

"Why?"

"Because I want to be your friend."

"I have friends."

"Please, for Frank's sake."

"I'll leave the door unlocked."

The clerk's gaze skimmed over her heavy walking shoes, her gloved hands holding a straw picnic basket. When he went back to his paperwork, Robbie decided he must have determined she wasn't a problem visitor.

When Jake's door swung open, she heard the shower running. Her mind scurried toward Jake standing naked under a flow of water. Ignoring the stab of desire, she focused on the task.

She dragged the flowered spread from the bed. The quilted fabric wafted Jake's scent when she shook it out and placed it on the floor next to the window. She unpacked votive candles from the basket and set them on a tray in the middle of the blanket. They didn't need the sprinklers going off because of a fire. If she weren't careful, her rising heat would set off the sensors. She fanned her face with a newspaper that had been on the end table. She hadn't been this warm at her parents. She unwrapped the fresh barbecued chicken, a baguette, assorted slices of cheese, some raw vegetables and dip, a bottle of wine, and finally, wine glasses.

She carefully eased her padded body onto the blanket, careful not to move the tray with candles. The steam from the shower seeped around the edges of the bathroom door and she breathed deeply, picturing a meadow where a doe and her fawn stood at the edge of calm, clear water. The maple tree branches created shade for the pastoral scene. Strange groaning and belching sounds echoed in the woods just before a buck displaying a huge antler rack crashed through the clearing. She shook her head. It's too soon for rutting season.

She poured herself a glass of wine with a shaking hand, then took a quick sip and nibbled on the vegetables and dip. *What was going on? Friends don't think about their friends naked with imagined groaning sounds.*

The bathroom door opened and Jake stood before her. Beneath the hotel terry robe she saw his long, muscular legs, his hair moist on his shimmering skin. Her gaze traveled past the loosely tied belt to the curly sprinkling of hair, which peeked out from the V front of his bathrobe, up past his taut neck muscles to his chin. She noted the frown around his lips, his puzzled eyes, and his furrowed brow.

"Robin?"

"I called, remember?

"You said Robbie."

"It is me." Her voice shook.

"Is this some sort of joke, or just another little experiment?" His voice was hard.

Robbie braced her body with a straight arm and stared up at him. "It's not a joke. I'm your friend."

He eyed her suspiciously and strolled over and sank down onto the blanket. "I'll play your little game for awhile. I've become used to having you around. Let's see how you deal with the feelings that are welling up inside me now as I glance at this chicken breast. Under the skin, it is smooth, white, and tasty." He spoke in a lecturer/scientist's voice as she watched him reach for a bunch of grapes. "Or how about these grapes you've brought, associated with the god, Dionysus, a deity of fertility and procreation. And grape juice which can be made into wine has aphrodisiac virtues."

Robbie gulped audibly.

"Consciously, Robin, Robbie, you may be saying 'friend' but subconsciously you're telling me a different tale."

She straightened her back, then placed her arms on her hips, her feet stretched out in front of her. As Robin, she really did take up a lot of space. "Men!" she cried. "Does everything have to be brought down to sex? Can't we just talk?"

"Sure, I'll try, but you're going to get a little experiment back. I see the way your eyes are lingering. Another part of your brain is wondering if, indeed, I'm wearing underwear, sort of like the proverbial question, 'What does a Scotsman wear under his kilt?' I'll share your picnic. We'll see who wins."

"Wins! Wins! This isn't a game. It's our lives." She banged her heel against the floral spread. Then a little voice nagged at her and she acquiesced. "You're right, a part of me does want to know what's under your robe but we have my suit to protect us."

"Hey, is that why some women are fat? Do you think they're actually trying to protect themselves from lust and men? Have they sabotaged themselves into believing that men are not good enough unless they're able to see past their body image?"

"Is that why your grandmother was fat?"

He took a big gulp from his glass. "I don't know. Let's just eat and get this over with so I can go back to sleep." He set his plate aside. "Unless you have other persuasive methods, my mood is suddenly and certainly gone."

She blinked back tears. "I know that I always try too hard but I wanted to be with you. I miss Frank, too. I tried to think of what I'd do for a female friend. Picnics are usually considered fun. People sit around in the sun, nibble food, and talk." She wiped her face with a napkin.

"Jake, would you tell me about the gathering at Care Manor? I couldn't stay."

He was silent for a long time, then said, "Granddad was a celebrity. Family members of past and present Care Manor residents sent flowers and shook my hand. Apparently he always sent flowers whether the family wanted them or not. It was his way of celebrating a life. I met past neighbors and his past coworkers and of course church members. It was gratifying to be hugged and shaking hands with those whose lives he had touched."

"Sounds like a celebration of a life well lived," she said.

"That's what it was. My head knows that it was better for him to be finally free of the cancer, but my heart is another thing."

He brought his glass to his mouth and sipped the red liquid, then held the glass in his hands and studied her. "Okay, if we are going to spend this time together, I need you to do something for me, too." His eyes narrowed. "I want you to start moving away from your disguise. How about taking off your wig"—he scrubbed his hand over his chin—"and . . ." He paused. "Let's see, shoes and socks? That way I can see some of you that I know is in there."

"But, I'll look like a clown."

"We all have to make sacrifices. I have to sit here in this robe because I'm not going to get dressed just to get undressed again. So you, too, can look a little foolish."

Robbie tugged off her wig, gave her head a shake, and ran her fingers through her hair. She slipped her shoes off without untying them.

"Why did you do that?" he asked.

"What?"

"Push your shoes off like that without untying them?"

"Oh," she said. "It's just easier than bending over. It's hard to get past this middle."

"That explains why grandma used to do that." His voice was thoughtful. "Her stockings were always in a roll at her ankles, too, and that sure didn't make her look like any of the other kids' moms."

Robbie nodded. "I know. The elastic usually slinks down to the narrowest point."

She watched him reach for some cheese and bread. "Would you help me with this sock, please?"

He reached over and removed her sock. Then dropped it as if it were burning his fingers. "Talk about body memory," he said. "I'd wince when Grandma would ask me to remove hers. Yet I'd watch Granddad as he would kneel and gently pull off her stockings then massage the ridges in her flesh. When I was young, I used to trace my finger around the grove and wonder at the dent in her skin. I'd ask if it hurt. She'd shake her head and laugh and tell me that I was tickling her with my fairy tracks. It made me feel special."

"What else do you remember, before you became aware that she was different?" Robbie asked as Jake rubbed the pads of his thumb along the sole of her foot.

"When she hugged me, I felt so safe and loved."

"There are advantages to being a larger size. For a long time women felt protected by big men." She closed her eyes and a small murmur escaped from her throat as she reveled in the contact between his flesh and hers. He slowly entwined his fingers between her toes. An erotic pleasure burst through her core. "No!" she said as she jerked her foot away.

"What are you doing?" His hand clamped down on her ankle.

"I'm getting up. Let me go." She tried to lift her foot.

"Not yet." He eased up on the pressure.

She looked into his eyes. "I don't think I can stand it much longer if you continue to tempt me. Who would have thought a foot massage could be so stimulating?" She attempted to laugh.

"You could give in." He raised an eyebrow.

"You're right. I could give in, but then what? I want something more, not just a bedmate."

"You're asking a lot from a man who just buried his grandfather today. I'd like to comply and be soft and sentimental, but right now, I'd rather just put my head on a women's breast and have her make nice to me."

"You want a mother?"

"Robin, Robbie. Damn." He stood and walked over and started to remove the belt on his robe. "Right now I'm not analyzing. I'm going to bed."

Robbie busied herself so she wouldn't watch. She slammed paper plates, chicken, and glasses into the basket. Her frustration dissipated as she turned to see Jake's back turned to her, wrapped in the blanket and sheet with his arm folded across his chest. The bedside lights were out. She quietly advanced, moved a chair beside the bed, then sat down. "If I could, I'd take away your pain. I'd help you feel like yourself again."

She heard his slowed breathing. His neck muscles relaxed. Light from the Christmas street decorations gave the room a warm glow.

"In your hours of deepest need, I wasn't there. I would have liked to be but I'm not sure how much my presence would have helped. Frank was your father." She slowly ran her fingers through his hair, massaging his scalp."

She rubbed her hand across her eyes and swallowed a lump of grief. "I wish we could cry together, and someday perhaps we'll remember his wit and you'll tell me more about the years you shared together." His shoulders were pliable to her touch.

Her breasts felt heavy and she was glad she had the body suit on because the temptation to crawl in behind him was immense.

She imagined herself in his embrace with her whispering words of love, but those words couldn't change the grief or mend a torn friendship. She would hold onto her resolve. She was going to demonstrate her friendship to Jake. She kissed him gently on his temple. She untied her laces, tugged her socks over each foot and slipped into her shoes, double-knotted them and left the room.

Robbie drove home and thought about what she wanted. She wanted Jake to accept her friendship and maybe it would lead to love. She wanted to love and be loved.

Jake was right. She needed to be herself. It was time to mend the split between Robbie and Robin. She would have to accept her own package and all the baggage that went along with it. She would need to be mindful of the advantages that it brought to her. As soon as she got home, she would pack up the torso of the body suit.

Jake rolled over toward the spot where he had felt warmth emanating while he slept only to see an empty chair. The folded bedspread now occupied the space. He wandered over to the window in time to watch Robin exit from the building, struggling as the wind whipped at her coat and pulled at the picnic basket. He felt as if everything had been a dream. She was a lithe runner but she was also a round fleshy woman, all breasts, abdomen, and thighs. But she had been there. She didn't run away from his grief. She didn't ask him to forget it. She accepted it. Accepted him.

Though desperate for some sleep, he found he couldn't. Instead he paced around his hotel room and finally his eyes settled on the old locker. He went through his grandfather's wallet and found a key, then unlocked the clasp and lifted the lid and found a-life-in-a-box. Jake was astounded to find a letter addressed to him in his grandfather's familiar script. Simple and direct, his grandfather was telling him to discover his own roots, rather than only those of ancient tribes. "Son, you'll be a better man for it."

Jake carried the locker over to the table and began an anthropological study, sifting through pages and pictures, attempting to make sense of his past. With a sense of distance and a professional attitude, he laid things out chronologically, in years and decades. His eyes skimmed photographs curling at the corners. There were yellowed envelopes addressed in fountain pen script, both of his grandparent's handwriting. Love letters, not spilling over with only sentimentality but of shared feelings of apology, and sorrow. It seemed as if Frank and Mabel had kept their love alive with this long lost art of communication.

He crossed his legs and poured some of the red wine that Robin had left behind. The red was like the breast of a robin, the light reflecting through the glass like the twinkle in a bird's eyes. Although this image was not what he predicted, it was a fitting description of the Robin he knew. She was flashy in an unusual way, with alert eyes that explored her world. She was strong. Even though he told her he couldn't forgive her deception toward him and Frank the most, she had honored Frank in the shape he trusted. Jake took a big gulp. She didn't stay away from his grief and approach him as if nothing of importance happened. She came to share his sorrow. His universe did not give him what he expected. He put down his glass and gathered his clothes quickly. He'd left her phone number in his office but he knew where she lived. If her lights were on, he'd knock on her door and tell her he forgave her and he'd like to start over. He understood that the immersion in a culture under study was important because it helped researchers learn. He should have understood that she needed to become less visible and lessen the observer effect. While he put on his pants, he also acknowledged, *I just don't like to be the observed.* Guess he'd had some of his own medicine.

Chapter 16

Once home, Robbie parked the car in the garage and pressed the button and the garage door groaned with metal against metal while it rolled into place. Mrs. Mitchell's Christmas lawn ornaments twinkled in the crisp night air. She carried the picnic basket into the kitchen. She didn't even want to look at it again. She turned on the stove light's soft glow. Why, oh why, did she have to go to extremes? If she would have visited Jake without the suit, she would probably be in bed with him right now. Her lips puckered with a desire to connect to Jake's. She leaned her forehead against the cool refrigerator. She could have followed her fingers that had massaged his scalp with kisses on his earlobes, his neck. If she hadn't resisted the temptation to capture his tongue as it slid across his lips while he relaxed, they both would be comforted by a warm, willing body, right now. Instead, she was home climbing the stairs to her bed all alone. She turned on a bedside lamp and shed her outer shell, her arms sliding from a sleeve that provided dangling triceps, and tugged the torso with a double-D cup away from her body revealing a B underneath. Her nipples were erect and ached.

Stop this. Yes, he is a handsome man, but I need to gain his trust. I want to be his friend first.

She stood under the shower and thought about the friends she'd made during different classes throughout her student days and during the semesters when they helped each other out and then they went their separate ways. Her relationship with Jake was similar to that, wasn't it? She and Jake learned from each other and helped each other for a time and now it was time to accept this. She vigorously dried her hair. No more thoughts about sharing a bed, a life together with a man she hardly knew. Sure he was kind. Sure he was funny. Sure he wanted a family.

He had traveled and experienced other cultures. Sure he seemed to like her, but so did many other people. He'd probably leave again. There wasn't anything to hold him here now.

While she cleaned the torso one last time, the cleaning cloth blurred before her eyes. The suit felt as if it had taken on extra weight when she positioned it on the hanger. She gave her teeth a cursory brush and promised to floss in the morning. Once in bed, she tucked the covers under her chin. Her forehead felt hot to the touch. Her stomach ached. She dozed fitfully, only to wake up with a gripping abdominal pain. She rushed to the bathroom and vomited. She lay with her cheek on the cool tub until she had the strength to shuffle slowly back to her bed. Was it something she ate? The moment she put her head down, the room started moving. *Great*, add sick to the list of things wrong with her. She reached for the phone and hit the speed dial for her parents' home.

Her mother answered with a groggy, "Hello."

"Mom, it's me. I feel terrible."

"Dear, you'd better take this. It's Robbie. She's sick."

She heard the phone clunk a few times as it changed hands.

"Talk to me," her father stated in his usual brusque manner.

"Dad, I've vomited and now I'm so dizzy I don't think I can stand."

"Do you have pain in your right side?"

"It hurts all over." She moaned.

"Listen to me carefully, Robbie. Get up slowly, put your head down, and take some deep breaths. Go to the stairs."

"Dad."

"Just go."

Robbie rolled onto her side and sat up. "I'm going to pass out."

"No, you are not. Breathe deep."

"Okay."

"Crawl to the stairs if you have to." She felt another wave of dizziness as she obeyed her father. "I'm holding onto the wall."

"Are you on the stairs? Robbie, stay with me here. Now hold onto the railing. Count out the stairs to me. Keep going, honey. Go to the front door. Unlock it."

Feeling the world swirling around her, she did as he asked, then said, "Unlocked."

"Good."

"Got-to-go-to the bathroom. I'm going to be sick."

"I'll be there as soon as I can."

She dropped the phone into her robe pocket and crab-walked up the stairs. She must not pass out. She must not pass out. Dad lived so far away. She wiped her mouth on tissue, flushed, then put her head down on the bathroom mat. *Just for a minute. Dad will be here in just a minute.*

Jake stopped at curb in front of Robbie's house. The lights were out.

He hesitated. What was wrong with him? Of course he couldn't go ringing her doorbell at midnight.

He'd probably scare her half to death. He put the car into first and eased back onto the street. He drove around the park where the fir trees swayed in the wind and past the Care Manor where most of the windows were in darkness. He felt as if he should turn around and go back. Grief did terrible things to the mind. He had the knowledge of death but he hadn't assimilated the reality into his being as he was being forced to right now. He heard the wail of a siren before he saw the lights flashing. He hoped no one was seriously ill at Care Manor. He watched the lights flash across the park and come to a stop.

Jake accelerated and arrived just as the paramedics were removing the stretcher from the back of the ambulance at Robbie's house.

"What the hell is going on?" he asked.

"Sorry, mister, you'll have to stand back." The man in uniform shouldered him out of his way as his team rolled the stretcher up the walk.

They opened the front door and called Robbie's name. Jake paced on the front walk. *You should have had her stay with you.* Moisture pooled in his eyes. He yanked the winter hat over his ears, shoved his hands into his pockets, and stood on the front stairs. Stupid pride. Robin, rather Robbie, had never hurt anyone really. Frank was happy. *It was you who felt betrayed. What did she really do to harm you? Nothing.*

He heard the paramedics on their phones talking to someone.

Just then another car pulled up to the curve. A man and a woman ran past him and into the house.

The paramedics exited carrying the stretcher. Robbie was covered by a blanket and belts held her secure. Her head was wrapped in a towel. He stepped forward. "Robbie, I'm here."

She moaned.

"Step aside, sir," an attendant instructed.

He moved onto the lawn and watched while they slid the stretcher in the back and closed the doors. The ambulance roared down the street with lights flashing. His head didn't want to believe what he had seen. Robbie was in an ambulance. Where would they take her?

He heard the front door close and turned to see the man and woman who had run into the house just minutes ago, striding toward their car.

The woman glanced over at him and stopped. "Are you Jake, by any chance?"

"Yes."

The woman called. "Ron, this is Robbie's friend Jake that she told us about."

The man advanced quickly, extending his hand. "Ron and Megan Smith. Robbie's parents. They're taking her to the General Hospital. I suggest you meet us there in emergency."

Ron put his arm through Mrs. Smith's and they turned toward their car. Jake shifted the Mustang to third gear following their taillights down the city streets to the hospital.

He damned the speed limits and held reins on the Mustang. When he arrived, he imitated the quick purposeful stride he'd witnessed at the manor all these weeks and followed the signs toward the ER.

Robbie woke to clatter. She wriggled her toes, stretched out her legs, flexed her buttocks, and contracted her stomach muscles. *Oh that's tender*. She stretched her arms and fingers. Where was she? She squinted against the bright light that obliterated the remaining dream fragments where Jake had fed her ice chips on a beach. She closed her eyes again.

When she opened her eyes, Jake was in the same room standing at the window with his back to her. She leaned over a bed rail, "Jake." He turned and took three giant steps. He scooped her into his arms. Cradling her head against his shoulder, his hand smoothed the muscles along her back. He kissed her sticky forehead. When the heart monitor sounded an alarm, he almost dropped her.

A nurse slid to Robbie's bedside. "Sir! I need you to step back. Miss Smith, lay back and relax. Your heart's going to jump out of your chest. Breathe deeply. Slowly. Close your eyes. That's it."

A steady beat beeped until Robbie opened her eyes and saw Jake.

"Maybe you'd better leave," the nurse said.

"No, don't go," Robbie whispered. "He's a friend," she explained to the nurse. "He surprised me."

She slid the covers up to her chin. She'd rather burrow under all of the blankets than have him see her like this. But she'd just defended her thesis that said packaging shouldn't make a difference. If he could see her at her very worst and not run for the hills, then maybe they had a chance. She felt like her bones protruded through her skin and her hair was all greasy and she probably had bad breath.

"A few minutes. No more." The nurse looked at the clock and then at Jake before she bustled from the room.

"I'm thirsty." Her tongue felt like sandpaper. "My throat hurts."

She drank from the blue plastic cup with a flexible straw that Jake held to her lips.

"Your throat will be sore for a couple of days. You were a very sick woman."

"I remember waking up and feeling awful. I called Dad and he wouldn't shut up. Kept at me to unlock the front door."

"While he was trying to keep you conscious, your mom called nine-one-one."

Robbie struggled to sit up. "Where are they?"

Jake ran his fingers through his hair. "In the cafeteria."

"This doesn't make sense. How'd you get here?"

"Guilty conscience." He shrugged his shoulders. "I couldn't sleep. I couldn't call. I still don't have your phone number in my phone book. I arrived when the paramedics took the stretcher into the house. I was there when they carried you out. I met your parents. They made it to your house and your dad told me which hospital they were taking you or I would have had to chase the ambulance." His fists opened and closed at his sides. "We were pretty scared."

"What happened?"

Jake's eyes connected with Robbie's. "Food poisoning is the educated guess." He waited a moment, then added, "I've gone over everything we ate. The only thing I didn't eat was the vegetable dip."

In that moment, Robbie knew the dip was the probable cause. "I ate nearly all of it. I nibble constantly when I'm nervous."

Jake chuckled as he leaned onto the edge of the bed. "The woman who defended her thesis in a disguise, nervous?"

Robbie raised an eyebrow. It was the only thing she had the strength to lift. "Last night was different and you know it."

Jake lightly touched her arm. He didn't want any more alarms to go off on the monitors. "We'll talk about that at another time. You need to get stronger."

"I'm working on it." She lifted her hand and covered a yawn.

Jake stepped out of the way when her parents came into the room.

"Sweetheart. I was so worried," Robbie's mother said while she cupped her hands around Robbie's face and kissed her on the forehead and cheeks.

When her mother stepped aside, her father wrapped her into his barrel chest. "I knew you'd pull through."

"This is my fault. If I didn't carry everything to the nth degree, you wouldn't all be standing here with sunken eyes from lack of sleep and worry." She smacked the sheet with her palm.

"As soon as they let you out of here, you're coming home with us." Her mother took charge in her usual way. "When do you think that'll be, Ron?"

Her father ran his hand over the top of his head, like he always did when he concentrated. "Usually within twenty-four hours if there aren't complications. We'll cancel our tickets."

"Oh, no. You're leaving for the conference tomorrow." Robbie gasped. "Dad, you've worked so hard on that paper. The conference can't replace you at such short notice."

"Don't worry, honey. They always have someone in the wings for unforeseen circumstances."

"No, I can't let you do it. I'll stay here until you get back. I can do with the rest." She covered her face with her hands and yawned.

"Honey, when you're discharged, you're expected to go home. This isn't a hotel." Her father's voice was gentle.

"I can't leave my little girl." Robbie caught a glimpse of disappointment in her mother's deep hazel eyes. She knew how much her parents needed this break and how much they'd looked forward to it.

"Don't cancel anything right now. Maybe I'll have a clean bill of health and everything can go as planned." She straightened her back, raised her chin, and tried to look like a woman in control in her baby blue hospital gown.

Jake stepped away from the window again. "I'll help out. I'll look after Robin, uh, Robbie at her house. I'll make sure she follows any orders." He met both her parents' gazes with a firm stance.

Jake stood in the middle of the hospital room and wondered what to do next. He'd made the offer. It was up to Robbie and her parents. Her father looked from him to Robbie and back again. "I'll track down the man in charge and see what he says. If there aren't any serious issues, it might work."

"But who's going to make soup and make sure she's safe in the tub?" Megan Smith patted her daughter's arm.

"I can," Robbie said.

Jake stepped closer to the bed. "The soup isn't hard and I'll listen at the bathroom door." He pictured Robbie leaning back in the tub with bubbles bursting across her chest. He smiled for the first time in many hours. "I'll even volunteer to feed her soup in the tub."

The rhythm of the beeping heart monitor sped past normal.

"Hold on there," Mr. Smith said with a stern playful frown. "Jake, come with me and we'll track down the information we need."

Jake followed Robbie's father from the room but turned for one last look at Robbie tied to her bed with tubes and wires and couldn't help grinning like an idiot.

"Robin, what do you think? Could Jake look after you?"

She'd been called Robin. Her mother was serious. She didn't call her Robin often. Robbie took some deep breaths and willed her heart to slow down. Visions of Jake spooning consommé into her mouth while she lay naked in a tub would definitely have the alarm bells going off. She concentrated on pleating the sheet. "Of course, but I might not need anyone. I could just crawl under my covers and sleep until you come home and then it will be Christmas. I'm exhausted."

They heard the men approaching. "Good news," her dad called. "Your electrolytes are within range. They'll discharge you after lunch." Both men were smiling like they just watched the winning touchdown in a Grey Cup game. "I've talked to Jake and I'm sure we can trust him Megan."

"What did the doctor say exactly, and not *you* the doctor, but *my* doctor? Do I really need someone to stay with me?" She sat up straighter, feeling awkward and slightly embarrassed.

"You do if you want your mother to accompany me on this trip."

"Oh, all right." She answered as if it wasn't a big deal but when the heart monitor started to beep faster, she lowered her head. "When do they unhook me from this thing then?"

"Are you sure, honey?" her mother asked.

"I'm sure, Mom. I'll be fine."

"I'll take care of her until you get home," Jake assured them. It was still hard to separate the brown-eyed Robin with the hazel-eyed Robbie, the voluptuous figured woman with the one in front of him now. She deserved to have him wait on her hand and foot. She'd taken time away from her thesis to be with his granddad and even spent time with him. Jake shook his head. How could he have refused to hear her explanation? He owed her big time and more than just the money they agreed upon. "I'll pack a bag, pick up a few staples, and meet you at home, Robbie."

She didn't want to think about Jake staying in her guest bedroom, all kinds of alarms would ring.

After the discharge order was received, Robbie's mother helped her with her coat and then her mother brought a wheelchair into the room. "Don't roll your eyes at me. The chair is hospital policy."

"Then let's get out of here." Robbie perched on the vinyl seat.

When her mother balanced the flowers in front of Robbie's face, she said, "I hope Jake's causing those rosy cheeks and not a fever."

"Actually I'm thinking about the state of my bathroom and kitchen and maybe having Jake so close."

Robbie felt her mom's hand on her hair, smoothing it as she had done when she was a child. "Take it slow, honey.

Some men just have to learn how to fit into another person's world."

Maybe Mom had a point. Jake did see how others fit in their worlds so now it was his turn.

When they arrived at her house, she looked fondly toward the park, where Frank used to whisper to the geese. How she missed him already. She shoved the negative thoughts aside. Dwelling on them would change nothing. With her mother's help, she changed into fresh clothes. Then she filled a bucket of hot water.

"What do you think you're doing?" Her father was at her elbow.

"Dad, you're the doctor. You know what happens when you have food poisoning."

"I'll do it. You go and keep your mother company in the kitchen." Her father nudged Robbie out of the way. "If you have a relapse, your mom won't come with me. So do what I say."

Robbie readily stepped aside while her mother scooped coffee into the filter and set out four mugs. "Perhaps you should have tea. Clear fluids," her mother said over her shoulder.

"You're right. I would prefer a cup of mint tea. It's refreshing." Robbie searched through her basket of flavored teas while her mother filled the kettle with water to bring to a boil. Robbie leaned against the counter and warmth spread through her tired body. How wonderful was it that her overprotective parents could be here when she was sick? She tugged at the sweatshirt slipping off her shoulder and her thoughts drifted to Jake. She used her sleeve to stop a tear. He wouldn't ever experience this kind of love from a parent again.

Impulsively she gave her mom a huge hug.

"What's this for?" her mother asked, surprise in her eyes.

"Thank you," Robbie said simply. "For being my mom, for being here for me."

Jake parked the Mustang in front of the house and scrutinized the outside, looking for evidence of the complex woman who had won his grandfather's heart and was slowly causing his to open. With his duffle bag in one hand and flowers in the other, he rang the doorbell. He was surprised by the woman whose sweatshirt hung on her like drapery. "Robin, Robbie, step back, away from the cold. You look terrible."

The smile that was there only seconds before disappeared. She looked down and stumbled back toward the hall. He rushed in and almost slammed the door against the winter air. He opened the closet and was met with her sweet, spicy scent. He hung his parka next to Robin's heavy black coat. Of course both Robin and Robbie had used the same fragrance. He should bang his head against the door. How could he have missed that? His profession was studying and observing people. On a subconscious level he hoped that he *had* noticed, but he'd examine that detail later.

He carried his bag through the small living room with its hardwood floors and set it at the base of the stairs. He followed the sound of voices to the kitchen.

Robin sat with her back to him, the neck of the sweatshirt drooped down exposing one bare shoulder and a fuchsia tank top. Didn't she have any sweatshirts that fit properly? Of course, it was a Robin sweatshirt versus a Robbie shirt. Had he really told her that she looked terrible? But she did. She looked like a scarecrow with the clothes flapping in a big wind. She could probably fly if a wind came up behind her.

Her mother, Megan, was washing up dishes and pouring coffee into mugs. Someone nudged him from behind.

"Make yourself useful and open the door for me, please," Ron said as he shouldered his way past Jake. "Megan, Jake's here. We should get going."

"Let me finish what you're doing, Mrs. Smith," Jake said, approaching her.

"Wish you'd have come just a few minutes earlier, then you could have cleaned up after my daughter," Doc. Smith said as he held the mop as far away as possible.

"I was going to do it, Dad, but you offered. I was going to do the dishes, Mom, but you just filled the sink."

Jake watched Robin's chin tip forward. Then she looked straight at him. "And you told me to get out of the cold and that I look terrible."

Megan said, "You do look terrible in the old, huge sweatshirt."

"I was afraid you'd have a relapse," her father said.

Jake handed Robin the bouquet of spring flowers he'd purchased along with a few groceries that he'd left in the car.

She smiled sweetly. "With these and the flowers Mom and Dad gave me, it'll look like a funeral parlor in here."

Jake felt as if he had been kicked in the groin. He turned on his heel. The hanger had his coat in a chokehold and rattled when it hit the ceramic tiled floor. He heard her call. "Jake, I'm sorry."

He didn't know grief could be like this. One minute he was fine and the next it was as if his granddad had just taken his last breaths all over again.

Robbie dropped the flowers on the table, then unfurled her legs and plowed her feet into her slippers. How could she have been so insensitive?

"Stay where you are. I'll check on him," her father said.

"Mom."

"Your dad's right." Her mother rescued the flowers. "Tell me where you keep your vases."

"Bottom shelf." Robbie kept her eye on the kitchen door. Why'd she say something so thoughtless?

"I'm not used to being told that I look terrible. How can I be twenty-five years old and a toddler within a few minutes?"

"You've been under a lot of stress and you're having a maturity lesson," her mother said in her usual counselor voice.

After her parents' plane took off from the airport, Robbie would tell Jake that he could leave. Until then, she would stay out of his way. She didn't want to hurt him anymore than she already had.

After Robbie put the vase in the center of the table, she hugged her mother. "Have a great time and don't worry. Jake will take good care of me."

"Remember, you're not too weak to take care of him, too." Her mother returned her hug squeeze for squeeze. "Our itinerary is in your email."

They heard the front door close and the men's voices in the hall.

"I'm going to my room," she said. "Tell Jake I've gone to bed. Give Dad a hug for me."

She held onto the railing for safety while she hurried up the stairs.

Robbie flipped the comforter back and slipped between the cool sheets. She listened to the steps on the stairs, wondering if Jake was coming up. Her heart raced at the knock, then she heard her father say, "I've come to say goodbye."

"Come in," she said, surprised at how disappointed she felt that it was her father approaching her, not Jake.

Her father sat on the side of her bed. "You're probably thinking as soon as the wheels of our plane leave the tarmac that you will tell that man to leave. I hope that you reconsider." He leaned toward and kissed her forehead. Her skin was probably pucker marked from so much kissing.

"I don't want to keep him from what he needs to do. I don't even know what he needs to do. As long as he's out of my way, he can stay." She couldn't think about the feelings that she'd had when they were in his hotel room. Was it only last night? That meant one day since Frank was buried. That meant a week since Jake had become an orphan. Her fingers nimbly plucked at the blanket. "How long exactly did my doctor say I needed looking after?"

"As long as it takes," her father said as he closed the door.

Chapter 17

When Jake opened the refrigerator, he was assaulted by odors from forgotten food items. He stowed the milk, fruit, eggs, and sliced ham. He'd clean up the fridge later.

He heard Doctor Smith's footsteps. "She's in bed. Maybe she'll sleep. Check on her in about an hour. Guest room is at the top of the stairs on the left. She has our itinerary in her email. See you in four days." He extended his hand for Jake to shake. Their grips were firm. They understood each other. Jake would keep their cherished daughter safe until their return. He could do anything for four days.

He was afraid that he'd find a tiny single bed for the occasional friend who came to stay but the guest bed was hotel size and layered with a plaid comforter and piled with pillows. There were dust bunnies under the dresser but there were good reading lamps on both sides of the bed. In the top drawer, she had packaged toothbrushes, travel-sized toothpaste, and deodorant. She was prepared for overnight company. He gave his head a shake. He'd promised not to make leaps of judgment without consulting her. Besides, if she had an overnight male friend, he'd share *her* bed.

He unpacked his duffle bag and placed his grandfather's locked box on the floor.

When he walked past her door, he thought he heard her moan. With his ear pressed against the door, he heard the sound again. He knocked. When she didn't answer, he opened it a crack. She was in bed, with the covers up to her chin, headphones pressed securely on her ears, and watching TV. The sound he'd heard wasn't discomfort but stifled laughter. He backed out and closed the door. She wasn't in any danger, but he could be, if his fast breathing and racing heart were any indication. He closed his eyes. All these symptoms were a delayed reaction to his grandfather's death, Robin's duplicity, the funeral, Robbie in hospital. These palpitations were well earned. Oh, yes, his name had been cleared, too. He shook his head. Just a few weeks ago, the threat against his reputation seemed so very important.

After returning downstairs, he noticed that the living room and dining room walls were cranberry with a white ceiling. He had noticed this nook, which probably used to house a buffet, when he was here for pizza. It held her computer desk and all the paraphernalia that went with it. He saw her neatly stacked pages of her thesis. If he hadn't been so self-centered he could have asked her about her thesis. On the mantle were pictures of a full-figured woman posed in a jeweled tunic and jeans, on a lounge in lace baby doll pajamas, and regally posed in a sequence gown. Every photo had Robin's face superimposed on the body. Who was this woman who didn't do anything by small measures?

The amber liquid in his glass, warmed by his hand, slid across his tongue and down Jake's throat. The contents of his grandfather's box were scattered on the coffee table. They brought back memories of his grandmother reading to him at bedtime, sewing costumes for Halloween, getting up in the night when he had a fever, and supporting his desire to go away to a university. His grumbling stomach forced him to remember the great meals she had cooked from scratch. His grandmother always told him that she loved him no matter what. He hadn't heard or felt those words in a very long time.

Robin's call startled him.

Upstairs, Robbie removed her headphones. Where was Jake now? She purposefully covered her ears and turned on the TV so that she wouldn't hear him moving around. She lay there and wondered what she'd do without her parents if they were suddenly gone from her life. No, she couldn't think about that now. They were getting on an airplane soon.

"Jake where are you?"

"On the sofa. Feet up. Drinking brandy. Staring at a great log fire."

"Stay where you are. I'm going to have a bath."

He walked to the hall and looked up the stairs. She was still in the old gray sweats. "Can I make you some tea?"

She licked her dry lips. "Thanks."

"I'll bring it up so you can drink it while you bathe."

Robbie knelt on the floor and turned the taps, reached round for her favorite bubble bath powder and scooped an extra portion. Even though her hair was greasy and her eyes were less cavernous, she wished for some of her other persona's fuller face. She looked down at her skinny wrists. She felt like a thirteen-year-old instead of a twenty-five-year-old woman who ran and lifted weights.

She wished Jake would hurry so she could strip out of her sweats and sink into the tub of hot water and wash her hair.

When he tapped at the door, she opened the door part way. The scent of the bath made the air feel more intimate than she expected. She gripped the door handle for support. He appeared with a tray containing a teapot, a china cup, milk and sugar, soda crackers with a dab of butter on a plate, and a jar of jam in one hand and a folding table gripped in the other.

"At your service."

She giggled.

He stepped into the room and flipped open the folding table, set the tray on it, and backed out into the hall.

Their eyes met. "Would Madame please leave the door unlatched in case Madame has difficulties?"

Her eyes widened. "If sir promises to enter only if he hears a cry for help."

"I shall stand ready for your cry until you remove yourself from the mass of bubbles." He bowed and retreated into the hall. She closed the door.

After quickly shedding her clothes, she slid into the tub and felt the water soothe her tired arms and legs. Her shoulders relaxed when she heard the water from the kitchen rattle along the pipes. Jake wasn't outside the door. She wouldn't have to stay submerged in the event that he decided to check on her. She plugged the earphones and turned on her tunes. The mint tea was washing over her tongue and soothing her tummy, the jam and soda crackers a reminder of a childhood treat.

After Robin closed the door, Jake listened until he heard her hands slide along the edge as she lowered her body into the water. Then he retreated to the kitchen for a glass of ice water. If he stayed in the vicinity, he might even imagine a cry for help and then he could charge in and pull her from the bubbles and carry her back to her bed.

He climbed the stairs to the bathroom and tapped on the door. "Robbie, I'm going into the living room so if you need me, you'll have to make a racket." He heard her singing. *She must be listening to her MP3 player*. Other members at the gym who ran on the treadmill or used the weight machine sang the songs that only they could hear, too. No need for heroics yet. He put the TV on low volume and kept one ear turned toward the stairs and hallway.

Robbie shifted in the tub. The bubbles had dissipated. The tea was cold. Her toes and fingers were like raisins.

When she stepped out of the bath water, she wrapped herself in a towel and reached for her robe, which wasn't on the back of the door. *Shoot.* She'd tossed it into the laundry basket. Could she make it to her bedroom wrapped in a towel? She opened the door a crack, looked both ways, and ran toward her bedroom.

Jake heard running feet nanoseconds before he heard the yelp and crash. When he reached the stairs, Robin was stretched in the hallway, her almost bare ass in the air.

"Robin."

"Don't come any closer," she said, sounding frantic. "Go back to wherever you were. I just need to catch my breath."

Unable to control herself, Robbie started to quiver and a snort escaped from her lips. What was it with falling with her rear end in the air in front of Proctor men? First, when she met Frank in the park, then Jake on their walk, and now in her own house. Admittedly, she had a few more layers on during the other two falls.

Jake didn't know if Robbie was laughing or crying. He advanced and retreated until finally he walked to the middle of the stairway and leaned toward the hallway. "Robbie."

"I was remembering that Frank found me in this same position, then you. What is it with landing with my rear in the air?"

"I'm sure granddad wasn't looking at the view the same way I am."

Robbie tucked the towel under her and twisted it tight. "I'm serious, you have to leave. It's not that comfortable."

"I promise not to look. Let me help you up."

"There isn't enough room."

"Turn onto your side. Take my hand."

Robbie twisted onto her side, gripped the towel edges with one hand and extended the other. She looked into his eyes and held them there while he placed her on her feet. His gaze dipped down to her lips and then her chest, her breathing deepened. He crushed her to his chest and she shivered.

"Robin, Robbie, go and put some clothes on you're shaking. I'll make more tea and some soup. You've got to get strong again." He set her away from him. She watched him disappear down the stairs where he kept moving toward the kitchen.

Jake paced in the kitchen. He was over thirty and not some erratic, hormonally charged teenager. He could keep his libido under control. He stared at the water rushing into the sink while he held the kettle in his hand. She was just out of hospital. Her parents trusted him.

When he collected the tea tray from the bathroom, he caught his reflection in the mirror and for a flash he saw his grandmother's smile play across his lips. He thanked her for teaching him how to make a great cup of tea. She said it was the perfect way to think things over. When you brought the cup to your lips, the steam floated past your face and cleared in front of your eyes.

Anthropologists weren't renowned for their quick action, so he was probably on the right track that gave them both time. He whistled while he made a light lunch because he looked forward to discovering much more about this chameleon who had come into his life a short time ago.

Robbie gathered the towel above her knees and walked carefully into her room. She shivered but her core was hot, her breasts heavy. She wanted to feel Jake's lips on hers and have his arms pull her to his chest. She had been mesmerized by the pulse in his neck. Where were they in this relationship? Jake had been ready to cross the physical line last night, but he was still grieving. She was ill. She dressed in her jeans and periwinkle blue long sleeve sweater, recalling he liked her in this shade of blue when they'd first met at the university. She had felt a connection then. He cared about her well-being. Would he still find her attractive and worthy of his attention now that he knew who she really was?

Chapter 18

Robbie opened the kitchen door to the heady aroma of bubbling soup. The air was moist from the boiled water. She jumped as the toaster popped.

Jake whistled under his breath while he poured water into the teapot.

"Can I help?" she asked from the doorway.

He turned and surveyed her. "You look better. Sit down, everything's ready." He brought the tea to the table.

He'd placed the table setting on the long end of the table as she had in the past, away from looking directly at each other. He pulled the chair out for her and helped her slide it close to the table. When she leaned back, she felt the warmth of his fingertips against her back. She dipped her spoon into her soup bowl and sipped, then nibbled the edge of her toast.

"This isn't enough for you. What else are you going to eat? I don't have many groceries." She watched while he brought the spoon to his lips.

"I thought I'd order pizza after you go to bed. I don't want to upset your delicate stomach."

"Thanks." She flexed her abdominal muscles. "Still tender."

But the way she felt could have more to do with Jake in her kitchen caring for her then being sick. She focused on his neck rather than his face, only to see his Adam's apple move. She felt as if she was back in a time when hand touches, ankle views, and sensuous necks were the causes of arousal.

He cleared his throat. "Your dad said four days. We'll need to have some sort of understanding."

"What would you suggest?" She gripped the chair seat for support. Her head felt hot. Maybe she was delirious.

"I'll prepare the meals and tidy up until you're stronger and then we'll talk."

"That sounds fair." She stole a glance at his face. He had his controlled professorial attitude in place.

Disappointment cooled her imagination.

He leaned back in the chair. "Tell me about getting suited up in the costume."

She sipped her tea. *Right, she could do this, too. She can keep a professional distance.* "The costume wasn't that hard when I found the right order. It could get pretty warm and if I knew I'd be indoors and doing small amounts of activity, I put gel packs in specially designed pockets. I couldn't have carried out this experiment in the summer. The hard parts were my face and hands. I used different brushes and makeup tones to give the illusion of fullness. On a good day, I could have been ready in an hour, but on a day when colors didn't blend or my wig wouldn't sit right, it would take more time. You met me on my first day. I'm not surprised that you were suspicious."

She spread her unadorned fingers wide. "I also acquired a lot of costume rings to add weight to my hands."

She swallowed a lump in her throat. "To be honest, I'm surprised you didn't recognize me. I saw so many similarities. I think Frank did. He called me Robbie during our last visit." She blinked at tears forming in the corners of her eyes. "During that visit, while you were out running I told him about my disguise and my research, but he was asleep. I was going back to tell him the whole thing the next day. I only hope he heard me, if he needed to. Maybe he was just being Frank and accepting me no matter why I was dressed up."

"He was astute. I wouldn't be surprised if he had guessed." Silence flowed around the table until he said, "Initially I thought you might have been ill. Your wig was obvious. But then you began to look better and I had other things on my mind." He paused. "I saw your photographs on the mantle. Cute."

Her shoulders relaxed. She understood. He wanted to keep the topic more general. "One of the women in my control group did that. It's called visualization."

"I'm surprised I didn't see them the night we shared pizza," he said.

She glanced up at his soft brown eyes, which seemed to be focused on her lips. She reached for the teapot. *Where was the bravado she'd had in Frank's room when she'd mimicked Jake's movements in order to be attractive to him?*

"I turned them face down on the mantle. Besides, as you just said, you had other things on your mind."

He nodded.

She heard him tinker with his spoon against the side of the bowl.

"Did you know there is an appetite suppressant made from the Hoodia Gordonii?" he asked. "The !Kung San used it for thousands of years to control thirst and hunger during their long hunting trips."

"You mentioned that during your talk at the dinner." She relaxed and rested her arms on the table. "There are so many advertised products that promise quick weight loss."

"When I was with the !Kung San, they discussed a lawsuit against drug companies that stole their ancient medicinal knowledge of the plant without consulting them."

"Women and men for that matter don't need another drug to spend their money on. Before my research, I would have advised a quick fix medication to drop pounds, but not anymore."

"What would you suggest?" He leaned toward her and filled her cup to the brim.

"Be healthy in the skin you're in. It sounds easy, but it isn't. Some of us are larger than others. The body comes in all shapes and sizes. We are not made from a cookie cutter." She felt rather than saw his eyes on her.

She teased her leftover cold toast apart, just as Frank had done for the geese so many times. "The fat suit had disadvantages but the advantage was that I took up space. I was noticed and some men just wanted to talk to me. There wasn't that whole pick-me-up challenge most of the time. I'm going to miss that feeling."

"I suppose you could always use the suit to go undercover and investigate discrimination." He picked up the empty dishes and took them to the sink. She felt the air around her cool her warm face. *She could do this if they kept their distance. He was right.*

He brought a cloth back and wiped the table surface. She slid her chair away from the table. "Initially I thought that as well, but now I understand my limitations. I'd need a whole movie costume team behind me if I wanted to continue. I know there are more sophisticated ways of changing appearances. When I begin my career in human resources, I'll cultivate staff to be sensitive to diversity." She yawned.

"Time for bed," he said. He shook his head as if he, too, was dispelling images that statement raised. "Do I have to? It's early." She imitated a whining child.

"I lit the logs in the fireplace. The living room should be toasty warm if you'd like to watch a movie."

"Same spaces. I get the sofa and you the chair."

"Deal. I'll be in as soon as I've washed the dishes."

She carried her teacup to the living room, snuggled into the sofa, then covered her feet with the afghan. She watched the flames lick at the logs. She listened to the various noises coming from the kitchen, the running water, dishes rattling, and Jake whistling. Sounds she found oddly comforting.

When Jake finished, he brought his cup and a fresh pot of tea to where she half sat, half lay on the couch. The remote was on the coffee table. Neither of them reached for it.

"Can I warm up your cup?" he asked with a smile.

"I can't remember when I've been so cared for."

After pouring her a fresh cup of tea, he settled into the chair and propped his feet on the ottoman.

When she bought her teacup to her lips the steam rose and cleared in front of her face. She rested the cup back on the table. "I wish I had been strong enough to stay for Frank's celebration of life." She glanced into Jake's brown eyes. He looked down at the floor for a moment. The curtains whispered when the furnace pushed more heat into the room.

"I'm glad that I met him."

"I know you made his last weeks happier as well."

"Thank you. That means a lot to me. I wonder if we would have become friends without my disguise."

He glanced at the photographs on the mantel. "It's as if you have a twin."

She saw the uncertainty in his eyes. "I wished for a sister, what about you?"

"I don't remember. I think I've always known my family was different."

She wanted to reach out to him but shifted her extended arms above her head.

"You seem tired. Let's save the movie for another time." He gathered the cups onto the tray.

She pushed her feet into her slippers, stood, and folded the blanket. She kept her voice light. "Sleep tight."

During the next few days, she and Jake continued to build on their friendship. As her strength returned, she helped make the meals and tidy up afterward. They often ended the day around the fireplace sharing stories about their youth. She no longer held her breath when she heard his footsteps down the hall when he went to bed or got up in the morning. She no longer trembled like a maiden if they passed each other on the way to shower. What she couldn't stop were the dreams of his hands on her body and his lips covering her lips. But other than a playful tap on the shoulder, they avoided touching each other. It was as if they both understood that if they crossed the line once, their tentative newfound friendship would change.

Jake spent an extra long time under the cold shower. He had to survive one more night under Robin's roof without touching her. He'd promised her parents that he would protect their treasure and he would do that. He planned his day carefully. Robin/Robbie was how he thought of her now. She was both rolled into one. Today she was Robin in his mind, because they had a foundation of the friendship they'd established with Frank in their lives. It kept Frank's memory between them. She was well enough that he could leave her for a few hours. Today he needed to pick up some groceries and meet with Jean Clifton about teaching the next semester. He needed to check out his new apartment. He also needed to do something for the Smith Christmas he'd been asked to share. He dressed in his jeans and sweater, then joined Robin for coffee.

Jake wrapped his fingers around a mug of coffee to keep his fingers away from shifting a stray wisp of hair from Robin's forehead. "You sound better this morning."

A smile floated across her face as she answered evenly. "Christmas and family always does it."

He was quiet.

"Do you have any traditions that you'd like my family to honor? A special type of food we can prepare?"

He shook his head. "This year will be the first year when I will eat a traditional Christmas turkey in a long time. Your family does have turkey?"

She nodded.

"I'm glad, I'm looking forward to sharing a Christmas dinner similar to my time with Granddad and Grandma. For many years, my schedule always included a research project during this time." He paused. "I'd call my grandparents from some far off land and say Merry Christmas around the general time. But I can't examine the past right now. I don't want to feel guilty. What do you have planned today?"

Glad Jake didn't want to dwell on sad subjects, Robbie said, "I'm going to decorate my Christmas tree. I'm not like my mother where every corner in her house and yard has to reflect Christmas." She carried her coffee cup into the living room and turned on the weather channel. She called over her shoulder. "We haven't had our usual snowfall. But I'm not wishing for a white Christmas this year."

She knew instinctively when he was in the same room. She didn't even have to turn around. He stood behind her at the window. "I pictured you with your nose pressed against the window watching the sky for snow clouds."

She heard the tension leave his voice.

"Where's the winter wonderland you said you wanted last night?" His voice flowed over her jangled nerves.

She wanted to say that she didn't want anything to keep them from sharing Christmas with her family, but she said, "This year I'll pass on mounds of snow. Many people drive distances in Saskatchewan to visit family and friends. I'd rather the picture perfect snowdrifts remain on the cards."

"I agree. I know I certainly would prefer to drive on a clear blacktop highway." Did she hear a chuckle?

"Are you laughing at me?" Her eyebrows drew together.

"Yes. I'm imagining you with your nose pressed against the pane with your fingers crossed and wishing against the thousands wishing for snow."

She turned and tipped her head. He really was getting to know her.

"Tomorrow, after church, I'd like to show you the park around the river. Mom and Dad won't mind," she said.

"I'd like that. What should I bring your mother?" He backed away from her. She knew he was creating safe space for both of them.

She thought about her parents' home. It would be easy to suggest a bottle of wine or an ornament to add to the collection but she thought that he might be the right kind of man to experience the real 'Smith' Christmas. Her family gave their largest gifts to the community all year instead of each other. During Christmas Day, while they sat around the tree, they shared a few examples of their good deeds and the feelings they experienced over the past year.

"Anything that shows you will help someone," she replied.

"That's cryptic." His eyes looked up and toward the left. She knew from paying attention to his subtle little moves that he was thinking.

"It'll give you something to ponder," she said.

"And a reason to go to the mall."

"I don't think you'll find it at the mall." She shook her head confidently. "Use your imagination." She tapped him on the shoulder. His reaction was quick and he held her hand in his. They were both breathing heavily when he brushed a kiss on her forehead.

"I've got some errands to run. Have fun." He turned on his heels and she heard the closet door rattle.

She was glad he was gone. She had to stay focused and

keep her hands to herself for less than twenty-four hours. She could do anything for a day.

The four-foot artificial tree took less time to decorate than she thought. Jake wasn't home so she dressed carefully. When she sat in her car, she moved the seat forward. The last time she'd been behind the wheel had been the night she got ill. But she was better now. She drove to the nut and candy store and health food store for her parents' gifts. She didn't know what to buy Jake that wasn't over the top like a muscle shirt or cologne, so she chose a CD of easy-listening rock hits. He seemed to enjoy her tunes whenever he worked around the kitchen.

Jake wasn't sure who he'd find at the university on Christmas Eve. He couldn't tell from these halls that it was a special season for some students. The university remained the politically correct neutral. He used his security pass and went up to the department. He hoped that Jean would be there. He needed to speak with her.

Luckily, her door was open into the reception area. She came out of her office door just as he opened the main office door.

"Hello there," she said. "I wondered if you left right after the funeral to travel somewhere warm and exotic."

"No, I completed my marking and I'm here experiencing a deep freeze that brings back memories of my youth. However, I don't seem to remember feeling the cold to this extent when I was young." He continued toward her. "Do you have a minute? I'd like to talk about next semester."

"Come in and sit down." She circled her desk and sat with her arms folded on the clutter-free top.

He sat in the visitor's chair. "I received a letter from the University of Ottawa and everything is cleared up. They found the missing funds and determined that I didn't have any knowledge of the use of the money."

"Who took it?" She leaned forward.

"I'm sorry, I'm not at liberty to discuss the matter." He felt a loyalty toward his team.

"Of course not. So what are your plans?" She sat back.

Jake gazed out the window to where the bright, blue sky filled the window behind her desk.

"If you still need me," he started, "I'd like to stay for the winter semester until spring. While my office at the U of O is available, I have a few loose ends to tidy up and I've rented an apartment for January first. I'm enjoying working with undergrad students." He placed his hands on the arms of the chair. He, too, knew body language signals and he wanted her to recognize that he was open to suggestions.

"First of all, you were right. I have received many positive remarks about Robbie's presentation, even though she told the committee that she conducted that part of her research without my permission. Second, I hoped that you would stay. I know the rest of the department would be pleased to have you stay on and finish the winter semester. Your evaluations from your students were very positive."

"Thank you for giving me a chance to teach. I'm honored." He stood up and approached her desk and extended his hand.

She received his handshake and sat down again. "On a personal note, do you have plans for Christmas?" She crossed her arms in what he suspected was a protective move.

"Yes, I have been invited to spend Christmas day with a friend's family."

"Jake, this is hard for me to say but I feel that I should get it out in the open." She took a deep breath.

He remained silent, just watching her.

"I have been friendly toward you, but I hope you realize that it was just to welcome you to our university. I never mix work and pleasure." She nodded, as if to second her proclamation.

His heart did a quick jump and he was tempted to smile, but he wanted her professional friendship.

"Thank you for your honesty. I agree that professional relationships are better if they are separate from personal relationships. I admire your professionalism." He offered her his hand again. She stood and walked around the desk and with a firm grasp they sealed their relationship.

"Merry Christmas, Jean. I'll see you in the new year."

"You too, Jake."

He left the office with a lighter step than when he had entered. Circumstances had a marvelous way of turning events around. Could he have misinterpreted Jean's attention, or had she decided that he was no longer necessary to her career advancement, or had she realized that he didn't respond in the way she had hoped? She was smart. He would learn a great deal from her.

The clock in the main corridor indicated that time was going by quickly. He could check on the final detail of his apartment on December twenty-seventh. He needed to organize his Christmas gift for the Smith's.

Robbie bought the ingredients for clam chowder for dinner and had chopped the celery, onions, diced the carrots, and peeled the potatoes before Jake came through the door.

"What smells so wonderful?" He placed two sacks of groceries on the floor and blew into his hands warming them.

"I hope you enjoy clam chowder and biscuits? It's almost ready." She had taken a page from her father's book and worked neatly, washing up after herself. The kitchen was tidy and so was she.

"It is one of my favorite meals. Grandma made it every Tuesday." He leaned toward her. His eyes widened with surprise when Santa's mouth on her apron opened and he said, "Ho, Ho, Ho."

"Cute apron."

"Thanks. It has a motion detector in the appliqué."

Plus, if perchance Jake wanted to come into her personal space, Santa would give off a warning.

"Something new?" His left eyebrow lifted.

"Yes." *I'm going to need all the help I can get tonight.* She turned toward the simmering pot. "Let's eat."

Robbie noted that Jake seemed preoccupied throughout dinner. But she, too, had been distracted while she watched him spoon the soup into his mouth.

"Great dinner," he said, setting down his spoon. "Thank you."

"I'm glad you enjoyed it and that I was strong enough to make it. I'm almost one hundred percent."

When they took their coffee and brandy into the living room, he said, "Great tree."

"Thanks."

"No gifts?"

"You sound surprised. My family exchanges small personal items, and they're all packed and ready to travel tomorrow." She twirled her glass and tried not to look at Jake's glass nestled in the palm of his hand because her breasts ached for the touch of his hand.

"Your parents must be organized to be able to host a dinner the day after they arrive home."

Christmas carols played softly on the stereo.

"They are. I don't know what I will ever do without them."

"Develop traditions of your own, because you might not always live close enough to share the holiday together." He seemed to be watching her closely.

"I know. We're much the same Jake. We're both old enough to have a family and traditions of our own but we don't. Instead you traveled, and I was content to keep my parents' traditions."

"Maybe next year you'll have a job somewhere and they can come and visit you." He leaned forward as if her answer was important to him.

"That's true. I'm going to enjoy this year's celebration as though it will be my last." She leaned forward as well and tried to memorize every little line on Jake's face, the shape of his brow, the length of his nose, the way his hair fell across his forehead, his straight jaw, his lips. She brought her glass to her mouth. He turned away as if twinkling lights and the fire reflected in the shiny balls was captivating his attention.

He rose to his feet. "And I'll enjoy it because it'll be my first with you and your parents." He stretched lazily. "I'm going to call it an early night. That way I'll be refreshed and eager like a young boy waiting for Santa Claus." He stepped close to her and put hands on the back of the sofa and bent over her and feathered a kiss on the right corner of her mouth then left. "See you in the morning, Robin."

Robbie remembered when he had told her that sometimes friendship was a cold place to be and now she understood because all she wanted was to wrap her arms around his neck and pull him down on top of her. Was he being honorable or since he'd spent this time with her, was this all that he wanted from her? Thank goodness she hadn't told him that she wanted so much more from him. He'd been calling her Robin all day. Robin, the name of his *friend*. Her heart sank. After tomorrow, Jake would be leaving and she wouldn't see him when she woke up and went to bed. Still, Jake was right. Who knew what the future held?

Chapter 19

Christmas morning dawned bright and clear. Robbie was relieved that she had had practice disguising her eyes and accentuating her cheeks because she needed every bit of talent to cover the ravages of a restless night. Jake looked rested when he gave her a Merry Christmas hug. She touched her right cheek to his and then her left to his while making the smooching sound. If he could be content with a platonic friendship then she would be, too. She could do anything for a day.

She locked the front door while he put her bags into the Mustang's trunk.

She looked up and saw Mrs. Mitchell's curtain flip. "One minute please, Jake. Will you come with me to speak with my neighbor?" They crossed the street together and she rang the doorbell.

Christmas carol music welcomed her on the stair while Mrs. Mitchell opened the chain. Mrs. Mitchell had on a sweatshirt with a decorated Christmas tree in the center.

"Merry Christmas, Mrs. Mitchell."

"Thank you, Robbie. Where are you going?"

"My friend, Jake, and I are going out to my parents for Christmas."

"I've watched that young man coming and going in that red sports car. I also saw the ambulance." Mrs. Mitchell seemed curled into herself clutching the walker. "I sure wish someone would have told me what was going on. There is Mr. Bell's invention, you know?"

"I'm sorry. That was my fault. I had food poisoning but I'm all better now." Robbie put her hand on her neighbor's shoulder.

"You sure have a lot of friends. I haven't seen that bigger woman, you know the other friend of yours recently. I suppose she didn't tell you to phone me."

"She did, Mrs. Mitchell. I just kept forgetting because I was studying."

"Well, no harm done, I suppose. How long is this friend staying?" She looked Jake up and down.

"He stayed with me until I recovered. I'm well again, Mrs. Mitchell." Robbie felt her shoulders slump.

"You look like a nice young man."

"Jake Proctor. Pleased to meet you. Thank you for watching out for my friend, here."

"Neighbors have to look out for neighbors, young man."

"Yes, we do." Jake replied.

"Wish your folks Season Greetings, Robbie. I have to go in now. It's cold with the door open," she said, backing away.

"I will. Can I come over for tea in the new year?"

"As long as you drink Red Rose. I don't keep anything in the house but Red Rose."

"Perfect. I'll phone you next week." Robbie leaned in and kissed Mrs. Mitchell on the cheek.

"Go on now."

Robbie waved and they walked down the stairs and across the street.

Jake held the door open until she slid into the passenger seat and fastened the lap belt. He drove with ease.

She slid her hand on the wood grain dash. "Tell me about your car. I suspect there's a story here."

"Frank and Mabel bought it for my mom when she turned sixteen. Frank drove it for awhile then he just parked it in the garage and I hung out in it until I was old enough to drive."

"Wow."

"You're right, wow." He drove to the corner. "I take it you haven't visited with your neighbor very often."

"Since I met Frank, I've been thinking about elderly people on their own and possibly how alone they might be. Mrs. Mitchell has been my neighbor for as long as I've lived here and I haven't even taken the time to get to know her. That is going to change."

"Your New Year's resolution?"

"Sort of, more like a Christmas gift."

A comforting silence fell and Jake turned on the radio. She sang along with songs on the radio, everything from "Rudolph the Red Nose Reindeer" to "Silent Night," while he drummed his thumbs on the steering wheel. The traffic was steady along the four-lane highway.

"I think you had your wish granted." Jake turned slightly and smiled at Robbie.

"Pardon me?" Her heart jumped in her chest.

"The highway is clear, not a snowflake, not a patch of black ice."

At least one of my wishes came true. "I'm glad."

About twenty minutes later, she and Jake surprised her parents at church when they squeezed in along the bench. She watched people file in front of them. Her heart slowed into a comfortable beat when she saw the familiar icons, banners, and the crèche. She thought of the young members of the congregation trying to quell their nervous tension before the big moment when they would carry the doll and lay it in the manger. Jake wrapped his arm around her. His down-filled parka nestled against her wool coat. She glanced up at Jake's intense eyes searching her face. His hand reached for her hand on her lap.

Her fingers splayed between his. She shouldn't be thinking that she wanted his lips to cover hers. She wanted to feel his tongue tapping against her teeth, seeking entry to one of her most sensuous spaces and she shouldn't be thinking that she'd let him in. Her thoughts were not appropriate for the time and place. She just wouldn't look at him.

After the service, Jake, watchful as always, stood with the Smiths in their circle of friends and neighbors. Robbie put a coffee cup into one of his hands and a cookie into the other. Finally, when he seemed to be more involved in observing rather than participating, she stepped on his toes, hard. "Earth to Jake."

"Sorry," he said, his eyes still following the frills on a little girl's dress disappearing under the tablecloth with her mother trying to retrieve her.

"We need a little participation here. Not every gathering is research." Robbie couldn't help but smile. She'd learned that his work was his passion too.

"Look who's talking." He tipped his head in the direction where she'd been observing the different generations of women filling plates with sandwiches and dessert slices while men carried coffee urns and filled teapots with water.

"Okay. Guess we're both guilty. Let's go for a walk."

Robbie's parents were in visiting mode and nothing was going to hurry them along.

"Mom, Dad, we'll meet you at home, okay?"

"Fine. Lunch will be ready." Her mother turned back to the group of women who surrounded her.

She and Jake raced down the stairs, hand-in-hand. They laughed into the wind as they sauntered across the street, down the road under the poplar trees, and finally onto the riverbank. The grass was brown and hard, with skiffs of snow on the frozen river, but it had a peace of its own.

"I feel as if this is a place Frank would whisper to his geese," Robbie said.

"Robin, you're not telling me you think of my granddad as a goose whisperer?" Jake teased.

"When I first met him, he told me his name and his nature were the same, Frank. So to me he was whispering to the geese and they listened. Don't laugh." She tugged his sleeve.

His boots flew out from under him and he landed with a thud that seemed to shake the earth. She watched him fall, land on his rear, and finally on his back. She rushed to his side, breathless. "I think he's dead, I think he's dead," she cried. "I'd better do CPR. C: tilt head, P: feel for a pulse." She felt his heart thumping under her fingers as she continued to play. "R: put cheek to person's nose and feel for breath, watch chest rise and fall."

His controlled breathing was warm against her cheek. His chest shuddered while he tried to control his laughter. She quickly pinched his nose and called out, "Two quick breaths." When her mouth reached to cover his, he brought his arms around her and cradled her onto his chest. Their closed lips met. She put her hands under his head and angled her mouth and pressed her cold lips against his. His hands pressed into the small of her back. This closed-lip kiss was great for starters but she wanted more. She opened her lips and explored his lips with her tongue. When his lips parted, she slid her tongue along his teeth and darted into his warmth for a taste of him, like a humming bird flitting against a flower. Her body tingled from under her fuzzy warm hat right down to her toes in her winter boots. She wriggled and settled into his down jacket. He held her legs between his. When their lips met again, he slid his tongue against hers and they explored with long sensuous tongue thrusts. Puffs of steam rose against each other's eyes, noses, lips, foreheads.

Robbie rolled away from Jake when a dog barked at their heads.

A woman yelled, "Unhand her, you, you, pervert."

Robbie looked up to see a woman standing with her cane raised, ready to strike Jake on the head.

"No!" she screamed. "Mrs. Lefcowitz, it's all right."

"Robin Smith, I thought you grew out of this tomfoolery."

Jake lifted up onto his elbows, eyebrow raised.

Darn, she'd have to explain that one. "My neighbor and her dog are protecting my virtue."

"I'll stay here and make certain that you both get up and act respectable. This is Christmas day, after all."

They both struggled to their feet. Jake kept his arm around Robbie, and his eye on the cane and the dog.

"Now, you let go of her, and if she wants to run free, she can. I don't always trust the first things out of people's mouths."

The stocky woman, shielded from the cold, covered from head to foot in a green snowmobile suit, motioned with her hand. "That's it, Robin. Take some steps away!"

"It's all right, honest," Robbie continued. "Merry Christmas. Is this your new dog?"

"Yes, this is Caesar. He's an English Mastiff, you know, powerful jaws," she said, keeping her eyes on Jake.

"Now, you're sure you don't want to be getting on home, Robin?" she asked.

"Actually, Jake and I are going home now. Thanks for calling our attention to our behavior and the time. We're supposed to be home for lunch."

"Looked like you were eating each other up," she said with a chuckle.

"Mrs. Lefcowitz, any of your kids coming home this year?" Jake asked.

She stared at him. "No, but how did you know I had kids?"

"That badge on your lapel states you're a proud grandma."

"I am proud." She touched the badge. "But they'll come home for Christmas on the Ukrainian Orthodox calendar, so I'll have to save my gifts until then. Merry Christmas, Robin and . . .?" She raised her brows so they touched her hat.

"Jake Proctor," he said, offering his hand tentatively. "Caesar won't jump me if I touch you, will he?"

"Not unless I tell him to. We have a secret little signal."

"If I shake your hand, that's not the signal, is it?"

"Certainly not!"

"Then, Merry Christmas today and next week."

Robbie's chest constricted and a wave of emotion rushed over her. She loved this man. She didn't think her ribs could contain the bubbling cadence of her heart.

"We need to go over there. It's our backyard gate." Robbie pointed toward a two-story brick house surrounded by a white fence. She and Jake simultaneously reached for each other's gloved hands and held on as they headed toward the Smith's backyard.

"Do you know how close you came to having your skull crushed?" Robbie's lips were surrounded by a cloud of mist.

"How come the guy's always the pervert and women never suspect their gender of being the instigator, Miss Smith?"

"Because we're innocent."

"Ha!"

He pulled her and she pushed away and shrieked in fright as her feet slipped out from under her. Jake's sturdy grip rescued her.

Jake looked down into Robin's dancing hazel eyes. A feeling of warmth, comfort, and love swept over him. His heart slowed as he felt the corners of his mouth pull up. "I don't want to pretend any longer. I love you and I need to be your lifelong friend."

"I love you, too."

"Thank you," he said, as his mouth captured hers. Her arms parted his jacket and she snuggled into him as he folded her to him. He longed to open her coat, to feel her body pressed next to his. But when she shivered, he lifted her into his arms and carefully picked his way past the ice and up the last remaining steps into the warmth of the back porch. He turned the knob and the white steel door swung open.

She clung to his neck, her legs dangled, her booted feet held inches away from his shins. But her thighs formed to him like a missing piece from a puzzle.

He held onto her until her feet were firmly on the floor. His hands shook as he reached for her wonderful rosy face. She tilted her head to one side, a smile spreading across her mouth.

"Robin, Robbie," he whispered. He was afraid to move, afraid to break the tenuous contact. He heard pots clanging and the Christmas carol recording seemed to have increased in volume. Robbie grinned. "I love my parents. I think we've had the equivalent of the porch light flickering on and off."

They hung their coats and scarves onto the pegs and opened the door, which led into a cornucopia of aromas, cumin, cloves, nutmeg, and pine. Sheer curtains on the windows were held back by bright red bows.

"I wondered when you'd unlock those lips. Mrs. Lefcowitz just phoned."

Megan Smith stepped forward and after wiping her hands on a Christmas towel, she shook his hand. "Thanks for taking care of Robbie."

"How was the trip, Mom?" Robbie sauntered around the kitchen with her hands behind her back as if she didn't have a care in the world.

"Great. It was just what we needed." Her mother gave her father a little smile while she placed an apron over his head, then tied a bow at the small of his back.

Her dad stepped forward and gave Robbie a quick hug.

Then he turned, his attention focused on Jake. "Welcome to our home." Ron grasped Jake's hand and looked straight into his eyes. Jake returned his firm handshake and nod with his own.

Robbie asked, "How do you do that?"

"Do what?" her dad asked with a satisfied tone.

"Communicate without words. I know you two agreed on something."

Jake draped his arm across her shoulders. "I'm afraid it's a male thing. The practice comes from centuries of hunting to feed the family, so we wouldn't scare the dinner before we captured it."

"Lunch is ready. The crepes are getting soggy." Megan shooed everyone to the table adorned with a white linen cloth and Christmas dinner plates.

"Jake, would you sit on the right side, please? Robbie, your place is on the left."

Her mother sat on one end and her father on the other.

Jake shook out his napkin. "In the early days, the hunters kept silent and used their eyes to indicate the location of their prey. It's suspected that this survival instinct became a genetic trait and is recognized in many of the best leaders."

"I suppose that you're going to tell us that women couldn't hunt because we need to talk," Robbie said, passing the plate of crepes.

"Not at all, all of the people in the hunting villages were needed to surround the animals."

"Nonverbal communication is my second language," Robbie said with a gleam in her eye.

"Robbie, keep your hands on the table and allow Jake to eat this wonderful meal. And you should eat, too."

"Yes, Mother."

"Do you cook?" her father asked Jake.

"I've had to learn my way around the kitchen."

"That's good because these two women eat for energy, whereas to me food is an experience." Her father spread his arms to include the food on the table.

"If your recipes match your great taste in wines, I'd like to experience your cooking."

"You're eating some right now."

"These delicate crepes?" Jake sampled another mouthful.

Ron nodded. "And the chokecherry syrup."

"I could teach you some exotic recipes. The Bushmen usually cook their local dishes. I've had roast snake on a few occasions." Jake's arms hung loose. He felt relaxed and sated.

"Your body language tells me that this is a story you're fond of telling," her mother said.

"This family is obviously very good at picking up clues," Jake replied.

Robbie moved her chair, stood, and began gathering the dishes. "We need to be. Mom is a counselor. She needs to know what her clients are saying as well as what they are not. And Dad, well, doctors need to be fluent in the nonverbal languages, too."

Robbie's mother cleared her throat before she asked Jake, "You study people, why didn't you see past Robbie's disguise?"

Robbie stopped clearing the dishes and moved behind Jake. She placed her hands on his shoulders and he took a deep breath. "Initially I thought she was ill but her disguise got better. I saw what my grandfather saw. He liked her because she reminded him of the love of his life. While Robin reminded me of the only mother I knew, she also brought back some unhappy childhood memories." He reached up and covered her hand with his. "She taught me many things when she was in and out of her disguise."

Robbie's father stood up. "From the way you two are looking at each other, I'd say you'd like to be alone for awhile. Megan, let's take a walk."

"We can't get away with anything in front of these eagle eyes." Robbie squeezed his shoulders.

Jake felt heat crawl up his face. "To be honest, I don't think it would be such a good idea to be alone with you right now, Robbie."

"Okay then, time to finish clearing the table." Her mother stood.

Mulled wine simmered on the stove while Jake stacked the dishwasher. They all went into the living room and sat in front of the fireplace. Jake excused himself. When he returned, they looked at him in sleepy contentment. His heart pounded, his breath was tight, and he was surprised that his voice shook. He sat beside Robbie on the sofa.

"Robbie suggested that your family tradition shares a small gift with each other and then a mystery gift that involves helping someone. I've made an educated guess what a gift like that might involve and I'd like to share my mystery gift with you."

Ron began, "It's not necessary. We usually keep it a secret until next Christmas but we can make an exception if you both agree."

Megan and Robbie nodded solemnly and lowered their eyes while Jake continued. "I would like to share that I have committed three hours a week for visiting the Care Manor residents during the dances and card nights. I'd like to know the ordinary men and women who built our province. I hope that they will benefit as much from my visits as I'm sure that I will from theirs."

Robbie flung her arms around his neck and planted little kisses all over his face. Then her eyebrows drew together. "You mean I'll have to share you with all those women at the Manor? Maybe I'll come, too."

"Sorry, this is my gift. You'll have to share. And I'm sure that you have your own commitments. I'd like nothing better than to have someone break the ice for me but, if I'm not misunderstanding, hard is part of the gift."

"This man learns fast. You'd better hang onto him," Ron said. "If you two aren't going to be alone, then come to the kitchen, we have a dinner to prepare. I know lunch wasn't that long ago but good food takes loving attention and time."

"Mom, Dad. Since Jake has shared his gift for next year, do you think we could share the results of our commitments over the last twelve months now?" Robbie asked.

"I'm ready if you and your mom are." Ron moved over to the tree and picked up a folder. "The committee I worked with raised the total amount necessary to purchase all of the equipment to adapt the elementary school and the community playground for children who need wheelchairs to move around. They will no longer have to sit on the sidelines during recesses or when they are out on a walk." Ron closed the file. His eyes were bright. "I'm proud of all of the residents in our town and those in the surrounding district who participated in all of the fund-raising events."

"Was it difficult?" Jake asked.

"Raising money is never easy, especially in these economic times but I assisted with the presentations and approached some of the medical organizations which scoured their budgets for funds. However the volunteers worked very hard with baking, dances, walkathons, etc. They deserve the lion's share of the credit. It was worth seeing the smiles on the parents' and children's faces."

"Congratulations, Dad. Any hints about your commitment for the coming year?" Robbie grinned. She knew the rules but Jake didn't.

"Jake, Robbie is being coy. Part of the gift is keeping our commitment to ourselves until the following year."

The furnace ruffled the pine needles on the tree and the aroma of outdoors mingled with the warmth from the fireplace.

"Thank you for allowing me to participate." Jake straightened. "I can see your point. It is the quiet every-day gifts that are lasting."

"You're right." Ron handed Megan her bright red folder then sat down to listen.

"I wondered why you always brought home so many trays of brownies and peanut butter squares." Megan leaned over Ron and patted his tummy. She sat on the edge of his chair and opened her file. "I didn't venture too far out of my field this year. Last year an elderly client asked for my assistance in contacting her adult son and establishing a relationship before she passed away."

Megan swallowed. "I'm sorry to have to report that even though we located her son, he was not ready to allow his mother back into his life."

Robbie and Jake leaned forward.

"What? How could someone do that?" Robbie's voice squeaked.

"There are circumstances where the scars are just too deep or the relationship has been left unattended for too many years. I can't tell you which it was due to confidentiality. However, the mother and I are working toward a realization that she may have to learn to love her son from afar and find other solutions to filling her present life with love."

Ron put his arm around Megan's waist and she snuggled against his chest. "Some gifts don't come easy."

"No, but we'll continue to work with what we have and hope perhaps someday things may change." She closed her folder.

Robbie stood. "My parcels are in the car. I'll give you a sketch of my project and then I'll fill in any details over dinner if that is agreed upon."

The disc player turned off at the end of the last song. The silence held for a second.

"I'm fine with that," Ron said.

Megan nodded.

"I worked beside the intellectually challenged who sort our recyclables."

"Pardon?" Ron pressed the CD player start button. "Jingle Bells" played on violins filled the background.

"I've been taking my plastic bottles and drink cans to the same recycle depot for the last four years. The same woman has been sorting and counting my bottles. I didn't even know her name. I admit I was curious." Robbie spread her hands. "She made short work of sorting and counting the bags and bags of product that were dumped into her station. I've watched the work conditions change over the years with little things that protect the employees."

"This was certainly your year for diversity." Megan shifted, wiggled out of Ron's chair, and walked over to Robbie. "I'm proud of you." Wrapping her arms around her daughter's shoulders, she kissed her cheek. "Merry Christmas."

"Thanks, Mom. I'll give you more details over dinner but I can tell from Jake's wide-eyed, deer-in-the-headlights look, he's not sure about us. Maybe we should change subjects for a bit."

Ron stood. "Great idea, there is food to prepare and dinnerware to be placed."

Robbie's fingers were drawn to Jake's like metal to magnets as they filled platters, water, and wine glasses. His pupils were large and his melted chocolate eyes seemed to follow her fork when she lifted it from her plate to her lips. She knew because her hunger for food had flipped to heart-hunger and she hoped that his had as well.

While the Christmas music filled the air and the Christmas lights reflected in the picture window, Ron spoke briefly about his conference on family medicine. "I wish you had become a doctor, Robbie. We could sure use you. This community is growing."

"I may be able to help out in some capacity, Dad. We just have to think around the box," Robbie said. "Perhaps I can help make the clinic as efficient as possible."

"Good thought."

"That's enough business talk for one Christmas dinner," Megan said.

Robbie shared her experiences at the recyclable depot and demonstrated her acquired quick addition skills. "The manager wasn't too keen on my community service, however he asked the staff and Alice offered to be my mentor. She rides the bus for an hour to come into work. The workplace is not a clean environment if you think about the spills and the noise but she does her job and is proud of the wages she earns and her part in cleaning up the environment. She lives in a group home where they share the duties and she's sweet on the man who sorts in the station next to her. She dreams of marriage and perhaps a family one day."

"Let's hope her dreams come true." Megan sighed.

"I'm going to . . ." Robbie clamped her hand over her mouth. "Sorry, that's my next year Christmas gift."

When the bowls of potatoes, turnips, and dressing were half empty, Jake folded his napkin, stood, and placed his arm around Robbie. He raised his glass. "Thank you, Ron and Megan, for including me in your celebration. Thank you,

Robin, for your courage and patience." When he ended, he felt in his pocket and retrieved the circle of gold. He turned to Robin, and helped her to her feet. Gently, he touched the edges of her cheeks. "Robin, Robbie, I love you. When I'm with you, I feel like I've come home. Will you marry me?"

Robbie drew back slightly, her eyes intent as she looked at him. She watched as Jake held a too large band toward her left-hand ring finger.

"This was my grandmother's ring. Granddad gave it to his best friend and I'd like my best friend to wear it forever."

Robbie took a long breath as she gazed in wonder. Like her, Jake had grown a little wiser, and she loved the man he was and who he'd become. "Yes."

He slid the ring onto her finger.

She leaned toward him and he kissed her gently on the right side of her lips and the left and slowly in the middle. Everything in her begged her to wind her arms around his neck and meld into him body and soul.

Her parents approached and brought their arms around them. "Family." Megan said.

Robin Mary Smith stood tall. Her eyes were bright with tears and her smile wide. She had gained more from her research than she ever imagined. She became like the women who shared their deepest secrets, hopes, and loves. She was a true woman of substance. She was someone Jake, the man she loved, had grown to love and now they would share their future, together, wherever it may be.

CPSIA information can be obtained
at www.ICGtesting.com
Printed in the USA
LVHW041813291020
670187LV00010B/935